Skintown

www.penguin.co.uk

Skintown

Ciaran McMenamin

Doubleday

LONDON · TORONTO · SYDNEY · AUCKLAND · JOHANNESBURG

TRANSWORLD PUBLISHERS
61–63 Uxbridge Road, London W5 5SA
www.penguin.co.uk

Transworld is part of the Penguin Random House group of companies
whose addresses can be found at global.penguinrandomhouse.com

Penguin
Random House
UK

First published in Great Britain in 2017 by Doubleday
an imprint of Transworld Publishers

A CIP catalogue record for this book
is available from the British Library.

ISBN 9780857524850 (hb)
9781781620397 (Doubleday Ireland tpb)

Typeset in 11/15 pt Goudy by Jouve (UK), Milton Keynes
Printed and bound in Great Britain by Clays Ltd, Bungay, Suffolk

Penguin Random House is committed to a sustainable
future for our business, our readers and our planet. This book
is made from Forest Stewardship Council® certified paper.

MIX
Paper from
responsible sources
FSC® C018179

1 3 5 7 9 10 8 6 4 2

For J. P. McMenamin,
poet, uncle, inspiration

Town

1

A RIVER OF Thousand Island dressing springs from my Hawaiian burger and plunges earthwards, a swollen pink torrent raging through the middle of my Stone Roses T-shirt. I care not. The seven pints that I have annihilated in order to develop the hunger in the first place are taking care of everything. Chippie Street has burst into song since closing time and I will gladly float along its tune, embracing its charms, if I can convince any of them to let me. Three hundred and fifty yards of baffled hormones glued together in an orgy of booze and bile and batter. Three chip shops and two Chinese takeaways standing shoulder to shoulder on one small street in one small town on one huge Saturday night.

The next hour will be crucial. This is a naughty boy's final crack at getting his fingers dirty amongst the neglected and rejected of the last-chance saloon.

I don't even like Hawaiian burgers. Only in Ireland can you take a sub-standard beef patty, bung it in a soapy bap, top it off with a slice of tinned pineapple, smother the lot in diluted Marie Rose sauce and get away with calling it a fucking 'Hawaiian' burger. I panicked when I got to the front of the queue. I was in a tiny sweltering cell being crushed against the filthy Formica counter, choking on a thick cloud of steam and grease and vinegar. I could literally feel the starving drunken hordes breathing down the back of my neck so, as my imagination pulled me under and the hordes proceeded to jump on my back and stamp on my testicles, I pointed to the first thing on the menu and accidentally ordered a sweet meaty tribute to an American-occupied Pacific island.

Post-stodge my world is a lamp-lit, frightening place, eight months pregnant with possibility. There is a knack to making eye contact with the right person in a highly combustible environment. It is an art form. Catching the eye of the wrong girl will end in a showdown with a vodka-soaked chimp, who will happily donate his last breath to kicking the education from your brains. It won't necessarily be her boyfriend. It could be some emotional retard who has pined for her for years from the other end of the school bus but has never had the balls to stand up and offer her his seat. Now, tonight on this street, demented by alcohol and wild with unrequited lust, he will punch your features flat until she eventually tries to stop him and in doing so sees him for the very first time.

As I wipe the detritus of al-fresco dining on the arse of my jeans I hear it beginning in the distance. A cheer first, then a bottle breaks, and as a stray girl begins to howl I turn and sprint towards the rising sounds of battle. If it isn't old Green Eyes it'll be the great big lie. We're hard for religion in these parts, especially after midnight and with a bellyful of lager.

I force myself into the back row of the scrum and spot a figure on the ground through the massed ranks of denim legs. It's bad to go down this early. Rule number one is to stay on your feet, and rule number two is to use those feet to run for your fucking life. As I squabble for a ringside seat I decipher that tonight's entertainment is a town-versus-country debate. Mark McGullion and the boys from the Mount View housing estate have taken it upon themselves to defend the metropolis from this unprovoked agricultural invasion. I recognise from school some of the faces huddled around their fallen comrade. These lads have travelled thirty miles tonight from a village on the border called Belleek, and they are about to get a serious hiding for their troubles. It is inconvenient being different around here, and these boys are certainly inconvenient. Culchies, munchies, bog trotters. Call them what you will, they're only country boys with country brogues. When we have gratefully legged it to Glasgow or Liverpool for college or unemployment we will all be inconvenient together. Micks, Paddies, porridge niggers. Irish boys with Irish accents from the far-western corner of our well-trotted little bog of a country.

The swarm of bodies grips me. I am carried forward and my feet momentarily leave the ground. Another surge, but backwards as the fray resumes and the townies push the country reinforcements aside and start kicking at the boy on the pavement. Above him his friends fight separate desperate battles in an effort to protect him, but these side-shows are manoeuvred away from the main event and the boy lies fully exposed and alone. His terror shines wet and black, the fully dilated pupils having devoured all of the white from his eyes. He is taking a horrendous beating. McGullion, Rat Kelly and someone I don't know are literally booting his brains out. Six feet, like a Lewis gun, hammering constantly on his undefended head and shoulders. They stop kicking for a second, and as one the crowd breathes in, but then the victors start taking turns to jump on his head and chest instead. Both feet high in the air, then the weight of a fully grown man landing on a ribcage and skull. I stare at my filthy suede desert boots and listen as a hammer slowly beats raw meat, the blows becoming less frequent but more precise. When I glance back at the boy his blood is pissing from his nose and mouth and his petrified eyes have taken on the resignation of a much older man. The crowd, erect and silent, do nothing but watch and wait for a glimpse of something grey that they have only ever heard of. A girl behind me sobs then gags, and as I turn towards her she vomits at my feet. I want to hold her hair back from her face and tell her not to worry but behind me the dispassionate thud of the mallet reverberates up my spine and into the base of my skull until I can stand it no longer.

'Gully, stop it, man. You're going to fucking kill him.'

The crowd parts and I step forward like a shit Moses.

'Leave it, lads. You've already won.'

Unaware of the thoughts as they form, I watch powerless as the words pass through my lips and spill onto the pavement with the blood and the vomit and the chips.

'Come on, boys. The bastard's not worth it.'

They momentarily step off the trampoline and McGullion glares at me, his face a web of veins fighting each other for oxygen through his tight plastic yellow skin. 'But he's from Belleek!'

I am momentarily relieved for the minorities of Europe that McGullion wasn't alive in the forties.

'He wanted it and he fucking got it.'

A shout goes up behind me from the car park across the road.

'Pigs! Pigs! Pigs!'

The pack splits up and runs for the hills. The Royal Ulster Constabulary tend to drop their customary discrimination when wielding batons in the middle of a crowd. I am left alone eyeballing a psychopath who straddles the body of a bloody beaten farmer's son. Nothing is said but his scowl tells me everything I need to know about my immediate future or lack thereof. I am a traitor who has let the town down. I am weak and artistic and I probably have a penchant for the cock. The air fills with affronted mechanical growls and as the paddy wagons descend I deliver my farewell.

'Forgive me, *mein Führer*.'

His face tightens and shrivels as rage sucks the air from his lungs.

'I don't speak Irish, you wanker.'

He turns and runs off towards Mount View, leaving me standing over a vegetable fighting for its life. Three armoured Land Rovers pull in at speed and I'm suddenly faced with a peculiarly Northern Irish dilemma. If I run I'm guilty and if I stay I'm guilty and will take a government-sponsored kicking on the house.

I run like fuck.

2

I NEED THE darkness. The sound of their boots drives me onwards as I pound up the steep hill towards the park. Anaerobic fear floods every muscle driving me up and over the ancient rusty wrought-iron gates. The crack of my knees on concrete is as loud as a gunshot, and then I'm up again and I'm tall and strong and I'm gone. The path circles the hill, snaking around it, crushing it over decades in its many loops. It steadies my legs and I cut sharply to the left onto the silent grass and head uphill for the white Victorian bandstand that squats at the summit. Straight through the middle of it I leap and now I'm a lightning bolt shooting into the hedge at the edge of the park. Just before impact I twist and land on my belly, sliding underneath the bushes where I roll onto my back and lie stock still. A Keith Moon sound-check is exploding from my chest and the pressure in my ears is unbearable. My heart will surely burst through my ribcage and forsake me. Breathe, hold, then count to ten. If my heart's escape bid is unsuccessful then it will be forced northwards into my throat where it will surely get lodged and choke me. Breathe. Hold. Count to ten. Keith's frantic solo begins to settle into the rhythm of an actual song and I focus on Daltrey's passionate voice and try to regulate my breathing. Out there in the fields, Roger? I had to fight for my meal in a chip shop! The Who are playing live in the Forthill bandstand. Who'd have thought it? The entire population of the town is packed onto the surrounding hillsides and hanging out of the ancient trees. If Townshend smashes that guitar I'm kicking for the front and fighting for every last fucking piece of it.

It's a healthy five minutes before I'm in control of myself. They won't find me. Lying down in the dark will always hide you. I know this park like the back of my bag and, if necessary, I'll push through the hedge and jump the wire down into the convent school below. As their voices reach out for me I can clearly distinguish their individual accents. Belfast mostly, and maybe one or two from Derry or Coleraine. You're not allowed to have local policemen in a war where people get shot in their beds or on the school run or in the car park after church in front of their kids. As their patter recedes, my fear is replaced by the smugness that accompanies the outwitting of the law. I am a guerrilla warrior at one with my terrain. Warm in my well-chosen hide, I consider the Viet Cong in the jungle and the French Resistance in the hedgerows of Normandy. I think about the Apache warriors in the Arizona foothills and the IRA drinking pints of Guinness in the Hatfield bar on the Ormeau Road in Belfast.

Takeaway tumbleweed and some pools of puke are all that remain of the most important night of our lives. There is another thicker, darker pool where his head used to be. Why is there never any black blood on the telly? Why is the blood on our screens always bright red? Accident and Emergency in the hospital is where they will be. Those poor frightened fuckers from the country, wondering if their friend will live and how the hell they will ever get home. McGullion will be tucked up in his bed by now, sleeping it off, his big fat lazy cow's tongue stuck to the roof of his mouth as he greedily tries to suck frozen Coke from a glass bottle in his dreams. I want to climb through his window and piss on his bloated bastard of a face.

The usual stragglers from out of town are stranded at the taxi office but only two of them are nearly female. A fog is beginning gently to cover the shoulders of proceedings as a few cars screech past at speed, showing off to an audience long since departed. Ghostly lone riders endlessly cruising a point-less one-street circuit. They never stop or talk to girls, they just roar around in an angry state of delusion that someone actually gives a fuck.

The old Ritz cinema sits slumped at one end of the street, and on my way home every Saturday night I stop here to smoke and reminisce. Our Friday-night Scout meeting would decamp to the flicks every third week of the month, and in the back row I would laugh and smoke myself sick with Fingers Fitzpat-rick and Jelly Flanagan. I fell in love in there for the first time, slouched in one of the big red velvet seats in the freezing damp mouldy stalls. She never found out but I really did love her. She had fallen already for one Indiana Jones, Esq., as he battled insects and snakes and religious fanatics in his desperate attempts to save her from the Temple of Doom. I was nine years old. When I got home that night and climbed into bed I fought thirty-seven crocodiles and scaled tall buildings and downed shots of whiskey and whipped evil, dark-skinned megalo-maniacs to death and I won her heart. I didn't know why I loved her or what I wanted her to do about it, but I wanted her to be mine and mine only, and I wanted other people, including Harrison Ford, to know this and to stay the fuck out of my way.

Every few days since the place closed down the letters on the advertising hoarding have mysteriously been changed to spell out something bold or profound or something completely and utterly pointless. No one seems to know who the culprit is and nobody has offered any explanation as to why he does it. Perhaps a comedian, perhaps a prophet, or perhaps just some arsehole with a ladder and a lot of time on his hands since he lost his job in the cinema.

IF JESUS COMES BACK
WE WILL KILL HIM AGAIN

I take my prized gold Zippo from my pocket and light a Silk Cut purple. Kill him again? As I roll the filter lovingly between my lips and wolf the second drag down into my stomach I'm grabbed roughly from behind and pulled backwards into some-one else.

A cold soft female hand takes the fag from my mouth and drops it to the ground, then runs itself slowly up my face to cover my eyes. 'Guess who, Vincent Patrick Duffy.'

'What do you think it means?'

'Jesus, Vinny, who fucking cares?'

She drops her hand and spins me around. 'Why are you smoking on your own outside a derelict cinema at three in the morning?'

Eileen Maguire. An all-singing, all-Irish-dancing, tin-whistle-blowing wee heartbreaker from the lough's shore. I glance at her ample breasts and consider toasting Our Lord next Saturday night when I'm drinking beer behind the leisure centre and pretending to be at eight o'clock Mass. We've kissed once before in the dusty recesses of an under-age disco, corralled together by eager friends who knew less about what to do than we did. I was thirteen at the time and was about as prepared for the task in hand as Denis Thatcher on his wedding night. To say that I embarrassed myself trying to force my tongue into a mouth that had previously only been frequented by various woodwind instruments would be putting it mildly. Now, more than four years later, here she is, offering me the chance to right all of those nerve-shattering, mortifying slobbery wrongs. She is flustered and out of breath and various bits of her wobble invitingly. She grabs my arm and in my heart we are already Riverdancing together round the Forthill Park wearing nothing but smiles and matching black brogues. Green eyes, auburn hair and a bearable freckle quota. I want her. I need her. She pulls me closer and I gag in a miasma of Head & Shoulders.

'Vinny, I need to ask you a massive favour.'

'And there was me thinking you found me irresistible.'

She smiles a little and I melt a little more, and then she hits me with it, hard.

3

FIVE MINUTES LATER and I'm climbing into the arse of a shiny black Ford Fiesta. There was genuine doubt between her ears while she waited for me to decide whether or not to accompany her home to the countryside with two mysterious older lunatics under the guise of being her boyfriend, then take a lift back to town all by myself with said lunatics. What she failed to grasp was that, having been put in that situation in the first place, I had no bloody choice. What was I going to say? 'You know what, love, I'm very tired, so take your lift when you're getting it. Sure it'll only be a bit of an oul gang rape and you'll forget all about it in the morning.' As I shut the door, trapping myself inside the vehicle, I realise I'm in a world of shit. Our chauffeur and his Hammer Horror co-pilot are both comfortably drunk. The driver swigs from a can of beer as he twists in his seat before requesting my name. There is a charming little game we play in Northern Ireland where the participants attempt to fathom the colour of the other's birth mistake by using only the other's names for clues. The problem is that after a generation of conflict everyone is so good at it there is nowhere to hide, and when your name is Vincent you might as well be the Pope's private fucking chef. I dive straight for territory that is neutral, bordering on the Orange.

'Mark.'

As I fasten my seatbelt I give Eileen a glare that leaves her in no doubt that if we ever come through this situation alive I will shove her tin whistle up her hole.

'So you're the boyfriend, are ye?'

They know the score, these two. They know I'm no more a Mark than I'm Ian Paisley's love child, and they know I'm definitely not riding Enya beside me here.

'I'm Kyle and this is Grant.'

Two true-blue geniuses hot off the conveyor-belt of hate. We're in the back of a car belonging to the men our mothers told us never get in the back of a car of. Eileen takes my hand and squeezes it hard, and as we drive out of town, away from the safety of other people and into an ever-thickening fog, I close my eyes and wonder how many girls will come to my funeral.

They talk amongst themselves in the front while we shit amongst ourselves in the back. I estimate that the two of them are currently drinking their way through their early thirties. Kyle the driver is clearly in control of the brain they share. He is the snide, bitter type, who specialises in bad one-liners about how drunk he is. Grant has a whole monosyllabic grunt thing going on and is far too big for the car. As we shoot up Garvary Hill, with the lights of civilisation receding into the grey veil behind us, the volume of the conversation in the front is turned up for the benefit of the passengers in the back.

'I'd fucking love to go into that Silver Star bar some evening, Grant, and give it the oul trick-or-treat treatment.'

Kyle is not professing an urge here to dress up as Dracula and collect monkey nuts in a Wellworths bag. He is referring to a massacre last year where the UFF shot eight innocent people dead in a 'Catholic' bar near Derry at Hallowe'en. One of the gunmen shouted, 'Trick or treat?' before they opened fire with a VZ58 assault rifle and an automatic pistol. He should have shouted, 'Tit for tat,' because that was what it was. The week before, the IRA had left a bomb in a fish shop on the Shankill Road in Belfast, killing eight innocent Protestant civilians. Why do they call it that on the news? Why not Kit for Kat? Two men were shot today in what is being called a 'shit for shat' sectarian killing. The Silver Star bar is a pub in town that is mostly frequented by thirsty Catholics. Kyle was just letting me know that he knows I get the old ashes rubbed on my forehead six Wednesdays before Easter Sunday.

'So what school did you go to, *Mark?*'

'Portora.'

Call me cheap, but I've taken a gamble on their fledgling intellect. Portora Royal is the Protestant grammar school. I figure these two might have passed a few Skodas in their time, but they haven't a fucking hope with the eleven-plus.

'Oooooh, a brainy cunt.'

Suspicion confirmed. Kyle turns and sneers at me for an uncomfortably long time. It's not so much the sneer as the fact that he's supposed to be driving. A silence of epic proportions ensues. I crush Eileen's hand in reciprocation and look at her face for the first time since leaving town. Tears slalom through those freckles as she mouths terrified sorries at me. Her parents have taken living in the middle of nowhere a bit excessively. By the time we reach her house my crippled sense of direction has been left somewhere behind us in the Transylvanian fog. I have never seen anything like it. You can barely see ten feet in front of the car, so Christ knows what driving through it after ten cans of cheap Continental lager is like. We come to a halt on the driveway and she steps out of the Fiesta and looks back at me with pity, or fear, or lust. She closes her eyes first and the door second, then dances up the driveway to her daddy's house as fast as her legs will carry her.

4

IT'S IN MOMENTS like these that I know Ireland is truly fucked. I am about to be murdered and she could have saved me by bringing me inside, but my mutilation or slow, painful death is easier for her to bear than her father's Roman rage if she brings a fella home after the watershed. Alone in the back of the hearse, I finally have the space to appreciate how frightened I am. The best I will get away with here is a free wheelchair from the NHS. Released from the shackles of a female audience, Kyle ups the heat from the front of the car.

'So, *Mark*, who do you know from Portora?'

Listing the names of lads I know from another school seems futile when the questions will only keep coming. Next up will be the words of 'The Sash', or upon which French battlefield did our grandfathers bleed for the Union, or did Mary ride the donkey the whole way to Bethlehem? My brain prolapses. *Come on, you know loads of Prods, just fucking think!* I can see them all lined up before me, all those perfectly symmetrical well-tanned faces, but the names seem as distant as the exotic destinations where they spend their Christmas holidays.

'Jesus, Grant, do you get that awful smell coming from the back of the car?'

'That's my trainers in the boot, mate. I've been meaning to bung them in the machine.'

'No, you prick. I'm talking about him in the back. He's a Fenian.'

It hangs in the air like a Guinness fart.

'A wee Taig hiding in the back of my car!'

There are many derogatory terms for 'Catholic' in Northern Ireland, and over the next twenty-five seconds Kyle displays an impressive aptitude for both knowledge and delivery.

I've never given much thought to divinity, never mind its powers of intervention, but as I sit in the back of a car preparing to forsake the blue skies of Ulster for the grey mists of a shallow grave, the good Lord Himself arbitrates and the Ford Fiesta levitates. We have been moving at speed under the influence through fog, and have arrived at and driven straight through a T-junction. We hang in the air like a steel eagle for what seems like for ever, then crash, beak first, into a field fifteen feet below the road. I've heard that when you're in a car crash everything happens in slow motion and your whole life flashes in front of your eyes, but on this occasion, due to extenuating circumstances, the entirety of my eighteen years and two months has already been screened to me in full Technicolor throughout the course of the journey. My ears are ringing and my mind is replaying the complete back catalogue of X-rated government seatbelt commercials, and the time that my mother came down our driveway at two in the morning and nearly crashed when she found my skinny white arse in her headlights as I rode Sarah Bishop on the lawn at the front of the house. My head is filled again with the stench of Eileen's shampoo and I'm carried backwards out of the car and dumped into a crowd in the changing rooms at the Gaelic football pitch as Franky Fivey rubs a whole tube of Deep Heat into his balls for a one-pound bet.

I lash out and grab hold of my mind with both hands. The car seems to have bounced on impact and is sitting flat in the bottom of the field. The only pain I can identify clearly is in my shoulder and chest and I know that that's from the seatbelt. Wiggling both legs shows no sign of paralysis and my immediate instinct is to open the door and run like fuck away from the scene and away from the men who mean me harm, but I just can't resist a look into the front of the car. Kyle is motionless, slumped forward on the steering-wheel. I can't see Grant properly as he's in the seat directly in front of me but there is a horrific gurgling sound coming from where I know his head should be. Unstrapped I shove myself forward between the seats to see if he'll make it. When my hand grabs his shoulder he sits up a bit and half turns so I can see that he's clutching his face. He groans, then that gurgle again as he's clearly struggling to breathe.

'Can you hear me, Grant? You're gonna be all right, Grant. I can't see any blood, Grant.'

He flails around, searching for my voice, then takes his huge hand away from his face and I can see that it still clutches a crumpled tin of beer.

'Grant, can you hear me? Can you breathe?'

He lifts his paw to his face again and, as the horrific gurgling noise resumes, I realise that it's him trying to suck warm flat beer out of the squashed-flat can. I start to laugh. You know when you know at the time, in the moment as the laugh takes hold, that it's one of those ten-in-a-lifetime numbers? I lie back in the seat and laugh and laugh at the ridiculousness of man and the beer in the can, at me hiding in the dark from the cops in the park, at the boy in the street with his head crushed by feet.

An odd strangled roar interrupts my reverie and Kyle is coming at me from the front of the car. 'What's so funny, Fenian?'

Jesus, there's nothing wrong with him either! Forsaken by reason and with my bowels threatening treason, I open the door and fall out into the field.

'What's so fucking funny?'

He has circumnavigated the crippled wagon and towers over me where I lie by the back left wheel. Despite the euphoric convulsions that twist and rack my body I cover up in preparation for a conversation with his shoes.

'What the fuck is so fucking funny?'

A switch flicks and I'm up and sharp and away to my left, leaving him stuck between me and the paralysed Ford. I eyeball him for a healthy second before my shoulder and head tear into his chest, buckling his back on the boot of the car. When he tries to rise I'm down and on him and I have him by the collar of his Saturday-night shirt. As I spit my roll call of honour into his face I punctuate every name with a desperate grateful shake.

'Dick Moffat, Stewart Lafferty, Ralph Brady, Paul Hogg, Neil Greaves, Danny Mills, Graham King, Billy Little, Ivan McKinnon, Josh Noble, Freddie Jones!'

He kicks upwards, pushing me off, then retreats rapidly around the car as I fall backwards then roll over and lie splitting on my side in the soaking-wet grass.

'You're mental, man! Seriously, you're not wise in the head. You need some fucking help!'

I can't get up for the laughing so I roll flat onto the middle of my back and I call out to him through the sobs and the fog.

'I'm sorry, Kyle. It must have been the bump on my head but I've just remembered the names of all the Prods I know.'

5

THEY ARGUE. I listen. Kyle's main bone of contention is that as Grant's head cracked the windscreen it will therefore be up to him to foot this particular part of the bill. As I survey the damage to the written-off car, it occurs to me that Grant will merely be picking up the tip.

'You will provide a new windscreen for this vehicle, fat boy!'

'You're worried about the windscreen? There's a hole in the sump bigger than your mother's!'

'Don't talk about my mother like that.'

'The car's squashed like a lemon.'

'A melon.'

'What?'

'It's squashed like a melon.'

'What is?'

'The car.'

'That's what I said.'

'No, you didn't, you said fucking lemon.'

I could listen to this gold all night but my Hawaiian burger is a disappointing distant memory, and having laughed myself sober I'm starting to get hungry again.

'Lads, we should ditch the booze.'

Grant looks at me like I've shat in his lap. 'Why in the name of fuck would we do that?'

'It's the scene of a road accident so we should ditch the booze before the cops get here.'

Kyle looks impressed. I sense a breakthrough. Perhaps he has a penchant for clever young Catholics in slightly flared jeans.

'He's right. I can hear a river at the end of the field: go and dump the beers.'

'Now, you just hold on one wee minute here, mister. I work like a bastard all week, and by the time I send my wages to that bitch in England to feed my son, these few beers are all that I have left for myself!'

I'm a sucker for a sob story but I can't help thinking that if Grant's son lives in England with his mother then he's clearly the bastard of the piece. I walk to the front of the once-proud Ford Fiesta and tap the concertinaed mess sagely with my toe, then spit into the field beside me. I know nothing about cars but I have watched my uncle tinkering with them for years and I know for a fact that in rural Ireland the language of the car expert is a toe-tap to the bumper followed by a lazy lobbed Clint Eastwood of a gob.

'The car's fucked, Kyle.'

'Well, listen to Nigel Mansell. Of course the fucking car's fucking fucked!' He's gone off me again. Maybe he doesn't like boys who spit. Kyle starts to cry. 'It's my sister's car, it's my sister's car! Jesus, it's my sister's car and I'm not even fucking insured!'

You couldn't write it.

'I've had enough. It's always me! Why does this shit always happen to me?'

Grant drops his beloved can and moves in for a man hug.

'Don't fucking touch me, mate. I am not doing this any more. I've had enough. I'm getting into that river myself and you two can't stop me.'

Kyle flounces off into the fog towards the river to take his own life and neither of us attempts to prevent him. After watching the fog in silence for some time Grant goes back to the passenger side of the car and liberates two cans of Bavaria 8.6. Cheap, nasty rocket fuel.

'What's your real name, son?'

'Vinny.'

'Nice to meet you, Vinny. He's always like this, you know. Total fucking drama queen.'

We find him on his knees at the back of the field, staring down into the river below. I say river but this is a more of a ditch. It is immediately apparent that a fully grown man could never drown himself in there unless he lay face down in it and drank like fuck. In preparation for death Kyle has removed his shoes and they sit neatly behind him with the fog-drunken moon reflected perfectly in their shiny leather uppers. I look down at Grant's feet and realise that he, too, models some lovingly polished ebony Sunday-bests. It occurs to me that this is the done-thing, to wear your smartest black shoes out on a Saturday night with your finest pressed shirt, when you go hunting for frightened young people of the other persuasion. It's a particularly Protestant trait, the old shiny shoe, but then it is a particularly shiny religion. Catholicism, on the other hand, has never really shone. Guilt and fear have a tendency to leave one looking rather harried and slightly worn.

After listening to a monologue on the terrible cards he's been dealt since some bint called Mandy ran off with a squaddie called Clive, we gently convince Kyle that his future holds more than a pathetic mud-gargling demise. Grant and I work well together, and as he continually furnishes my hand with new cans of beer, I'm ready to suggest the pair of us teaming up to do some counselling work for the Samaritans. When Kyle asks me tentatively about the uncle I mentioned, who is a mechanic, I point out that he doesn't work miracles and can't work at all with a Browning automatic pressed into his neck, and the three of us nearly fall into the river from the laughter.

Ours is indeed a strange little country. We can kill each other for decades on end, but never accuse us of not being able to laugh at ourselves. It is decided that knocking on doors in the middle of the morning is not the best idea in a country where people get shot in their beds, and we strike out for home with the remains of the bag of beer to fuel the journey. By the time we see the lights of the town winking at us at the foot of Garvary Hill we have been on the move for three long, gruelling hours. Shiny shoes are shite for walking.

6

DESPITE SOBERING RAPIDLY in the face of multiple varied attempts on my life, I have a head like a foot when I wake on Sunday afternoon. I know that my mother is not my friend. She rarely is, but every sinew of my poisoned frame tells me that today will be something special. You can measure the ferocity of her moods on the door-slamming Richter scale, and today the whole house is shaking and my heart is breaking at the inevitability of the nuclear fallout. It is one thirty and she has returned home from Mass pissed off, hungry and pious. The monsignor in the church up the town can take your average mother, feed her five pints of righteousness in the sermon bar, and send her home drunk on devotion and with the inner strength to shatter outer entrances. My mother hates a lot of things, including Americans and my father, but mostly she hates the drink.

'Drink, drink, drink, drink, drink!'

She may in fact not even hate my father. It may simply be the fact that he drinks. Or perhaps she only hates the drink because of my father. Either way it was an alcoholic chicken-and-egg apocalypse from the moment they collided. In the end he left and she quickly modified her tenses to remind the world how he drank, drank, drank, drank, drank. Personally I don't mind his imbibing, it makes him smell nice and tell shite jokes, but then I never had to sleep beside him or try in vain to stimulate dialogue about money or children or responsibility. Most of my Saturday nights begin with a few hours in the Market bar with the oul boy and his friends. He's not a bad man; he has never raised his voice in anger, let alone his hand. Neither is my mother a bad woman; she just married the wrong man. She married Peter Pan instead of Peter Perfect. Enid Blyton, Jane Austen, Catherine Cookson and the BBC have a lot to fucking answer for. No man is perfect and no man should ever be called Peter. Peter is a wanker's name.

The kitchen is like a sauna, thanks to the steam coming from the Sunday peas. They freak me out, these Sunday peas. Nothing that has to be soaked overnight to have any vague hope of being edible should ever be trusted.

'Hi, Ma, how was Mass?'

'Don't "How was Mass?" me. How do think Mass was? Isn't it always the same?'

'Why do you go if it's always the same?'

'It's you who should be going instead of pretending. Do you think I'm stupid?'

'I don't believe in ghosts.'

'Where were you last night?'

'Out.'

'Doing what?'

'Messing about.'

'Do you think I didn't hear you coming into this house at seven this morning, stumbling about drunk?'

'I wasn't drunk.'

'Jesus, you are just like your father!'

For the millionth time I refrain from pointing out that I'd had no choice in the matter. She'd decided to copulate with the man and I am merely the end product. Somewhere deep down inside herself my mother still loves me, but it's been hidden away since I've grown because all she can see now is the youthful reflection of the man who broke her heart.

'Where are you going?'

'Work.'

'Is that what you call it?'

'No, that's what it's called.'

'Balls.'

'I can change it, if you want.'

'You don't know what work is.'

'How about "giraffe"?'

'You've never done a day's work in your life.'

'All right, Ma, that's me off out to giraffe for the day then. Enjoy your fucking peas.'

I slam the front door too hard and one of the small panes of glass falls out and smashes on the driveway. I don't look back. If I did that she would see the tears in my eyes and she would win.

Recently my life has been full of dramatic exits. Four months ago I took the head-staggers and dramatically exited my education. I was being schooled by priests and lay Catholics who had never actually left the education system. Seven years at school to gain the required qualifications to do three years of teacher training to earn the qualification to go back to school for some money. Couple that with some soutaned celibates who have devoted their lives to a fairy tale and you don't exactly get a bubbling crucible of input from the University of Life. A school for Catholic boys who have passed the eleven-plus exam, or for Catholic boys who have failed the eleven-plus exam but have parents wealthy enough to pay for them to attend anyway.

Confusion from the outset. In this particular seat of learning, the learning didn't actually matter as long as you excelled at Gaelic football. In fact, you could fail all of your exams in your vital year and be brought back the following September anyway if you were good enough for the school team. Every lunchtime the playing fields are policed by a gang of intimidating sixth-years, with full beards and cocks down to their knees, who are re-sitting their GCSEs for the third year in a row because they can kick the ball over the bar from forty yards.

An institutionalised conveyor-belt the sole purpose of which is to drop as many troops as possible into the middle-class clerical occupations that have for years lain in darkness behind enemy lines. We don't need musicians or poets or thinkers. We need as many dentists and doctors as possible, and thousands more teachers to create as many more dentists and doctors as possible. Individuality is a threat to such values.

I was far from a bad student, but I couldn't keep my mouth shut. The end of my final year and I stood alone in a well-buffed corridor, expelled from a biology class for asking pertinent questions in an impertinent fashion. There was an inevitability to what came next. Many laws, including Murphy's, have determined that if you are thrown out of a classroom and have nowhere to hide it will inevitably coincide with the singular journey of the school's headmaster along said corridor that week. True to form, that was exactly where Father Hogan, Darth Vader to Bishop O'Grady's Emperor, found me standing alone scratching my arse for the third time in as many months.

'Duffy, Duffy, Duffy.'

I looked around me for the other two Duffys but as far as I could see I was pretty exclusive.

'It's always you, isn't it, Duffy?'

He's changed his tune: there were three of us a second ago.

'You always know best, don't you, Duffy?'

When it comes it comes fast.

'The big man Duffy.'

There are several different versions.

'You think you're something special, don't you, Duffy?'

But I am never in control. I wouldn't say that it always involves a full out-of-body experience but there are usually two of me involved. The one on the outside that is doing the talking and the one trapped inside who is screaming, *Stop fucking talking!* That particular day I did float off in some capacity and I remember clearly looking down on myself ten feet below as he looked down on the man of the cloth.

'Jesus thinks we're all special, doesn't he, Father?'

'Come with me now, Duffy.'

'I think I'll stay right here, Father, and enjoy the light coming through yonder window.'

'You will do what you are told, boy!'

'I won't, you know, Father, which is why I'm standing in the fucking corridor.'

Horrified yet amused, both of me watched the scene play out in slow motion through the crimson mist.

'You've done it now, Duffy, and for the last time, boy!'

Both of me knew that the situation was deteriorating beyond redemption but only one of us has a voice and he always makes sure it's heard. 'What are you going to do, Father? Beat me round your big office?'

When he grabbed my collar I grabbed his back, when he

raised his voice I screamed something in his face that included the words 'bullshit' and 'theocracy', and when he told me to get off the premises and never come back, I told him to go and fuck himself, and I got a job in a Chinese takeaway.

It is a sunny Sunday afternoon and the further I get from the house the brighter my disposition becomes. Barry will sub me a tenner for a few pints tonight and I'll pay him back when my dole cheque shows up in the week. His father owns the establishment where I work, and for three years now Barry has been running it in the family name. Unbeknown to Barry, however, thanks to my best mate Jonty and myself, the only place the restaurant has been running is firmly into the ground.

The Wang family arrived from China in the early seventies and opened an eating establishment on the Falls Road in west Belfast. After a slow start the word spread and the locals went buck mad for the chow mein. The Wangs simply couldn't keep the place in thick noodles and bamboo shoots. Chicken fried rice and curry sauce became the signature dish for freedom fighters throughout the city, and the Protestants in the east grew so jealous they started eating chop suey by the bucketful themselves and admitting that there was possibly room in the Union for people who hailed from further east than Norwich. An army marches on its stomach, even a clandestine republican army, and from '74 onwards there wasn't an off-duty policeman shot in front of his children, or a greengrocer delivering turnips to the Brits blown up in his van, before the boys had finished their Peking ribs and Cantonese beef in black-bean sauce. They were unstoppable. You simply can't beat troops armed with RPGs and AK47s and fuelled by MSG.

By 1980 Daddy Wang was exhausted and left the city, taking his culinary experiment along the M1 to the country folk near the border. Within three months, having previously tasted nothing more exotic than potato croquettes on Christmas Day, the entire population was hooked on chicken, onions, Peking sauce and free delivery. After several years word filtered back to the Chinese community in the Big Smoke that the spud people out west couldn't get enough crispy duck into them, and Oriental eateries started popping up all over the town. By the nineties, though, the Wangs' flagship Chippie Street establishment, the Shatin City, was well past its sell-by date. It was possibly the competition, possibly the introduction of pizza into Ireland in 1991, but probably the fact that certain members of staff were constantly stoned out of their minds.

I landed the job handy enough. Jonty was working there and he brought me in to meet Barry. Wang junior gave me a suspicious once-over, taking my hands firmly in his and checking my palms for evidence of hard labour. He had a smoke hanging from his gob and a severe stare thing going on that put me in mind of the Russian-roulette referee in *The Deer Hunter*. He stopped short of checking my teeth and told me I could start that evening on a trial basis. He looked like Bruce Lee and he sounded like George Best, and that was good enough for me. Four months later I was still doing six shifts a week and eating all the chicken fried rice with curry sauce I could get my hands on.

Jonty and I work as a team. We are prep chefs and spend the afternoon chopping chicken and onions, prawns and peppers. We dissect racks of ribs and blanch bags of chips. We wash tons of rice, chop mountains of garlic, quarter fields of mushrooms, scrub piles of pots and smoke forests of marijuana. There is a system. Two hours of graft, then out the back for a treat when Barry pays his daily visit to the bank. At first the system worked. We would only have a couple of joints a day, but being stoned is a wonderful thing, and as the intake markedly increased, productivity went totally and utterly out the window. The chicken was showing up in the beef, the mushrooms were hanging out in the bin and the customers were turning off in their droves. By the time I had completed my second month, the business was in deep trouble. To make matters worse, increased pressure from his family and decreased interest in Chinese food have driven Barry utterly demented. He has become increasingly moody and irrational, so we stay out of his way now as much as we can until our shifts are over.

After work he brings us to the pub and plies us with pints out of guilt for his moods. It is a perfect arrangement. Today is ribs day. The intact sides of twelve dead swine are dumped out the back of the kitchen beside the bins every Sunday. I have never laid eyes upon the supplier but I assume that he is a reputable butcher and a standard cog in the official food chain. Twenty-four entire ribcages wrapped in black bin liners to be dragged inside, rinsed, sectioned, chopped and flavoured by two hung-over fuckwits.

I am barely through the door when Jonty winks at me and heads out the back through the kitchen and into the long, thin scullery, soon to be transformed into a piggy morgue. He sits on the edge of the yellowed old Victorian bath and produces the makings of a joint.

'I feel like death warmed up, Jonty. I can't face the pigs today, man.'

'Well, you are facing them, cunty, cos I'm not doing them all meself.'

He has a way with words, our Jonty, though admittedly only with a few and most of them are of the swearing variety. He can put five expletives into a sentence and it will roll off his tongue so naturally that you won't even hear the profanity. He is short and dark and angry. When he is stoned he is short and dark and mellow. When he first discovered the calming effect that the green machine had on his filthy temper, he vowed to stay stoned as often as humanly possible. He hands me a packet of red Rizlas and I lick and stick three of them together in a crude rectangle. I hold it flat in my hands and Jonty takes out a Regal King Size, runs his tongue over the glue on the join, peels off a perfect strip of paper and lets the tobacco fall out into my little nest. I break it up into a nice shape for rolling, then Jonty takes a lighter and begins to burn small sticky bits of hash off a little black block onto the tobacco. I tease the cocktail patiently between the fingers of both my hands until it blends, and when I feel that the nap of the paper is ready to turn I roll a neat chubby little jazz cigarette the shape of a small baseball bat. When he puts the flame to the end I suck the smoke right down to my balls and hold it there for as long as I can without choking. Four long, deep pulls, but not rushed for fear of throwing up on the hangover. When I exhale, only a little smoke escapes from within me, and when it hits me a second later it doesn't mess around. As I watch the hot end of the joint burning angrily closer to the V of my fingers, Jonty burns a hole in the middle of my left eardrum.

'A cock-tease, Vin, she's a fuckin' cock-tease. I'm telling you, man. Wouldn't even touch it last night. Not even a handshake for Mickey Joe, never mind getting the lanyard into her. I'm going off me fuckin' nut, Vinny. She's just playing with me head, the wee cu—'

He inhales like a Hoover, oblivious to the fact that I have shoved the joint roughly into his mouth to cork his waterfall of filth. I watch him closely, both of us perched on the edge of the battered old enamel bathtub. He wraps his lips around the joint like a baby on its mother's nipple and sucks the milky goodness down into his belly. As the buzz infiltrates his bloodstream his eyes fade slightly from black to not so black, and his shoulders slide down gently an inch or two closer to his hips. He takes the joint from his mouth and stares dreamily at it as it fizzes happily between his rough yellow fingers.

'Fuck it, man. I still reckon I'll get riding her sister.'

I look down at the years of stains on the sides of the bath and wonder what rich man used to lie in this thing, looking down over his expensive belly at his wee dolphin of a dick winking back up at him. Old Lord Cole and his big fat hole. I wonder if anyone ever died in the bloody thing. I bet there's been some riding done in it over the years. One hundred years of biting and humping and grinding as the water sloshed out all over the elegantly tiled floor. I hear a servant girl screaming because her mistress has gone to town to play bridge and can't save her as Lord Muck pulls her into the drink and shoves his banjo up her doo-da. Jesus, I'm fucking stoned. My empty stomach turns over and sprays bile upwards into my throat. I push myself off the side of the bath and stumble over to the bins. Everything turns upside down, then sideways. My knees buckle under me and I sit down on one of the sides of ribs.

'I don't feel too good, Jonty.'

'You're all right, you bollocks. You're just having a whitey.'

I look behind him at Lord Banjo and the servant girl dogging away in the bath. She stops crying now, finally accepting his rhythm, and then she smiles at me over the top of the brass taps, and suddenly I see the bath behind her as it will appear in an hour's time, full of blood and raw pig ribs and sweet brown Cantonese sauce. My stomach panics, lurches, and I gag violently and vomit down the front of my Charlatans T-shirt. Jonty starts to laugh and falls backwards into the bathtub just as Lord Banjo blows his muck into wee Mary Moffat, creating another forgotten angry bastard of a mouth to feed.

Barry completely loses his shit when he finds Jonty hysterical in the bathtub and me sitting on a bag full of dead animals covered in my own stomach lining. He storms off upstairs to find me something else to wear, after screaming at Jonty that if he hasn't pulled himself together by the time he returns he'll be fired. Two minutes later a very slightly more composed Barry Wang returns and hands me a Michael Jackson *Bad* T-shirt.

'It's a Michael Jackson *Bad* T-shirt.'

'And?'

'You want me to wear it?'

'Yes.'

'But it's a Michael Jackson *Bad* T-shirt.'

'No one will know.'

'I will know.'

'What's wrong with Michael Jackson?'

'Where do you want me to start?'

I spend the rest of the afternoon stoned out of my mind cleaving raw meat, while a paedophile with bleached skin and a nose job moonwalks up and down my chest. Chopping ribs with a massive cleaver is a precarious enough pastime without the influence of drugs, so we take twice as long as normal people for fear of losing some fingers. For three hours I don't even look up from my station. I focus intently on the block of wood and the slicing steel and the visceral angry pig mess. Every twenty minutes or so Barry rants about our lack of hygiene and announces loudly to the ether that I am a useless cunt who pukes on himself, and each time without fail Jonty loses it all over again, like an irritating broken novelty record. Once the sides have been dissected into hundreds of individual ribs, the stomach-churning reality of what must be done can be put off no longer. They are dumped in Lord Banjo's lusty old bath, along with four buckets of Barry Wang's secret sauce, and then they must be stirred vigorously for an hour with an old fibreglass canoe paddle. In truth, ten minutes' stirring and an hour of marinating would be sufficient, but Barry, in his infinite wisdom, is convinced that exactly one hour, not a minute more or less, is the secret and the science behind the ribs' unique tangy taste. I refuse on principle to point out the correlation between their unique flavour and the ever-present sputum in the bottom of the filthy bath, and I begin to stir in earnest.

By six o'clock we are ready to rock, and the two Chinese chefs arrive for the evening rush. Two portions of chips and four battered sausages with curry sauce later, I am finally rescued from my stoned pork/Jackson nightmare. By eight o'clock we have sold only two chicken-fried rice, one beef curry and two cans of Coke. At exactly half past eight I announce to the ether that Barry Wang is a useless cunt whose business is finished, and we close up early and go to the pub.

7

SUNDAY NIGHT UP the town is a multifarious collection of miscreants and loners who haven't stopped guzzling from the night before, or the night before that. We choose the Bramble bar, which squats halfway up High Street. There are four people in the pub. Two English fishermen, Chalky the barman, and a well-known alcoholic substitute teacher. We place ourselves on high stools and are two pints into the future when Barry announces that he's closing the Chinese for a month to get his head around 'the financial end of things'.

'It'll take you a month to get your head around nothing?'

'I've had enough of you today, Vincent.'

'Don't call me Vincent.'

'The shite only hit the fan when you arrived.'

'Only my mother calls me Vincent.'

'You two stoned out of your trees all day is the problem.'

'Stoned? Us?'

'I'm not fucking blind. How am I supposed to run a restaurant with Keith Richards and Betty Ford on the books?'

'I'd better be Keith Richards.'

'Are you listening to me, Jonty?'

'We aren't on the books.'

'Yes, you are, Vinny.'

'Keith Richards is a legend.'

'You don't put anyone through your books!'

'What would you know about my books, Vinny?'

'Who are you, then?'

'What?'

'If I'm Keith Richards and Vinny is Betty Ford, who are you?'

'I'm the fucking boss.'

'So you're Bruce Springsteen, then?'

'Who said I was Betty Ford?'

'I'm not being a chick, Vinny.'

'She didn't smoke gear, anyway. She was a beer monster.'

'Would the pair of you just shut the fuck up?'

Chalky bangs three pints of Harp down in front of us on the bar. 'On the house. Now why don't all three of you shut the fuck up?'

Barry hands myself and Jonty twenty quid each to tide us over, and apologises for not being able to do any more. He looks completely miserable as we sip in silence and the English fishermen sit in silence and the well-known alcoholic substitute teacher dances in silence beside the broken jukebox in the lounge.

'Come on, Barry, you're not totally skint, are you?'

'Mind your own business, Chalky, and get us another pint.'

I wink at Chalky, telling him to ignore Jackie Chan or he'll have a tantrum and wreck the place. He winks back at me to say he knows the score but if Hong Kong Phooey gives any more lip he's going out on the street on his hole.

Chalky is the best barman in town. Six foot two of effortless ginger composure. I worked with him myself in this very bar when I was only fourteen. It was my first job and Chalky, although five years my senior, took me under his wing with aplomb. He taught me how to pour pints and how to drink them. He taught me how to handle money without freaking out and how to handle drunken arseholes without getting punched in the mouth. As it's a Sunday and dead, he closes early and joins us at the bar for a pint. The English fishermen sit on by the fire, discussing bream stocks, while the alcoholic substitute teacher undulates by the silent jukebox for the enraptured audience that lives somewhere in the malted depths of his imagination.

'He looks like someone trying to get out of a jumper that's shrunk.'

'Does he come in a lot?'

'Saturday and Sunday night without fail. Gets his drink and heads straight to the jukebox. Whatever type of music is playing he slithers around to it like a big brainy eel.'

'Does he only dance like Jagger?'

'To everything. You want to see him grinding away to that rave stuff. The kids feed him drink and put weird music on all night for the craic.'

'And he dances for them?'

'He dances for himself. Never says a word to anyone, just drinks Powers whiskey all night and gets his freak on to the tunes.'

'But there are no tunes.'

'Jukebox has been broken for two weeks but he comes in and dances beside it anyway.'

'Begs the question that, doesn't it?'

'Which particular question would that be, Jonty?'

'The "Is the music in the jukebox or in his fuckin' head" question, *Vincent.*'

'Right. I'll let Jagger know the encore's over. Barry, get rid of Birdseye and Pugwash, and, Jonty, you can roll one of those wee Christmas cigarettes you two boys are so fond of. You got a jumper to cover that T-shirt, Vin? There'll be fanny hanging around up town.'

It's cold outside after the fiery embrace of the pub. The sudden change of environment exacerbates the effects of the marijuana and alcohol, and we traipse and giggle our way up High Street past the town hall and into the Triangle, which is a square at the top of a hill. Why it's called the Triangle I have no idea. It's clearly a fucking square. Teenagers hang around here during the day, smoking and looking moody, and drunk men hang around here at night, smoking and looking horny. Surrounding the square are a Woolworths, a bank of phone boxes, an off-licence, and Maguire's, a massive barn of a pub that sells booze to anyone old enough to wear shoes. It's still open, and we fall through the front door laughing hysterically at nothing in particular.

We are received like the Four Horsemen of the Apocalypse on their night off. Silent indignant stares guide us to a snug opposite the bar and, like naughty schoolboys, we try not to catch each other's eye as we park our arses on the cold wooden benches. There is an upstairs section, which at weekends bulges with drunken teenagers, and this vast downstairs affair, which every night acts as a pseudo members' club for Round Table associates and Masonic Lodge affiliates who think they own the town. They wear Polo by Ralph Lauren and they only drink gin with tonic. They smoke large cigars and talk in loud voices about golf handicaps, provincial rugby and their business interests.

There is a handful of them in tonight, standing holding court at the main bar. It is considerably easier to generate volume and to talk down to peasants when you stay on your feet. Beneath them a chastened spotted teenage barman scurries about fetching drinks, emptying their ashtrays and mopping up the waste and effluent that gets spilled on the bar from all the shite they're talking. I'm transfixed by this downtrodden acne-ridden servant as I walk towards the bar to get my round in. No one has ever had this many spots, have they? Not just on their face, anyway. I mean, if you took all the spots off their back and arse and grafted the fuckers onto their face you might just about end up with this septic pus-ridden Third World trauma. I order my round in stoned slow motion, and I'm thinking about the personal health implications of drinking anything from a glass that has even flirted with this freak's fingers, when I become aware of a low, monotonous humming in my right ear. I turn slowly in that direction, and after a few seconds my eyes refocus on the bloated porcine face of Finbar Regan, self-anointed king of the knob jockey rugby fraternity. The incessant boring satisfied drone is coming directly from his snout.

'I had to head south this morning, Cormac, to WD a new meat supplier. I woke late with a stinker, jumped in the wife's Beamer and drove to Galway in less than two bloody hours!'

'Finbar, you mad bastard, what do you mean by "WD" a new meat supplier?'

'Wine and dine, Alistair. I mean wine and fucking dine.'

The hash has given everything new meaning and detail but my senses are only capable of functioning in single file. My ears shut down as my eyes pore over Regan's fuchsia-toned well-fed face. My God, he actually is a pig! I no longer see a red-haired, red-faced bullshit merchant and restaurateur. Before me stands a large, arrogant pink swine, snuffling and snorting and farting all over the bar. With a sudden jerky flourish, Pig Man whips his Hamlet cigar to his snout and takes a long, cool drag. For the second time in a day my stomach lurches due to the close proximity of an abundance of pork.

'What is it with today and all the fucking pigs?'

Half of the people in the bar are staring at me and the other half are looking nervously around for the law.

'You having trouble with the cops, son?'

The power returns to my ears and I'm back in the room having a conversation with Pig Man. This is more than anyone needs, four pints and five joints into a Sunday evening. I hadn't even meant to speak. My senses are so confused that I voiced a thought that was only meant for myself. I've spoken to none bar the other three Horsemen of the Apocalypse in the last four hours, and they understand my special needs. Regan takes another drag on his cigar and blows a tart blend of smoke, mozzarella and garlic into my eyes.

'What have you done, son?'

As I stare at him for ever and a couple of days, Jonty joins me at the bar. 'He hasn't done anything, Finbar, sure. We're just having the few pints!'

'I am not talking about drugs, son. I meant what did he do to annoy the pigs on a Sunday?'

Jonty kicks me hard behind the knee and I open my mouth to speak, but instead of words a little bit of dribble runs off my tongue and lands on my chest, momentarily blinding Michael Jackson.

'The usual, Finbar. Four fellas wandering up the street at night and they can't help stopping us and giving us grief.'

'Barry, I didn't see you there. How's business? You know, you really should try the oul pizzas. I can't sell enough of the fuckers.'

'Business is grand, thanks, Finbar. Same as your own, I'm sure.'

Pig Man sees straight through Barry's noodle-based bravado and Pig Man smirks. 'Don't worry about the cops, son. Do you know which officer it was that gave you hassle?'

My mouth opens again and this time Jacko's perm gets a proper dousing.

'You see, I have the cops in my pocket, lads. There are only seven men in this town that matter, and I just happen to be one of them.'

'Who are the other six?'

Regan smiles, impressed that I've finally spoken. 'You're Kevvie Duffy's cub, aren't you?'

'Yeah.'

'Your da's done a lot of work for me.'

'For which he has never been paid.'

'A big fucking mouth. Well, the apple never falls far from the tree.'

'I'll pass on the compliment.'

I pick up one of our pints off the bar and throw the contents at him, extinguishing his stinking cigar and ruining his expensive brown suede loafers. 'Don't blow smoke in people's faces.'

I hear Barry groan and I sense Chalky rising in anticipation as Jonty picks up an empty bottle and moves forward to stand beside me. Regan hops daintily out of the lager puddle that he finds himself standing in and stares down at his soggy Italian-shod trotters. 'You little fucker . . .'

'One step closer, Fatty, and you'll be back on the bottle.'

Spotty the barman squeaks in panic and twelve hundred zits burst simultaneously, spraying the bar canary yellow. 'We'll have no hassle, lads. Please just calm down and leave.'

'We were leaving anyway, Clearasil, don't you worry about that.'

'You'll pay for this, Duffy.'

'Well, at least one of us will have paid for something then, Pig Man.'

We roll through the Triangle, laughing until our chests burn. The Raven is a bar like any other, but on a Sunday night it has a disco upstairs and you can drink until two in the morning. We are riled up and excited now. Fired by bravado and alcohol, all thoughts of our imminent unemployment have faded, and the prospect of music and girls and more booze drives us up the narrow flight of stairs to the sticky-floored heaven above. Three stonewashed middle-aged women dance around handbags on the windswept overly lit dance floor.

'Smells of divorce in here.'

'I thought you said there'd be fanny, Chalky.'

'Unless I'm mistaken, no matter what shape it's in or how many children have climbed out of it, each of those women is technically in possession of a vagina.'

I take the twenty Barry gave me out of my pocket, hit the bar and order four large vodkas with Coke. 'What's this music, mate?' I have to shout to be heard even though we're the only people standing at the bar.

'It's the Jive Bunny megamix.'

I have to get out of this town. I down the vodka, ignoring the Coke, and order another. The heat hits my belly and quickly moves towards my brain. The bar fills slowly with men. We drink at a steady pace and watch farmers making fools of themselves to music their parents made fools of themselves to.

'You wanna dance, Vin?'

'No, Jonty, I don't want to dance to Eddie Cochran.'

'You're a music snob, Vin, that's what you are. What does it matter what it is if you can move to it?'

'It matters to me.'

'Didn't you ride Sonia Burns out the back of here at Christmas?'

'No, I didn't.'

'Lying cunt. Barry saw you leaving with her.'

We had huddled between the building and an empty skip, saying nothing and smoking fags for warmth. When she pushed her face into my neck and rocked me back against the wall I could feel the beat of the music reaching through the bricks and climbing up my spine.

Will you walk me home, Vinny?

I suppose I'll have to, Sonia.

We had sex in her mother's kitchen. I panicked half-way through, frightened of her da coming down and chopping it off with one of the readily available sturdy knives. She told me she hadn't seen her father in ten years and then she cried as I came inside her. Afterwards we returned to the silence as we smoked more fags in her garage for warmth. I walked home through the early-morning snow, knowing I never wanted to see her again.

'You're lying, you boned her.'

'No, mate, honestly. She wouldn't let me.'

The world stops suddenly and I step off it backwards as the squealing guitar intro to the Stone Roses' 'Elephant Stone' cuts swathes through off-duty policemen and middle-aged women alike, and the dance floor empties.

'I'm dancing now, Jonty, come on!'

I grab him and we hit the floor hard. The Roses are playing just for us and we whirl and spin in demented circles, like a pair of wheels that have been cut free from a speeding bus. Jonty closes his eyes and I swing him round and round, then let him go and he careens off towards the DJ booth, out of his head and out of control. I close my own and suck in the music. It speaks to me. It sets me free.

I stop swirling and stand stock still until the beat fills me and I begin to rock, then step backwards and forwards, like a pendulum, like a metronome, like Ian Brown.

I look at the bar and find Barry and Chalky beaming out at us from a sea of angry, threatened faces. Three minutes, people, that's all it takes. Three little minutes and then you can escape back into the charts and the safety of your little minds. Jonty grabs me by the waist and pulls me to the floor as the track ends. There is total silence as we get to our feet and look at the DJ on his little raised pulpit. The Raven's record-spinner-in-chief is known as 'the Visitor' because he looks like he's merely sojourning on earth as part of an all-inclusive extra-terrestrial package holiday. He is one of the oddest-looking individuals I have ever seen. A pale aberrant gentleman with tiny eyes magnified to the onlooker out of all proportion by the prescription lenses of some hard-core industrial space-age spectacles. The Visitor stares down upon us like the judge in an intergalactic court of music. The people at the bar stare down upon us like the inbred participants at a Mississippi lynching. There is an aching silence, and suddenly the Visitor smiles. He takes off his glasses and his eyes completely disappear, but there's no masking his big cheesy grin as he gives me and Jonty a thumbs-up with one hand and drops the needle on his next record with the other. The keyboard intro to the Happy Mondays' 'Step On' explodes through the silence, lifting my feet off the floor and punching the fuckers at the bar in their stomachs. Barry and Chalky hop down into the arena, whooping and shrieking, like little boys on a bouncy castle, and we meet in the middle and throw each other all over the music.

It's good to dance. For the length of one song I am somewhere and someone else. By the time the first chorus kicks in we are one. We link arms, shutting out the mediocrity of the world, and bounce for all we're worth.

We've had our moment and it's enough. After prostrating ourselves at the feet of the Visitor and sending him up a pint in thanks, we hammer another round of vodkas at the bar. When we've skulled two more Smirnoffs each, Barry announces that he's hungry and we float down the stairs and out into the night.

Chippie Street is pointless on a Sunday, as there are no chips, no girls and no fights, so we'll have to take our chances at the takeaway van that appears after dark in the Triangle. It looms in front of us at the top of the hill. Even in the paltry streetlights its exterior is visibly greasy.

'I am not eating that shite. You'd get the skitter for a week.'

'Stick to the chips and you'll be grand. Don't risk anything that used to swim or walk about.'

The queue is not long but when we get close enough to the front to peruse the array of rancid delights on the menu there is a rush behind us as the Raven empties, and the familiar claustrophobic panic begins to rise through my legs. I order chips, peas, stuffing and gravy and close my eyes amongst the huddle as I wait for Christine to cook it. Everyone knows her name.

'Can I get a battered burger there, Christine?'

'Cowboy supper and a can of Coke there, Christine.'

'Cheeseburger and chips and a battered sausage there, Christine.'

Hurry the fuck up so I can get out of this crush and breathe again, Christine!

I could go down under these feet. Drown beneath the narrow selection of footwear offered politely but at great expense by the town's three archaic copycat shoe vendors. If I had lived in Belfast, would competitive pricing have spared me the annual September fight with my mother, brought on by the soaring price of Adidas Kicks? I recognise a voice behind me as it joins the throng, but I don't focus on it for long enough to put a face to the tune. My mind casts my body onto the ground, but before my imagination can really run riot I'm rescued by Christine as she shoves a heavy paper-wrapped gravy-soaked mess right into my face. 'There ya go, love. Chip, pea, stuffing, gravy.'

As I open my mouth to thank her I'm grabbed roughly by the hair from behind and pulled onto my back on the ground. Calloused skin scratches my cheekbone as hard fingers manoeuvre for a stronger grip on my roots. In a peculiar moment of clarity as it begins to rain boots, I consciously debate whether or not to abandon my chips. Debate complete, I launch them skywards at my invisible foe and roll over onto my stomach where I stare point blank at the cold grey pavement. As I lie here on the lovingly laid council paving stones a solid kick behind the ear awakens something within me and I'm vividly reminded of the crowning glory that was Norman Whiteside's Cup Final goal for United against Everton back in '85. Big, lumbering Northern Irish Norman, God bless him. Another decent boot to the bottom of the back and I retreat to foetal, and wrap my elbows around my ears.

'You're not so fucking smart now, Duffy, are you?'

It was McGullion's voice I'd recognised joining the crowd behind me. If only I'd turned around.

'Not the big hero man now, ya cunt.'

I'm frightened. The rhythm of the kicks and his voice remind me of the hammer on the meat from Saturday night.

We'd had only ten men in that glorious sunshine after Kevin Moran became the first player in history to get sent off in the final. A proper smash-and-grab job, that! That's definitely my kidneys. I'll be pissing blood tomorrow for sure. I keep my arms tight around my head and my focus on the commentary from the Cup Final as I sacrifice my body to the pounding.

Whiteside's onside, Strachan's in the middle.

Biology never grabbed my attention in school but I realise now that I know exactly where each of my vital organs is as they take turns soaking up the barrage.

Olsen is up as well. A goal! Whiteside! That is incredible. How on earth did he get that past Neville Southall?

There is the very loud screech of a car and a lot of screaming from the crowd. Then the kicking stops. Jonty and Chalky drag me to my feet, and as I rise I smile when I see Grant and Kyle at the edge of the footpath. I try to call out to them but I make no sound and then I can clearly lip-read what they're screaming at McGullion as they smash his face repeatedly against the side of the chip van. All I can hear, though, are the United fans as they scream in ecstasy at big Norman from the terraces back in '85. Grant grabs the hair at the back of McGullion's head and slams his nose into the foetid aluminium one more time before letting him drop unconscious into the pool of his own blood that is beginning to mix with the excess grease spilling from the overflow pipe at the bottom of the van. I stare at his pulped bloody face as the lads pull me backwards into a car. When the doors are firmly closed we leave at speed with the FA Cup trophy stashed safely behind us in the boot.

8

MY THIRD MEETING with Kyle and Grant is to be less of a surprise than its predecessors. Jonty and I are to meet them in the Vintage bar at four, as they have a proposition to discuss with us. On Sunday night they'd been cruising town when they happened upon our sorry little scene. They weighed in and made the difference as Chalky, Barry and Jonty fought McGullion's friends, and I took my oil on the ground. Afterwards we'd fled to Chalky's flat to smoke grass and break down thirty years of sectarian barriers. I'd slept on the sofa, assured by all that I only needed Dr Weed to lick my wounds. When Kyle and Grant had consumed all of our gear and listened to the Carpenters' greatest hits three times in a row they kindly taxied everyone home. Once Jonty had sneaked me to bed at my mum's, they explained to him at length what stellar little Catholics we were and how they would like to cut us in on a sizeable drug deal they were putting together.

*

En route to the rendezvous I tell Jonty how fortuitous it was that the two lunatics and I became model friends for a peaceful future, and how they might well have kicked me inside out if not for the crash. We get there early and take a quiet table near the back, praying that no one will see us drinking with Hitler's favourite henchmen. I bite hungrily into the first pint. Sour vapours from the pipes it was sucked through shoot down my throat and claw at the back of my eyes. As I swallow slowly I gag violently. There is nothing to bring up as I haven't eaten since teatime yesterday. I bring the glass back to my mouth for another try and realise that it is Harp lager that gives my dad's farts their unique personality. I hold my nose, open my gullet and pour a liberal splash of Northern Ireland's pride and joy directly into my belly. Hold your breath and count to ten. Pour again and count to ten. The alcohol works fast on an empty stomach and it's kissing me better by the time the glass is half empty.

'I have got to get out of this town, Jonty.'

'Why would you do that?'

'My mother hates me, I have no job, Mark McGullion wants to kill me, and to be honest, mate, because the cripplingly narrow mindset and the pathetic selection of shoe shops are doing my fucking head in.'

'When McGullion gets out of hospital he is not gonna be happy.'

'They didn't let him out?'

'I was chatting to Fiddle Wilson this morning – he's a porter in Casualty. Reckons he'll be in for days. Probably get transferred to Belfast for facial restructuring, whatever the fuck that is.'

'Don't wind me up!'

'Nose smashed, cheekbone shattered, load of stitches where he bit down on his tongue. Right fuckin' mess. Never look the same again, he reckons.'

'Jesus, Jesus, Jesus, Jesus.'

'Calm down, mate.'

'Don't tell me to calm down!'

'Vinny, calm the fuck down and drink your pint.'

The second one smells much nicer. I relish the bubbles as they tickle my insides and a warm glow gradually takes hold of my balls. 'He'll find me and kill me, Jonty.'

'It's a distinct possibility, Vinny.'

'And we live in a town the size of your dick, so it'll take him five seconds to find me when he gets out.'

'He could be cabbaged.'

'What do you mean?'

'If he's brain damaged the cops will get involved, but it's still your best bet. He was beating you up and some Prods he has a history with intervened and vegetablised the cunt, and now society is a much safer place. Might be worth asking Fiddle if he'll let us into the hospital tonight so we can give him a good dig in the head just to make sure.'

Kyle and Grant come through the front door and head for the bar.

'Do you really think they're in the UVF?'

'They're in the UV-fuckin'-something, Vin.'

They materialise at our table with four pints and two huge smiles, like we've been reunited by Cilla Black after unwittingly spending years on separate continents.

'You feeling a bit rough this morning, Vinny boy?'

'I'm feeling pretty black and blue, Kyle, and my head's melted from the vodka. What about yourself?'

'Never better, son. Never better. Right, let's do some fucking business.'

Ecstasy. I know nothing about it apart from the fact it's twenty quid a pop. Jonty, however, is something of an expert. Grant and Kyle are giving us three hundred ecstasy tablets to sell for them at a rave in Portrush on Friday night. When we return six large to the Brothers Grim we get a handy five hundred each. They're quicker than they look and they've done their homework. They need to get rid of the pills as they 'shouldn't have them'. That's all they will say on the origins of the merchandise, but it isn't too hard for us to fill in the blanks.

Jonty explains to me that, in true Northern Irish fashion, not even the loved-up dance scene escapes the constraints of a suspicious psyche. Young Catholics and Protestants go to the thing together, get off their faces together and dream of a brighter future together, but at the start of the evening they split up and frequent separate sides of the nightclub to buy their drugs from their own brand of terrorist.

'You have to be kidding me, man.'

'No, Vin, I'm telling you,' says Jonty. 'I've been three times now, man. The last time me, Fat Davy and Long Jim headed up in Mickey McCann's Nova. When we hit Ned's, me and Mickey turned left and bought our Es off the 'RA and the two boys turned right and bought theirs from the UVF. Then we met on the dance floor and no one said tickety-fuckin'-boo about it.'

'Fat Davy and Long Jim that used to beat Catholics up for having Protestant girlfriends? That Fat Davy and Long Jim?'

'How many other Fat Davys or Long fuckin' Jims do you know?'

'You're off your head.'

'I'm telling you, Vin, they're sound. They're not into that

bollocks any more. All they're interested in is bodybuilding and raving.'

'Bodybuilding and raving?'

'They lift weights all week so that they look hot with their tops off at the rave.'

'Hot?'

'What?'

'You said "look hot with their tops off".'

'So?'

'Do you take your top off when you're dancing?'

'Everybody takes their tops off when they're dancing.'

'Do you look "hot"?'

'Fucking right I do, man. You should see me move!'

'You take pride in your dancing?'

'When I dance people watch.'

'You should charge, then.'

'What?'

'If you take your clothes off and dance and people watch it's generally accepted that they pay for the privilege.'

'You taking the piss?'

'You drive ninety miles with three men to a nightclub where you take drugs, get naked and admire each other's gym work. I think these lads may be into a little bit more than the body-building and raving, Jonty.'

'Shut up, man. I'm warning you.'

'I'm just saying, mate. It sounds highly suggestive.'

'You know nothing about the rave scene because you're into all that indie shite where every cunt's in a bad mood and the birds even wear woolly jumpers in the summer.'

'Do the girls at the rave take their tops off, too, or just all you big bodybuilding boys?'

'Some of them do, yes.'

'There are girls at the rave, dancing about with their tits out?'

'Yes, Vincent.'

'You're full of shite.'

'Dancing about with their tits out, off their faces on pills, getting off with random strangers like me, Mickey McCann, Fat Davy and Long fucking Jim.'

'Is there any room left in the Nova?'

It's well-paid madness but madness all the same. I've never seen five hundred quid, let alone had it in my pocket. Grant and Kyle must have stolen the three hundred ecstasy tablets from their Loyalist paramilitary drug-dealing friends. They can't knock it out to their own side because their own side will torture whoever is selling it and find that the story leads back to Grant and Kyle. So who do they sell it to? The Catholics at the other end of the nightclub. Only they can't do the selling themselves because they're two big sore Prods, who will stick out like two big sore Prods. So they'll pay two young idiots to go to the rave and sell the gear to people they know right under the noses of the IRA. I can see it all before me. I can see that they have offered us a figure we can't refuse. I can see all the girls dancing with their tits out and I can see a world of pain and replacement knee joints and us driving straight towards it in a Vauxhall Nova full of naked bodybuilders.

With their pitch complete, Grant and Kyle leave us in the bar with a crisp-twenty donation to seal the deal.

'Can't we just offload them now and avoid mysteriously disappearing?'

'There's no market for it away from the rave scene or they would have knocked the whole lot out in one go. The only way to get full whack for them is to sell them at the venue for twenties and they need us to do that.'

'Do you think they'll really give us a grand?'

'Once they give us the pills, they already have. We're giving them five grand change and keeping the rest and that's fuckin' that.'

'You really think we can show up in Ned's and start selling pills out of the blue with no one noticing?'

'No. I need to think about that bit, but we have plenty of time.'

'Five hundred quid, man. I could get out of here with that.'

'Where to?'

'Belfast. That's enough money for a deposit and a few months' rent. I could crash on my sister's floor for a week until I find a room, get a job in a kitchen somewhere.'

'You serious?'

'What is there here?'

'You know what, Vinny, I never thought I'd say this but you're right. What is there here but the same small-minded wankers arguing the same small-minded arguments in the same small-minded pubs week in, week out?'

'That was pretty profound.'

'Do you think you have the monopoly on the bigger picture or something?'

'You just did it again.'

'I know a few things, Vincent, and I've seen a few things in my time too.'

'That was truly beautiful.'

'Fuck up.'

9

THREE PINTS LATER we leave the Vintage behind us and head towards the Bramble bar. As we take our usual stools, Chalky appears from the kitchen at the back. 'We're all barred from Maguire's. Barry, too.'

'Barry will be raging.'

'You reckon?'

'About his "professional reputation".'

'Professionally, he has the reputation of someone whose employees have ruined his profession.'

'You just can't get the staff, these days.'

'Well, you can tell him.'

'Finbar Regan went mental when we left last night, and the first thing he did this morning was to go and find your dad, Vinny.'

'You're winding me up.'

'Your dad told him to go and fuck himself with the big wooden pepper mill from his pizza restaurant.'

'That's my da, all right.'

'I couldn't give a shite. It's a dump anyway.'

'Good man, Chalky, that's the attitude. Put us on a pair of pints there.'

'Jukebox is fixed, lads. Stick a few songs on there, Vincenzo, while I change the keg.'

I whack a fifty in the slot. Songs, songs, 50p, none for you and three for me. Van Morrison, Michael Jackson, *Now That's What I Call Music*. Now that's what I call shite. Bomb the Bass, Erasure, Snap, Take That. I panic and hit 'Moondance' by Van the Man. The piano slides in and I relax and begin to slow down. Two songs left, Vin, so don't sweat, son. Two plays, pint on the way, happy days. All the time in the world, my son. Wet Wet Wet, Prince, Alison Moyet, the Shamen. Shite, shite, shite, shite. The Cure, bingo! I run my eyes down the list of songs. 'Just Like Heaven', you wee dancer! One song left. Can't wait for that bass line. Jonty starts towards me from the bar. Panic rising now, he's got suspicion in his eyes and a repetitive beat in his soul. Not on my fifty you don't, rave boy. East 17, George Michael, Duran Duran, MC Hammer, New Kids on the Block. I can feel him closing through the floor. Soft Cell's greatest hits. Fuck me. Marc Almond probably would. Yes! AC/DC! Get in! 'Thunderstruck'! It's not Bon Scott but it'll do. Three songs, 50p, no rave for you, no rave for me.

'What you put on, Vin? Some of that baggy-jumper shite?'

'No, bit of DC, just for you.'

'"Thunderstruck"?'

'"Thunderstruck"!'

'Happy days. Pints are ready.'

There's a smattering of people drinking and most of them are teachers. Finish work for the day, then sink as many pints as possible before retiring to your bungalow at a reasonable hour.

Is everyone in this town a teacher? Where do they all work since the factories closed? Does everyone employed in the education system wear the same jumper? V-neck, diamond pattern. Christmas presents from their kids, who spend the year at school looking at their own teachers in exactly the same jumpers. It's a vicious fucking jumper circle.

'How's the head, Chalky?'

'Better than McGullion's, from what I've heard.'

The well-known alcoholic substitute teacher appears beside me, orders a double Powers whiskey and downs it in one.

'Get him another there, Chalky.' I hand over the money and watch Jagger slither towards the jukebox. He doesn't thank me for the whiskey. He swivels, winks and gives me the finger. At least he's consistent. I bought him a pint last week and he smiled after the first mouthful, then told me to go and fuck myself. Silence follows Van. Sensing the tirade that will accompany the intro to a Cure song I slink off to the Gents. What an intro. The bass thumps in from the get-go in perfect sync with the tom-toms. A guitar joins second time around, mimicking the bass note for note but in a higher, smarter falsetto voice. Third time around and the rhythm guitar kicks, dropping in those big expansive vibrating open chords. The synth asks a question this time, holding chords back by the hair so they're almost out of time and, wait for it, wait for it, wait for it . . . Jesus, it's unbearable, give it to me now – every fibre in my back aches for the release.

'Come on!'

The lead guitar cries in pain, weeping crippled broken drops of gold in a Gothic heart-breaking lament.

'Hey, arsehole, where's AC fucking DC?'

Stay seated during the performance. I like that. Written

boldly in black marker bang in the middle of the toilet door. It's one of the better pieces of bog graffiti I've seen in a while. It's nestled perfectly between *Melvin Hopkins takes it up the arse* and *Shauna Maguire is a RID Harry Maguire is a COUNT*. I stare at this for a time as Robert Smith caresses my soul with a cheese grater. *Shauna Maguire is a RID Harry Maguire is a COUNT*. Maybe I'm reading it wrong because I'm blocked. Does Harry Maguire live in a castle and wear a cape? A RID? ARID! Focusing on Shauna Maguire for a second I conclude that she is certainly fertile enough to support vegetation and that I would definitely plough her furrow and then the penny drops. Shauna Maguire is a RIDE. This artist was clearly kept behind for 'extra' classes. He is trying to explain his lust and need for Shauna while convincing us of his hatred for her brother Harry, but his spelling has let him down badly when it mattered most. The reality of Harry in a Bavarian castle eating Black Forest gateau, however, is a much more interesting visual image than him just being another cunt. The rest of my door is scarred with the usual suspects: UDA, UVF, IRA, LFC, CFC, MUFC, INLA. We live in a country obsessed with abbreviations. Perhaps most of the morons loyal to these groups and football teams can't actually handle more than four letters and therefore it's a necessity. A country full of dyslexic homicidal sectarian counts. The main toilet door bangs and I'm no longer alone. My father coughs outside my cubicle. I know for a fact that it's him from this one barely audible vocalisation.

'You having a shite, son?'

'No, I'm making a pizza.' His piss sounds heavy against the stainless-steel urinal. 'You've had a few, then?'

'Just a few after work, son. You know how it is. See you at the bar. What are you having?'

'Pint of Harp.'

This could go either way, but I'm not getting out of here tonight without some semblance of a conversation about my future. It's been an important movement. I know now what I need from life. To live somewhere with a better standard of toilet graffiti. I step out of the jacks and into a musical void. The Cure have left the building and Jonty is standing beside the jukebox in silence, a pint in one hand, the other thrust to the heavens extolling youth to make the ultimate sacrifice. There is the sound of distant thunder and the well-known alcoholic substitute teacher appears beside Jonty carrying an imaginary Gibson SG guitar. As I pass them, Jonty pokes me in the eye with contempt. 'The Cure? Bender!'

A fresh pint slides in beside my half-finished one. 'Why are you limping?'

An afternoon's drinking and the excitement of my new-found career as a purveyor of class-A narcotics have relieved me of any pain awareness, and I'd completely forgotten that I am in fact a cripple. 'I fell.'

'Why are you pissed on a Monday?'

'Why are *you* pissed on a Monday?'

'I am not pissed. I was looking for you, and I've had to drink beer in order to find you, as you seem to dwell mostly in pubs since you got kicked out of school.'

Touché.

'You watching the United game tomorrow, Da?'

'Probably.'

'The Vintage has a new big screen so you can watch Eric up close and personal.'

'We'll walk it this year, with Cantona playing like that.'

He takes an educated mouthful of beer and lets it settle. His eyes search mine for inebriation. He sucks his moustache. That does not necessarily mean he sucks beer from his moustache.

He could well be pondering his next move. Some people sniff or stroke their chins or stare into the middle distance but my father sucks his moustache. It can also be a temper indicator, but tonight's game feels more like chess than all-out war.

'Where do you get the money to drink all day?'

'Work.'

'Bollocks.'

'Work and the dole.'

'Bollocks.'

'Does it matter what answer I give or will you just say "bollocks" to everything?'

'It seems that you've already said "bollocks" to everything, doesn't it, son?'

He's on form tonight. Ginger, I guess. Yeah, you could only describe that 'tache as ginger. A man with black hair veering towards grey and a vivid ginger beard.

'Spoke to your sister much?'

'No. Spoke to your daughter much?'

We drink for a bit. He has a hard, angular face, but underneath is a soft rounded man. His eyes are shrouded beneath two small forests of tough auburn wire. I guess I have that coming too, angry, out-of-control eyebrows and hairy fucking ears. Angus Young is at full pelt, melting the inside of the jukebox with his nuclear guitar riffs. Jonty and his beanpole of a lead guitarist punch the air in tandem to every guttural scream of 'Thunder!' The majority of the workforce has left. A couple of men are sitting by the fire and I realise that they are the English fishermen from Sunday night. 'How's the fishing, men? Any bream?'

'It's very slow, boy. Won't take a big catch to win the Classic this year.'

'I'd heard that all right.'

'There's a good head of roach around if you can get them in

and keep them feeding, but the big bream are thin on the ground. Do you fish, lad?'

'Used to fish the competitions when I was younger. Me da here used to take me down. We used to catch some serious bags of bream between us, right, Da?'

He smiles as he warms to his favourite subject, the snow-drifts under the big red wiry bowers beginning to melt away. 'Good fun, all right. We'd be more trout and salmon men, you know, but the craic the cub here used to have catching the bream on a roach pole was something else!'

Jonty is on his back now miming Angus's guitar solo, note for apoplectic note.

'You still hanging around with that eejit?'

Our eyes are the same. Maybe grey, maybe blue, maybe bloodshot. I suck on my upper lip. 'How's work, Da?'

'I've put in for early retirement.' He glances along the bar to make sure our chat is still private. 'I'm going to get the pension and go back on the sites. Gerry has a few big jobs coming up that he wants me to foreman for him. One of them is in Dublin for five months. Do you fancy it?'

'Dublin?'

'Maybe you could learn a trade.'

'I don't know, Da. You said yourself I have hands like feet. I couldn't hammer a nail without breaking a fucking window.'

'Well, what are you going to do, then?'

'I'm thinking of heading up to Belfast. Get a job and a flat, see somewhere else for a while.'

He stares at me. Looks deep into me as only a parent or a two-year-old child can. I want to look anywhere else but I'm caught in the tractor beam of a black-and-ginger Death Star. He holds it for long enough until he knows that I'm asking myself questions and then it is over. He looks towards the TV and smiles wistfully. 'Some spot, Belfast. Just watch yourself up there, son. They take their murdering very seriously.'

He'd escaped it all, my father, or had chosen to escape it. His best friend Maurice was in the IRA and Dad had known something was going on. They lived in a small town similar to this one but even more split down the middle by religious hatred. They can all do the hating part but very few of them are actually bothered with the religion. Maurice had decided to fight for Ireland and that was that. He never said it out loud but everyone knew. Bombs started going off a little closer to home than before. The creamery was blown up. A device was found in the post office. One Sunday afternoon the two of them went walking through the fields to the river. They saw two figures by a ditch bordering a couple of fields that lay in their path. As they got closer Dad recognised two local Protestant lads their own age who were now UDR men, part-timers in the British Army. They were hunting rabbits with a couple of terriers and were waiting over a warren for the dogs to resurface. The men watched them approach until they could all clearly distinguish who was who. There was a somewhat pregnant pause while information and reputations were processed, then the hunters panicked. They grabbed their shotguns and jumped over the ditch into the further field and ran. They kept running like their lives depended on it and they left all behind them, nets, coats, dogs, the works.

'They thought we were going to shoot them, son. They had guns but they ran away. I grew up with them, played football with them, drank and danced and chased women with them, and they thought I was willing to murder them. I was guilty by association.'

*

I watch my dad watching TV in a bar and I imagine walking through town knowing that Jonty was a terrorist.

'How's your mother?'

'Angry.'

'I'm not surprised, the way you're getting on. Have you been eating at all or just boozing?'

'Been eating in the Chinese.'

'Yeah, well, that's not going to happen any more, is it? What happened last night in Maguire's?'

'Finbar Regan was giving me shite and pointing a cigar in my face so I poured a pint over him for the craic.'

'That fat prick showed up at my work today. It's one thing getting chucked out of school, but now you're up the town drunk and getting chucked out of bars?'

'So getting thrown out of a pub is worse than being expelled from school?'

'Don't put words in my mouth.'

The snow will freeze over again if I'm not careful.

'You walked away from that school and never forget it. Untouched and untampered-with, thank Christ, which is a lot more than can be said for half this country. Catholic education system's a disgrace. Have you noticed how priests all drive German cars, these days? Every Sunday at Mass we put money in those little pink envelopes so the priests can drive around in big silver BMWs. What happened to giving up your worldly possessions and following the word of God? Wee numbered envelopes, no less. Wee numbered envelopes so they know that you know that they know exactly how much you're donating every week. Fear and guilt. The Catholic Church is one of the richest organisations on the planet!'

He downs the last quarter of his pint and looks to Chalky, who is already pulling his next. I look at Chalky myself and he winks back to let me know I won't be going thirsty. We have an audience now. The English fishermen have slid their stools a little closer, aware they're getting gold dust here that isn't in the guidebooks. Jonty has returned to the bar, fresh from his heavy-metal sabbatical. An older gentleman I don't recognise comes in and takes the seat beyond my dad underneath the television as the dramatic music for the BBC news kicks in and Moira Stuart appears, resplendent in royal blue. Look at her sitting there proudly as always, as she reads us the news from the heart of London Town. She has her collar turned up and her deep blood-red lipstick on. She often reads the news with her collar turned up, like some sort of vampiric Oxbridge Shirley Bassey. Maybe her neck is covered with love bites.

'Bring an apple with you next time, Moira, and let him tear into that, love! I've never been to London, Moira, but I bet it's amazing. So vibrant and modern and stylish. Just like you, Moira. You're positively dripping with style. Unlike that ginger gobshite Witchell that stands in for you sometimes.'

'Vinny, snap out of it, son. Are you pissed?'

'No, I was just trying to hear the news there.'

'Bugger all on the news, lad. We had Radio Four on this afternoon down at the lough. No news and no bream!'

'Do you know who's certainly not on the news?'

'Who, Mr D?'

'I'll tell you who, Jonty. That bastard Father Brendan Smyth is not on the news.'

He's on a roll now and it doesn't matter who's listening.

'That monster is not on the news because he's still on the run over the border in the south. In fact, he's not even on the run. He's living in comfort in Kilnacrott Abbey, being waited on hand and foot by the very Church that kept moving him around and enabling him to abuse those children in the first place. We spent eight hundred years getting the country back from the Brits – no offence, lads, it's good to have you over for the fishing – and then we handed it straight back to the fucking Church?'

Two new pints hit the bar in a percussive amen.

There is total silence, punctuated sporadically by a wet, asthmatic snuffling noise, which is making the hairs attempt evacuation from the back of my neck. I look to the end of the bar and the stool under the television where the older gentleman I don't recognise is crying as quietly as possible into his pint. Tears are dripping from the end of his nose and plopping into the thick layer of cream at the top of his untouched Guinness. Dad walks over to him and puts a hand on his shoulder. 'Did our chat upset you?'

'Bastards.'

'We're just talking about it because it's true.'

'Not you. The Church.'

He weeps openly now and it's terrible to watch. Chalky brings him some tissues while the rest of us stare respectfully at the myriad stains on the old oak bar top.

'In 1976 my son told me something so horrific about our parish priest that I brought him outside into the yard, took off my belt and beat him almost unconscious. A year later he went into the shed, took off his own belt and hanged himself. This year I have finally realised that my son was telling me the truth. I thought he killed himself to escape the madness in his head. He did, but it wasn't his imagination. He came to me because I was his father and he had nowhere else to go. He came to me and I beat him for coming.'

10

MY FATHER HAS three cassette tapes. One has Leonard Cohen's *Death of a Ladies' Man* on side A and various Ry Cooder songs on side B. One contains Bob Dylan's *Highway 61 Revisited* and the best of Van Morrison, and the third contains a selection of rare tracks from Mr Cohen. They are all he needs. I tend to agree. As 'Famous Blue Raincoat' caresses me from the stereo in the kitchen I begin to flirt with feeling an inch less hung-over. The smell of the bacon and eggs helps, and the tea is working to boot. It occurs to me that Mr Cohen as a Jewish gentleman has possibly never sampled the life-saving qualities of fried bacon.

'The flat looks well, Da.'

'It's a kip. When your mother buys me out I'll buy somewhere else.'

We grew up with Leonard. When Dad drove, Cohen's songs punctuated every mile, and when Mum took control of the wheel it was purely Neil Diamond. Either way, our imaginations were in the hands of a melancholic North American Jew. We didn't get it at first, the two of us on the back seat fighting for attention while some gravel-voiced grandfather whinged in the front about a bird called Suzanne with a citrus-fruit fetish, and another bird stuck fast somewhere on a wire. 'You'll appreciate the lyrics when you're older. You'll be glad you listened to Leonard.' Really, Da? Who eats oranges when they're drinking tea? The trippy opening to 'Paper Thin Hotel' floats through the morning and I lay my head on the sofa's arm, close my eyes and picture my dad at the frying pan preparing to sing along. You're getting used to these hangovers, bucko. That's three biggies on the bounce. The side of my head throbs where a boot kissed it two nights before, while the other side of my head throbs just for the sake of it. I let Leonard's voice massage my temples as the sofa sucks me deeper into it, like the needy embrace of a lonely fat girl. The kitchen door swings open and I mouth my father's words in perfect sync as he shouts them over the music.

'"I heard that love was out of my control." Genius, that is, son. He summed the world up in nine words, nine fucking words, son.'

More strong tea and I'm feeling almost human. The thick egg yolk coats the acid in my throat as it trickles slowly towards my stomach.

'That's the good dry bacon I get from Gary in the butcher's.'

'It's the nicest breakfast I've had in a while.'

'You'd still be snoring and farting if I hadn't booted you off that sofa because you drink all night like an alcoholic and sleep all day like a teenager.'

'I *am* a teenager.'

'With nothing constructive to do on a weekday.'

'I have a jobseeker's interview at twelve.'

'A what?'

'You know, a dole meeting.'

'No, I don't know, because I'm forty-five years old and I've never been on the dole. Do you know why?'

'Will I make more tea?'

'Because unlike yourself I am in possession of something universally known as a work ethic.'

'Well, that's what they call it now.'

'What has seeking a job got to do with being on the dole, anyway? Last I heard the two things were not mutually inclusive.'

'It's an effort to get people off benefits quicker. You have to prove you're looking for work in order to qualify in the first place.'

'That's ridiculous.'

'Every few months you're called in to provide evidence that you've been actively seeking employment.'

'Fucking Tories.'

'They can also send you on job interviews in whatever field you've chosen.'

'What's yours?'

'Banking.'

'You can't count.'

'Jonty deduced that there are never any jobs available in banks so they won't be able to send us to any interviews.'

'He deduced, did he? Has he an interview today as well?'

'He does.'

'The pair of you haven't the brains you were born with.'

'It's worked so far.'

'Get off your hole, son, and sort yourself out. I don't want to see you drinking all day and doing horses, like half the bums in this town. Before you know it you'll be in your thirties and you'll have aspired to nothing bar conning the benefits system. And make up with your mother. She's just worried about you.'

He goes to work and I go back to the sofa. I bring the stereo and the two cold bottles of Harp from the fridge with me. *Highway 61*. 'You can kick-start proceedings, Mr Dylan, sir.' Jesus, but the bubbles are great with the first smoke of the day. 'Take it away, Bob.' Beer from a bottle really is something else. It's so cold it takes my breath away between mouthfuls. As the tingle spreads outwards along my limbs into my hands and feet, I stop fighting and sink deeper into the sofa's arms. Think I'll put in for a crisis loan while I'm down at the dole office and go on the session again tonight.

Buoyed by the bubbles I step out into the day and glide towards whomever. As I float past the Railway Hotel bathed in sunshine, a familiar unscratchable itch begins by the third vertebra in my lower back. I know that the itch is linked to the single green car parked on the other side of the road, and I know that no matter what's in the boot or magnetically stuck to its fuel tank I must pass by it in order to get on with my life. Just keep walking and ignore the impact. If it comes you'll feel nothing. You'll be obliterated and will feel no pain. Why is it only single cars that make you feel like this? It could be parked between two others, the one that takes you. I screw my eyes shut until they hurt. Keep moving, just speed up and keep moving. I bang into someone at the back of the queue for the cash machine. Eyes open again, I realise that I'm far enough away from any potential impact to minimise the mutilation. The sweat from my back has run down into my arse and I'm aware of it as I move away again.

When did this start? It must have been after the big bomb. When we sat in silence listening to the screams of our neighbour bringing her toddler down the driveway so that my mother could stare at his raging head wound. My sister and I trying in vain to spell the word 'cenotaph' as my father rushed us upstairs and out of the way in total shock himself and out of control of his mantra.

'It's a dirty act, a dirty act, a dirty act, a dirty act.'

The toddler lived. Neither of our neighbours on the other side did.

A girl I recognise saunters through my reverie, and when the angle between us is wide enough for a sneaky peek at her arse I swing my eyes to the left and find the red cords and stained brown loafers of Finbar Regan exiting the post office across the street. The Market bar is fifty yards in front of me, and before I've had time to deliberate I'm crouched, hidden at the far end of the counter. I can make the back exit beside the toilets in two seconds if he bursts in.

'Vinny, what are you doing, man?'

'All right, Turnip. I'm hiding from Finbar Regan. Stick your head through the door there and see if he walked past.'

Turnip is a barman who is built like a tank that can withstand direct hits from the majority of conventional weapons.

'He's gone past and into Johnson's Jewellers. Come on out.'

'Thanks, Turnip.'

'Heard you threw a pint round him the other night.'

'He was asking for it, man.'

'You want a beer?'

'Haven't a bean on me, Turnip.'

'On the house.'

He pours the pint slowly. It looks great as it turns the boring empty glass into a golden dancing angel. The door opens and a tall, skinny man enters. He takes the stool beside mine. 'Hi, Vinny. How are you, son?'

'Feargal. I've not seen you for ages, how the hell are you?'

It's a stupid question if ever there was one, as the man is clearly very ill.

'Great, Vinny son. How's your da?'

'Do you two not still have the odd pint together?'

'Now and again if I bumped into him we would, but I've been away for a long time. You still fishing with him?'

'I haven't been for a couple of years. I should really get back into it.'

'You have plenty of time.'

Turnip sets a double whiskey with no ice and a wee jug of water in front of Feargal. 'I'm taking the boat out after lunch, Vin. More than welcome to join.'

'Maybe, Turnip, maybe. I have to hit the dole office first, though.'

'You wouldn't pour us a drop of water in there, Vinny, like a good cub? I have a fierce oul shake in me arm.' Feargal tries raising the lightly watered whiskey to his mouth and I watch mortified as the tremor takes control. Turnip has the good grace to turn to a shelf and pointlessly move some bottles around. Racked and twisted from the booze, Feargal can't get the glass to his mouth to take the sip that will actually stop the earthquake. He was close that time. One more go and I think he might make it. The closer to his mouth the glass gets the more violent the shaking becomes. It's as if some intrinsic instinct is trying desperately to stop him ingesting the substance that is slowly but surely killing him. I can't watch this any more. Without saying anything I take his elbow and forearm and guide the tumbler home. He takes half the whiskey into his mouth and savours the burn on his tongue before allowing it carefully down through the sluice gates and into his belly. Together we raise the glass for a second pass and he takes what's left straight down into his gullet, no messing about with taste this time.

'Thanks, son.'

'My pleasure.'

Turnip brings him another double and this time he lifts the jug and gingerly waters the whiskey himself.

'Where have you been, Feargal?'

He spills a little water on the way but it's a totally different arm. He raises the glass to his mouth and drinks, a completely different man. The miracle juice disappears down his gullet and he slams the glass on the bar, like a cowboy, then holds his arm straight out in front of him, pointing his finger and thumb at me like a gun. 'Bang, bang, you're dead. That's some stuff, eh?'

We laugh deep and hard. Turnip disappears beneath the counter, doubled over in joyful pain.

'Where have I been, son? Where have I not fucking been?'

We go at it again, the three of us together. I leave my stool and laugh myself into little spinning circles at the corner of the bar.

'Put young Duffy on a pint there, Turnip, and have one for yourself.'

The second half of my pint is tossed liberally into me as I prepare for its successor. I feel tipsy already, as I'm topping up from the night before and the night before that.

'I was in Cambodia for a while, son. I ditched my practice and headed out there to doctor for a while. I felt like I could do the Cambodians and myself some good, but they have drink on that continent too and I wasn't long draining my welcome dry.'

'When did you get back?'

'I've been in Ireland since Christmas, but I've been down outside Dublin in a drying-out unit with the nuns.'

'Was it any good?'

'Does it fucking look like it?'

Round three really hurts. The laughter from the bottom of the barrel. A dry trapped silent explosion. I grab my new pint and as much of it goes up my nose as into my mouth. 'I think my ma mentioned that you'd upped sticks, all right.'

'How is your mother?'

'She's grand.'

'You still fighting with her?'

'How do you know that I fight with her?'

'Your dad told me you rub each other up the wrong way.'

'Doesn't matter what I do, it would never be right.'

'You've just been thrown out of school. She's probably worried.'

'How did you know I was thrown out of school?'

'It involved telling a priest to go and fuck himself, Vinny. It's hardly a state secret.'

'I'm moving to Belfast to try a change of scene.'

'Your mother is a fine woman. Best social worker we have around here. The people she helps would consider her a bit of an angel. You should sit in on one of her counselling groups some time. You'd get a totally new perspective.'

'You never know, Feargal, maybe I will.'

'The fishing bug will come back too, you know, when you're older and the booze isn't so fresh. Though I've been waiting for the novelty to wear off for forty years myself.'

When I hit the street the fresh air hits me. Not a punch as such but more of a two-pint slap. The twin spires loom before me at the top of the hill, the svelte Church of Ireland clock tower on the right and the recently added pointless monument to Catholic insecurity on the left. Fifty feet between them but a million miles apart. I've wasted too many hours of my life and layers of knee skin in the cold, unwelcoming building on my left, and once, a week after the big bomb, I had a brief peek behind the enemies' walls on the other side of the road. Reconciliation, they called it. Services, sermons and sing-songs for a community united in grief. A community that needed eleven violent deaths even to consider unifying in the first place.

There was a third service that week in the Methodist church at the other end of the town. Catholicism is utter lunacy but at least they keep it simple on the denominational front. The poor oul Prods don't know whether they're coming or going. Methodist, United Methodist, Church of Ireland, Church of England, Presbyterian, Free Presbyterian. I enjoyed the Church of Ireland offering the most. They had cushions for the kneeling-down bullshit, and their choir was actually in tune. No padding on the left-hand side of the road, of course. It's all about hard wood and pain over there. The Methodist church was adorned with Union Jacks and old regimental flags from the Somme. It was more like a war memorial than a place to worship a god. No doubt my Methodist neighbours were equally horrified by the bleak imagery on the walls of St Michael's. It's a strange world where children aren't allowed to watch television after nine p.m. but are forced every Sunday to behold images of a man in a crown of thorns being beaten and nailed to death while his mother watches on, comforted only by his girlfriend, who is a prostitute.

It stinks inside the dole office. Sweat and damp and desperation. John Major's millionaires club. Jonty and I sit in silence with one other punter in a prefab hut outside the main event, waiting with our numbered tickets to be invited into the circus. Mingin McGrath sticks his head round the corner, scans the room for potential spies, then plonks himself down on the plastic seats opposite us. He is clad head to foot like someone who carries speakers around before and after a Guns N' Roses concert. Cowboy boots, sleeveless black T-shirt with effigy of frightened, scantily clad woman on the front, ripped black jeans, and a big angry belt with brass bullets all over it. He is quickly followed by three identically clad heavy-metal benefit bludgers.

'All right, Mingin. How's it hanging?'

'Vinny, what about ye, cub? You got a good story ready for these bastards?'

'Usual bollocks about the bank.'

'Snap. Works every week, man. What about you, Jonty?'

'Allied Irish all the way, Mingin. What about the rest of the band?'

'We're going to count all those dollars together, baby.'

I turn to the punter in the seat beside me whom I have never met. 'What about you, mate? What are you telling them?'

'I haven't figured it out yet, but this banking thing sounds pretty tight.'

'So we're all gonna say we've worked in a bank?'

The door into the main office opens and Barbara the Bastard's prehistoric face enters our collective nightmare. 'Number fourteen.'

The bloke beside me gets up and heads for the door. As he pulls it closed behind him he winks at me gratefully.

'That fucker just nicked our idea, then thanked us for it.'

'Barbara the Bastard gets angrier every week.'

'She gets bigger every week while she's at it. So, what's the band called at the minute, Mingin?'

'Fudgegrinder, Vin. You know the lads, don't ya? This is Weasel, Virus and Simon.'

'You still playing the bass, Weasel?'

'Still keeping it real, Vin. We're playing in the Mirage tonight. You should come. There'll be a proper crew of nutters present and the warm-up act is a hypnotist.'

'If I get this crisis loan I'll be drinking somewhere, that's for sure.'

'You know, Mingin here actually has a wee notion of Barbara. Says he'd love to get her on her own for half an hour and put some rock and roll inside her!'

'Number fifteen.'

OK, don't look at the floor. Just look at Barbara. Look into those frozen bulbous eyes and exude something akin to confidence. 'Which cubicle do you want me in, then?'

'Number three. I'll be there in a second.'

She'll be there in a second? She's going to interview me herself? She never interviews people herself. She just breaks down doors and grunts out numbers. Breathe, man, they have nothing on you. Maybe Barbara knows about the Chinese and that's why she wants to interview me personally. She's clearly packed away a few sweet and sour balls in her time. Maybe she got wind that I was in the kitchen cooking up the double. She appears on the other side of the desk and I jump clean out of my seat.

'Did I frighten you?'

'No.'

'You look frightened.'

'I just wasn't expecting you so soon.'

'You seem very nervous.'

'Nothing nervous about me, Barbara.'

'How do you know that my name is Barbara?'

'Everyone knows that your name is Barbara.'

'So people talk about me behind my back?'

'Jesus, no. I mean, it's just common knowledge that your name is Barbara, like it's common knowledge that my name is Vinny.'

'I didn't know your name was Vinny.'

'Really?'

'Not exactly common knowledge, then, is it?'

'I guess not, Barbara.'

'Stop calling me Barbara.'

'Sorry.'

'Sorry, Miss Clark.'

'Sorry, Miss Clark.' I smile sweetly and refrain from telling Miss Clark that the collective community has subconsciously changed her surname to 'the Bastard'.

'So what have you been doing to find work, Vincent?'

Ten minutes later I'm leaving with a smirk on my face and three crisp tenners woven through my fingers. It means that next week's fortnightly cheque will be lighter, but I'll have the five hundred by then and my smirk will have flowered into a large cheesy fuck-the-lot-of-you grin.

'How did you go, man?'

'Barbara genuinely believes I want to work in the financial sector.'

'She interviewed you herself?'

'In a cosy wee cubicle. This is your big chance, Mingin. Just don't call her Barbara when you're shooting your load inside her.'

I smoke outside while Jonty acts his heart out for a lonely civil servant. If we were in any way organised we'd have an address across the border in the Republic and we could be picking up the Irish dole as well as the British one. That's what most people do. The Irish lift is twice as much, too. You get paid double time in a free country for doing fuck-all. He appears beside me wearing a grin and waving a ready-rolled joint. Afterwards we float back to the Bramble bar for a quick one, and Chalky has them on for us before we even get to our stools.

'Crisis loan, lads?'

'You'd better believe it, Chalkster!'

'Have you heard the news?'

'What news?'

'It's nearly one o'clock. I'll let Moira tell you herself. Prepare yourselves for a shock.'

He turns the telly on and leaves us to our pints. The first shock is visual. Instead of Moira's magnificence we are greeted from the London studio by the scarlet pimp himself.

'I can't fucking stand Nicholas Witchell.'

'Why do you hate him so much?'

'I don't like the way he looks at Moira.'

I down half my pint in a oner and watch Witchell as he first coughs politely, then drops the largest news-based bombshell for twenty-five years: 'The IRA has announced a ceasefire after a quarter of a century of what it calls its "armed struggle to get the British out of Northern Ireland". The statement came just after eleven a.m. and said there would be a complete cessation of military operations from midnight tonight, and that the terrorist organisation was willing to enter into inclusive talks on the political future of the Province. There is scepticism in the Loyalist community and celebration in the Catholic areas of Belfast and Londonderry. The Irish foreign minister, Dick Spring, said the statement was historic and met his government's demands for an unconditional end to IRA violence.'

'Only the Mexicans down south could appoint a foreign minister called Dick Spring.'

'The war's over, boys.'

'For now.'

'Another pint to celebrate?'

'Fuck that, I need some fresh air. Let's go fishing, Jonty.'

11

MUM ISN'T HOME. There is half a cardboard box in the door frame, covering the hole left by my recent tantrum. It looks like the patch on the glasses of the kid who always used to piss himself in primary school. At the back of the garage I pull away some sheets of fibreglass and uncover my old fishing-tackle box. When I open the lid the comforting smell of ancient ground bait rises to greet me. On Friday nights we would mix it with water and roll it into big moist balls and dump it into the lough beside the pier to tempt the fish into my swim. 'Another bag of bream this week, Da, and no one's gonna stop us! We're going to win the league!' We did win the league. Some said it didn't count as I had help from my father, but I didn't care about the winning. It was those evenings with him that mattered.

'Do you remember the Pet Shop Boys' song "What Have I Done To Deserve This?", Jonty?'

'Load of shite.'

'It used to float up the lough from the fairground when I fished the summer leagues with my da.'

'Pair of fruits, aren't they?'

'It was pure anticipation, waiting for the float to disappear.'

'With a pair of keyboards.'

'They were always playing that song and "A Little Respect" by Erasure.'

'There's a theme developing here.'

'The float always disappeared too. We were some team.' I let the lid of the box slam shut again and then I kick it as hard as I can.

'You all right?'

'Yeah, I'm all right. Are you all right?'

You drew lots for a different pier each week, the sun beating down and no school for two whole days to come. Good song, that. Good song. 'I think you'll find that only one of the Pet Shop Boys is gay, Jonty.'

I smash an old windowpane that is perched beside the fishing rods. Foot clean through it, electrifying screech as it shatters, satisfying crunch underfoot. A hammer now. I don't remember lifting it but there is a comforting weight to it in my hand, and nobody will be messing with Hammer Boy. It rips cleanly into the back of the old TV but stays there, and I really have to yank the fucker to get it back out again. Like one of those bayonets with teeth sawn into it, nice clean entry but your guts and sundry are coming with it when you call it home to yours truly.

'Vinny, stop it, man. What are you doing?'

A smashed uppercut hammer blow to the bottom of a shelf next. The whole shebang goes skywards in slow motion. Solid garage things hang like balloons in the oily garage air. More feet now, heavy feet: going to kick the life out of this cabinet with my heavy wrecking feet. The door's tough but a hard-heeled one-two in the middle bursts it clean open, lock and all. A swinging leg now, almost gentle, a deadly pendulum up through the line of shelves from bottom to top.

'Stop it, Vin! Please, stop it, man.'

'Sure the war is over, Jonty!'

Bottles and jars on the floor now, up and down, up and down. Who keeps jars? Who needs fucking jam jars? He's on my back trying to stop me but I shrug him off and kill the jars. The hammer's weight sings to me. 'Use me, use me, use me.' One vicious blow and the saddle flies off my bike, up over my left shoulder towards the daylight beyond the garage door. Power surges through me: an unstoppable force for bad. My hammer sinks into the side of the old canoe again and again and again. It sticks hard this time and as I fight to release it for another attack I feel the energy drain from me and I know that my work here is done. Jonty is hunkered down to my left with his arms over his head as I scream as loudly as I can and throw the hammer through the closed back window of the garage.

'It's all right, mate. I'm only having a laugh. I'm only messing about, man. I'm only having a fucking laugh.'

Turnip's boat is moored at the back of the police barracks. You can still see the patches of new tile where the IRA mortars bit into the roof in '85. Eighteen home-made rockets out of the back of a lorry. Nine of them found their mark. Best guerrilla army in the world, the posh British general on the news said. I was proud at the time, even though I knew I wasn't supposed to be. No one was killed that day but there were plenty of other days to make up for it. One of the quietest parts of the Province, as the Troubles go, but we've had our share. The cop gunned down outside the church in front of his kids. Bubbles Love shot dead walking home one night because he lived on the Catholic side of town. The two farmers stabbed to death by British soldiers with a pitchfork. The cop eviscerated by a radio-controlled bomb in a bin outside the toy shop. Eleven innocents crushed by a wall on a Sunday morning. It's more than enough. It's too much.

'Nice fucking boat, Turnip.'

'Let's go up to the mouth of the Ballycassidy River first. The harvest trout will be running the rivers after that flood on Saturday. We'll get as far up the river as we can and we should have a good chance of hitting a big brownie.'

The boat is open-ended with no cabin at the front to protect us from the wind. Jonty sits in the prow with his tongue hanging out, like a small dog, I slump in the middle with my demons either side of me, and Turnip steers from the engine at the rear. We pass Portora Royal School on our left, the last collection of buildings on the edge of town. We pull in to the side and navigate the lough gates, a massive concrete expansion that spans the lake where it narrows, controlling water levels for the town. Man's last effort before we mean nothing on the other side. We wave to the gatekeeper as he disappears behind us and head off out into open water. My back loosens as civilisation recedes. Not had the rage for a while now, Vinny. Thought the black mist had passed now, Vinny. Got to keep the head together now, Vinny.

A startled heron appears out of the rushes in front of us and slopes off over the water, like a pterodactyl. Nothing has changed here for ever. One hundred and fifty-four islands, twenty-six miles of open water and no people. The August breeze is lukewarm and we strip to the waist to let it under our arms and into our pores. The rushes stand proud, burned brown against the vivid green hills. The big lough stones reach out from the low summer waters, bleached altar white by the sun. It takes half an hour to reach the mouth of the river. Turnip snaps the engine down two gears and we move upstream and away from the lough. When we can go no further by boat we tie up to a tree and hoof it to the pools and shallow runs where the trout will be lying in wait.

Jonty decides to stay in a large meadow above the river to smoke a joint in the sun, and Turnip will walk to the road that crosses the river to fish the pools above the bridge. I will fish from the first streams upwards and meet him in the middle. It's just you and me now, Mr Trout. I know where you'll be. I'm going to sit downstream behind you and wait for you to show. I slide down the steep bank to the river, using the friction of denim on grass to slow my descent. The nettles sting my naked sides and back, but I ignore them as I'm focused and here in this moment. Under a hanging tree at the bottom of the bank I crouch by a long, slow pool that rolls calmly past my toes. Upstream to my right the water flows fast into the pool's head before steadying out as it deepens. This is where you are. I'll smoke and watch and listen and wait. Wee fish take surface flies at the back end of the pool but I'm not disturbing proceedings for small fry. You're running hard now, Mr Trout, gorging yourself on little roach before heading upstream to make little trout. I sit on the stones and light a smoke. There is no rush. I could try an exploratory cast and maybe hook a fish but I prefer to wait. No sound of the road from this side. Turnip crossed and shot along the far bank like a man possessed. Summer birdsong and an audible hum off the heat. There! A swirl in the water at the top-right end of the pool. I can't cast from here in case it falls short and you get spooked and run. Jeans rammed into socks, I move left to the bottom of the pool. Have to climb in gently, and far enough away so you don't feel me coming. Nothing at first, then a cold shock as the water finally soaks through the suede of my desert boots. It's ice cold but I acclimatise quickly and the water soothes my feet and calves. Gotta go deeper, Vinny, gotta go deeper. Up to my balls now. It's so fresh and cold that I'd love to just take off and swim. Here is perfect. Rod above my head, like a Japanese soldier in a Burmese river. My first cast is short. I've got to pull the spinner past your nose. It's working well on the retrieve. Twisting and dipping, the little silver blade spinning on its axle as the water is pulled fast over it. That's got to look tasty, Mr Trout. A handsome little silver fish. There is a rock at the top beyond where you showed. If I bounce this off the face it will fall right in front of your snout. Perfect. Quick flick to attract your attention. Now reel. Bang! I lift the rod tip over my right shoulder so that the pressure keeps you hooked. You rip your head from side to side, desperately trying to throw the bait, then tear off down the pool past my left leg. Give him line, give him line, don't try to horse him or you'll break the lot. You make a strong run and my reel becomes an angry wasp spitting venom by my wrist as you strip yards of line from its spool. I can feel you, Christ, I can feel you. You leap from the river and are framed moment-arily, buttery gold against the dark brown chocolate of the riverbank.

'I'm in, I'm in! Turnip, I'm in!'

You take another run up the pool towards me and I retrieve line fast, desperate to leave you no slack. The herd of elephants crashing through the undergrowth behind me tells me that Turnip is on the scene.

'No way, man. You in?'

'Big fish, man, big fish. He ran straight at me and now he's gone deep.'

I can see Jonty's head bobbing above the tall grass as he runs towards us. When he reaches the bottom of the bank he looks like he might be sick. One should never exert oneself after smoking an entire joint.

'I thought you fell in.'

'No, I'm in, into a fish, a good fish.'

'It's kinda the point of fishing, isn't it? I ran up here like a fanny because I thought you were drowning.'

'Just shut up and get ready in case I land him over on your side.'

'I'm not touching your fuckin' fish, mate.'

Turnip has gone to the far end of the pool and has his landing net off his back and ready. 'Is he still on?'

'Think so. He's sitting on the bottom or under a stone and I don't want to risk pulling the hooks out of him.'

'If he's as big as you think he'll run again.'

His sentence is still warm when you come off the bottom and rip through the middle of the pool like a motorboat that has lost control.

'Look at his back, Vinny! He's a brute!'

I hold on to you for dear life as you begin to panic and thrash.

'Vinny, that is a cracking fish. Do not lose that fish!'

I feel every bump and twist along the line and through the rod as you shake your head, like a dog with a dying rabbit. You run to the back of the pool again and I know that your strength is ebbing.

'I'm going to try to get his head up and glide him over your net.'

Turnip enters the water and crouches with his net submerged. When I drag you over its mouth he lifts and your race is run. You are dead by the time I come ashore, dispatched quickly with a rock to the back of the head.

*

Twenty minutes in the boat and we're tying up to the pier on Devenish Island. A short walk inland, then a few hundred yards sideways and left, and there is a little cove with fishing options and a spot for a fire. I take Turnip's knife and gut my trout at the water's edge. Head off first, then a clean slice from his throat to his cock and his guts spill out easily. Knifepoint run along the spine to release the sac of hard black blood and he's ready for eating.

'How big's your pan, Turnip?'

'Take his tail off and we might get him into it.'

'Sure if we don't we can saw him in half.'

'Some fish, man. Some fish.'

I put him in a plastic bag and leave him in the shallow water to stay fresh with a big stone holding all in place.

'Where will we put the baits?'

'One on each side next to reeds. The pike love a bit of cover.'

Naked I swim to the reeds, holding the head, tail and guts of the trout above my head. I sink them here as the smell will attract any passing monsters. I swim to the bottom and hold on to a large rock, letting the silence wash over me until my lungs can take no more. On the surface again I float on my back and let the cool water kiss my battered body. The middle of my back is still very tender from McGullion's kicks, and the bruising on my legs has turned a dark urine yellow. Ashore I sit in my finest as the late-afternoon sun does its best to dry my jeans and boots. Jonty sleeps nearby in the grass, knackered from all the excitement and marijuana. Turnip sets up two pike rigs on heavy rods. Half a mackerel secured on a couple of treble hooks suspended under a big red float. He dumps one expertly where I had dropped the guts and casts the other at distance to the other side of the bay.

'I could never have thrown it that far, Turnip. You're a beast.'

'Flat-out training three times a week, man.'

'Sleeping Beauty there was talking about bodybuilding and rave dancing the other day.'

'Yeah, sure, I've seen him up there leaping about like a buck eejit. Stripped to the waist too, the skinny wee bastard.'

'You go to Ned's?'

'Ned's is a religion, Vinny. It's bad manners not to go once a month.'

He heads off for a mooch around the island, and I sit in silence and stare at the big red float.

There is a ceremonial quality to our dinner. Our noble sacrifice does himself proud in death, and Turnip is quite the cook. Butter, black pepper and garlic do justice to the solid pink flesh. We chuck spuds into the hot ashes and let them cook slowly. Two tins of baked beans are set into the embers until they start to bubble. On our plates the potatoes break open, like big balls of flour, soaking up the tangy juice from the fresh fish and the sweet sauce from the beans. When the plates are licked clean, we drink tins of warm beer and tell Turnip about our change of career.

'Do you think we're mad?'

'Don't try and sell them in the club.'

'Where else are we gonna sell them? Outside Mass?'

'The woolly faces will have the club boxed off.'

'But they won't know who we are.'

'You try and get rid of even ten pills in there and you're dead men.'

'Should we not take the drugs from these two at all?'

'Take the drugs. Just don't start selling them until the club is over. There'll be an all-night party at the caves or the White Rocks. That's where you get rid of the Es.'

It's beautifully simple, though still incredibly risky. The paramilitary dealers will be hanging around the after-parties too, but they can't control the outside the way they can a nightclub.

'There is another issue here that we haven't even considered, Jonty.'

'Your latent homosexuality?'

'What if the drugs are duds?'

'Oh, I've considered that all right, don't you worry.'

'He tells me you're off when you get your money.'

'Belfast, I think, Turnip. Bit of a change. There has to be more to life than here.'

'There's always more to life if you keep looking.'

'Guess so.'

'But if you're always looking you never actually see anything.'

'Do you ever dream about women?'

'I used to, before I started jerking off.'

'Not those kind of dreams, Jonty.'

'Dreams about the woman of your dreams?'

'Yeah, Turnip, that kind of thing.'

'However perfect she is in your dreams, she'll still take half of your house in reality.'

'It's always the same dream, man, exactly the same.'

'Do you wake up sad that it's not real and it takes a few hours to shake off the disappointment?'

'Always. I can never properly see her face but it's the same girl every time. She starts to look at me over her left shoulder but I always wake up before I can see her properly.'

'How will you know her if you ever meet her, then?'

'From the sound of her laugh.'

'I want to get away from here too, you know. You're not the only man with dreams and aspirations.'

'Where to, Jonty?'

'The States. I've always been fascinated with the States. The women, the food, the cars, the works.'

'You should go, then, mate. It would suit you: they're all really loud and full of shite.'

'Vinny's right there, kid. You'll be running the country for them in ten years.'

'I've been thinking about it today. Could use the five hundred to get on a plane. I know lads in New York working illegally. Reckon they could get me a job in a bar no bother.'

'I'd never have thought that you'd want to leave here.'

'What is there for me here, Vin? New York would be grand but San Fran is the dream ticket. San fuckin' Fran-fuckin'-cisco.'

'Not the first place that springs to mind for the repatriation of Ireland's biggest homophobe, Jonty, but each to their own. What about you, Turnip man? You ever think about getting away?'

'Sometimes I get the bug all right, Vinny, but every time I've tried to leave something happens and this place calls out to me. I'm meant to be here and here I will stay.'

'Heavy, man.'

'We should go, lads. I'm working tonight.'

'Yeah, and in a few hours we're picking up the pills from Torvill and Dean.'

'Now that's fucking heavy, man.'

12

THERE IS A police road block at the library so we instinctively skirt the island to avoid the pigs. The law is out in force tonight, though, and as we step onto the East Bridge we're waved to a halt by a bearded officer of the peace.

'Where you headed, lads?'

'Just up the town for a pint, Officer. What's happening?'

'There is the Loyalist parade coming through, last one of the season. We're expecting trouble, boys, so keep your heads down.'

We'll be keeping our heads down all right. The night of an IRA ceasefire that was greeted like a triumph and the Orange Order are in town. There'll be blood on the streets tonight for certain. We wander into the Bramble bar for our final drink before becoming purveyors of all things illegal. Chalky pulls us a couple of pints. We are the only punters in the house, bar an older couple sitting in the silent wake of bad decisions.

'Quiet tonight, Chalk.'

'What do you expect with the circus in town?'

On cue the din begins in the distance. The bass drums send huge deep shells far out over no man's land, while the Lambegs and snares hammer an angry staccato of hatred out from the trenches. No one speaks as the creeping barrage approaches. They will have gathered at the bowling club on the outskirts and will slowly parade through the town to remind the world who really wields the power. Chalky puts the news on the telly and turns the volume up to drown out the distant rage. It's Moira o'clock, and she looks cracking tonight, framed perfectly between impressive blue shoulder pads as she informs us with a twinkle that the Russian Army has left Estonia and that the Irish Republican Army is indeed still observing its ceasefire, ten hours after first declaring it. More importantly, she tells us that this evening Wimbledon Football Club chased shadows as United beat them comprehensively, three–nil, at Old Trafford. King Eric, Brian McClair and Ryan Giggs. As the news comes to an end, the cacophony of hatred peaks as they stop outside and leather their drums for all they're worth, beating our brains out for God and for Ulster. They will repeat this little ritual at the front of every Catholic-owned pub tonight. With the curtains drawn and the doors locked we sit in silence, individually contemplating violence as the hairs stand solid all over our bodies.

'Here's two quid from the till for the jukebox, Jonty. Whack on as much rave music as you want. It can't sound any worse than that shite.'

We meet them in the Vintage bar. They smile out at us from two petrol-blue marching-band uniforms with red and white and orange piping.

'Were you watching the bands, lads?'

Grant thinks it's the funniest thing he's ever heard. Kyle

knows it's the funniest thing he's ever said. Grant hands Jonty a ten-spot and sends him off to the bar for pints.

'I didn't have you two down as musical types.'

'Well, we're not really, Vinny. Grant clatters a big drum and I throw a baton up in the air and catch it now and again.'

'Right.'

'Gives us something to do bar the pub, and sure the camaraderie is brilliant.'

'Cool.'

'I got the insurance all sorted on the sister's car, Vin.'

'How?'

'No one knew who was driving.'

'Right.'

'She said it was her so that the insurance will pay out. When her premiums go up I'll pay her the difference.'

'Handy.'

'You're full of chat tonight, son. You nervous or something?'

'No.'

Jonty arrives back from the bar with four golden pints on a silver tray.

'How's your injuries from Sunday night?'

'Fine.'

'We saw your friend today, limping through town with a head like a watermelon. We considered getting out of the car and finishing him off.'

'McGullion's out?'

'Don't worry, we have your back.'

'Right.'

'His face is hilarious – he'll never see out of his right eye again. It's like a piss hole in the snow.'

'I'm sure he can find me with his good eye, Grant.'

'Want us to sort it?'

'What does "sort it" mean exactly?'

'Sort him.'

'I get that he would be the person involved in the sorting, but what exactly does a sorting constitute?'

'Doing the cunt.'

'Yeah, again it's the terminology I'm struggling with here, Kyle.'

'You know where we are if you want it sorted. Just give us the nod.'

'No, honestly, I don't want it sorted, it's fine. He got his rewards on Sunday night so let's just leave it at that.'

'Whatever you want, son. Whenever.'

He means it too. It's wholly heartfelt. When you have survived a near-death car crash together, what harm is the odd sorting between friends? It's his gift to me. A violent, capable, benevolent big brother dressed in a rainbow-coloured military uniform, like the wanker on the lid of the Quality Street tin.

'How do we know the drugs are real?'

I stare shocked at Jonty as he stares coolly at Grant and Kyle. He seems calm, relaxed, a Zen master at one with the situation.

'That's a very fair question, son.'

'Yeah, Kyle, so what's the very fair fucking answer?'

'The Es are real. Doves, strong ones. Trust me, this shit's the real McCoy.'

Two lads I went to school with enter from the back and head upstairs towards our table. I see them preparing their hellos when they spot me, but their greetings stick in their throats when they see who I'm sitting with. They say nothing and hurry past.

'Let's do this. I want to get home before your brethren start a drunken witch hunt.'

'There'll be none of that tonight, Vinny. Sure it's just a bit of music and a wee march through the town. It's our culture, after all.'

'Yeah.'

'We can't be fighting with you anyway, now that you've declared a ceasefire.'

This produces their longest laugh so far. I give up trying to read into it when they double over for the third time.

'You got a bag with you?'

'No.'

'Right, Vinny. Here's another tenner. You're going to the bar this time. When you stand up, take your jacket off but hang it on the back of my seat.'

'Got it.'

'Your concern about the gear was understandable. Our concern is seeing our two favourite Fenians in here with our money at three o'clock on Saturday afternoon. We know where you both live and who you live with. So don't fuck it up.'

The Triangle is empty. The gentlemen from the marching bands are drinking now. When they are told they can have no more they will step out of the pubs and fight with anyone who didn't get dressed on a time-machine excursion to 1865. The town is crawling with policemen and I have three hundred ecstasy tablets stuffed down my balls.

'Where are we heading?'

'Let's get Turnip's keys and hang out in his house until we can get our shit together.'

'If I'm lifted with this lot I'm looking at ten years easy so let's get the fuck out of here.'

Dad is drinking in the Market bar and has beers on for us before we close the gap between the door and his moustache.

'All right, Da?'

'Good, son. You?'

'Grand, grand.'

'Jonty?'

'Grand, Mr D, just fuckin' grand.'

'Right, well, I'm glad we've established that everyone is grand. Here's a pint to celebrate.'

Turnip winks at me as he puts the drinks before us. There is a sea of sweat gathering on Jonty's forehead. Before he gets the beer to his mouth the salt will have blinded him.

'Did you watch the match?'

'I didn't see it, Da, but Moira told us all about it earlier.'

'Who's Moira? Your girlfriend?'

'Moira Stuart that reads the news.'

'You drunk again?'

'I've only had two pints.'

'Cantona's first class, just first class, lads.'

'He's the man all right. Da, I caught a brute of a trout today.'

'You did not!'

'Up the Ballycassidy River. It was the guts of four pound!'

'Get away outta that!'

'He did, Mr D. I watched Turnip there land it for him.'

'Did you eat him?'

'We did surely. Gorgeous flesh, much nicer than salmon.'

'Where are you two coming from anyway? The sweat is lashing off you.'

'Just walked through town there, Mr D. Sure you couldn't relax. The place is crawling with Prods.'

'I know. They stopped outside there and performed a wee private concert for us.'

'Cops said there'll be trouble tonight, with the ceasefire and all.'

'Yeah, son. Only country in the world where a ceasefire is a fucking problem.'

'You should go into politics, Mr D.'

'The Prods are annoyed because they don't believe the ceasefire is real, and we are annoyed because the Prods are still up the town banging their drums and intimidating everyone.'

'I'd buy you a pint back, Da, but I'm skint until Friday.'

'Always skint but always in the pub, son. You should sell your secret and solve your problem.'

Turnip puts three new pints on the bar.

'We really have to get going, man. We only popped in for your keys.'

'Drink this first. That was the boss on the phone. Cops are going to close off the housing estates. Everybody's out on the streets and the petrol bombs are being filled as we speak. Burn, Hollywood, burn.'

He throws his head back and bellows like a bull, or maybe a lion or maybe just a fucking mad man. When we've necked the pints Dad heads off to try to make it home before the world ignites. Jonty takes a couple of plastic bags from behind the bar to the toilets and splits the drugs into two smaller prison sentences. Better five years apiece than one man growing old alone. We plot a route to Turnip's house that might just enable us to avoid the law. When the lads in the estates start rioting the pigs will search everyone found out on the streets. If we head past the cinema and up through the back of the hospital we might just be able to sprint across the main road and up into the safety of Catholic Cornagrade.

13

ULSTER SAYS NO
BUT THE MAN FROM DEL MONTE SAYS YES

THERE IS NO standing outside the cinema discussing mysterious messages tonight. We take it in as we pass, stuck somewhere between a jog and a run in a vain attempt not to look too suspicious.

'At least it's topical.'

'Whoever he is, he's smoking more than tobacco.'

We leave the Ritz behind us and head towards the back entrance to the hospital.

'He must have worked at the cinema.'

'Not necessarily.'

'He has access to the letters and a set of keys.'

'All right, Kojak, we have exclusive access to Magilligan Prison stuffed down our trousers here, so hurry the fuck up.'

The police are at the bottom of Mill Street beside the Gaelic football field, and as they see two figures turning into the hospital driveway they start to shout and run towards us. We sprint uphill towards the Victorian workhouse. We need cover, we need to lie down. In a steep wet cleft between the hospital car park and the Gaelic football pitch we suffocate quietly as the police pound by just above us. Ten seconds later there is a loud whooshing sound and the roar of a crowd and the police come sprinting back past our heads again.

'Petrol bomb?'

'Think so.'

'Jonty, what if it's a woman?'

'A policewoman?'

'No, the cinema sign, dude. We've been assuming that it's a man.'

'It's a man, Vinny.'

'How do you know?'

'Chicks aren't funny.'

'Fuck me.'

'Women are not funny, and this person has shown an aptitude for humour with a limited supply of letters.'

We smell it first. The caustic stench of burning tyres. A torched car shoots tongues of greeting into the night as we haul ourselves from our trench and crawl towards the fray. From our stomachs under the fence at the edge of the road we watch as the petrol tank explodes, then listen with our faces in the dirt as parts and pieces bounce and fizz along the tarmac. In the darkness beyond, a hundred voices soar and a primal war cry rises in triumph above the roar of the flames. The car groans again, spitting and farting angry sparks, livid at the abrupt unconditional end to its journey. On the far side of the road lies a steep grass bank. If we can scale this and cross the wooden fence at the top we can take our places in the rioters' choir and scream ourselves dry. Fingers grip the tarmac lip of the road as we prepare for the short sharp burst of energy that will carry us to freedom. The car whimpers and shimmers one hundred yards to our left, casting eerie shadows onto the riot shields beyond. Three hundred yards to our right two armoured cars block the road and protect the line of policemen who are sharpening their bigotry as they bristle for a fight.

'We're piggy in the middle here, Vin.'

'I'm gonna shout across and let them know we're coming in.'

'Coming over.'

'Coming in, coming over, what's the fucking difference?'

'You've been watching too many Vietnam films, mate.'

'Laaads! Laaads, we're coming over from the hospital. Don't throw anything until we get across.'

'They can't hear you over the fire.'

There is a loud pop and a plastic bullet bounces down the road ten yards beyond our noses.

'They're firing baton rounds!'

'Well, they're hardly gonna throw fucking eggs, Jonty.'

A voice now screaming from the top of the verge: 'Who wants to cross our road?'

'Vinny Duffy. It's Vinny Duffy and Jonty McManus.'

Another plastic bullet bounces in front of us and bites into the wood above my head.

'Hope you've brought us some Peking ribs, lads! We'll provide covering fire from up here. Run like fuck when I shout, "Up the 'RA."'

As we rise and cross the fence the cops charge us.

'UP THE 'RA! YOU BLACK BASTAAARDS!'

A battalion of masked figures appears along the opposite fence, hurling stones and bottles and bitterness at the approaching police. Like Butch and Sundance, we break cover and pelt across the hard black road, which doubles in width the second our feet find it. In my peripheral vision I find a blurred line of men crouched under plastic shields as bricks and planks and paving stones rain down on them from above. A plastic bullet bounces once to my right and flies through the gap between us, inches from Jonty's arse and a millisecond from wiping out my future family. Uphill now, calves burning as we push hard into the grass. Hands stretching out for us, strong, urgent, friendly hands. Four hooded men jump across, bellowing, and we're grabbed and pushed and kicked up and over the fence to freedom.

'All right, lads, did you drop the chicken curries on the way over?' He pulls his mask up off his face and gives his trademark howl.

'Turnip! Jesus, Turnip! Some buzz, man! Some buzz!' I grab him in a bear hug and we fall again, laughing like mad men. 'You were only in the bar half an hour ago!'

'When you left I closed up and legged it before they cordoned the whole place off.'

'Come on, let's give this filth some stick.'

Turnip turns to address his troops. There must be a hundred men and boys lying along the fence, armed to the teeth with shattered public property. 'What do you reckon, men? Two more volunteers for the Cornagrade Brigade?'

The scream is deafening. We're pulled and pushed and hugged and congratulated for our daring mission across the hospital road. It has already entered the folklore of the night. I take a rock from someone's hand and run at the fence, tossing it as hard as I can in the direction of oppression.

'We need to lie low with all this gear, Turnip.'

'No bother, boys. Let's stash it at mine. There's a wheelbarrow up there too, and a few hundred bricks, so we can start to supply the front lines.'

We cover our noses and mouths with ripped towels from his bathroom. The Lone Ranger and Vinny the Kid. Turns are taken on the wheelbarrow but it ends up being quicker to let Turnip do it himself. The police have made ground and now occupy the T-junction around the burning car. The Toyota Corolla had been hijacked coming out of the hospital gates and immediately set alight. The bricks are dumped at the spot where we crossed the fence, and two men with block hammers start breaking them up. Half a brick is a better missile than a full one. Other men bring other weapons. Sticks, bottles, bits of lead pipe, roofing slates, anything that can be launched by hand in anger. A team with a hosepipe siphons petrol from cars on the estate and sends it directly to the factory that someone has set up in a garden. When the petrol bombs are brought to the front they're carried in plastic lemonade crates. Crate upon crate of Molotov cocktails. The kids have collected these bottles from houses on the fizzy-drink run and stacked them lovingly back in the crates they arrived in. There will be tears in the morning when they realise they won't be getting any ten-pence pieces for the broken charred glass that coats the hospital road.

A masked man runs crouching along the fence towards the enemy line. He lights the rag at the top of the bottle and waits. After five seconds he rises and bowls it towards the government forces. 'Have some Fanta, you bunch of cunts!'

We roar and run at our foe. We have the high ground but they have the riot guns. The deadly plastic projectiles rain down amongst us.

'Take cover! Take cover!'

We bury ourselves in the earth behind our fence and listen to the officers screaming at each other below.

'Cease fire! Cease fire!'

The second the popping stops we rise again and hurl for all we're worth. They retreat behind their riot shields and reload their weapons. Ground has been made and ground shall be held. The crates are passed along the line to the men closest to the Crown. Fifteen, twenty, thirty orange vapour trails arc towards the men in uniform. The sound of smashing glass, then *wump, wump, wump* as the petrol ignites. With the road ablaze we scale the fence and throw ourselves downhill towards our foe. Smoke and flames shield us from view, but they only have to shoot in our general direction and they'll find soft targets. The rounds smash into the road and bounce up amongst us.

'Man down! Man down!'

There are men down everywhere. A boy of around fourteen gets up from the ground beside me but collapses beneath his own weight. His right knee has been shattered by a plastic bullet and he screams in agony as Jonty and I drag him to the foot of the hill. A new roar erupts above us. Reinforcements. A large group of lads from the Mount View Estate surges down the grass verge and advances rapidly in the other direction towards the line of police at our rear. With our ranks and confidence swollen, we leave the boy where he is and stay on the road.

'SS RUC! SS RUC! SS RUC!'

The police at both ends retreat. They take refuge by their armoured cars and beyond the burning Toyota. We surge forward again, a wave breaking on the thing that it hates. Most of the infuriated faces are covered with the scarves of football teams from the very country they rage at. Tyres screech out of control behind us and we scatter, sure that we have been out-thought. It is not a police vehicle, though, but a shiny new Mercedes that has turned into the road from Mill Street and found itself wedged between two lines of riot police. It tries to reverse but gets nowhere as our boys spill back onto the road and surround it. Trapped in the ring, it spins and panics, a shiny silver bull that can smell its own end. A brick shatters the back windscreen and the driver slams down hard on the horn, which cries shrilly like a frightened piglet, but is instantly drowned in the human bay for blood. A second brick bounces off the front windscreen, creating an intricate spider's web of cracks, and Finbar Regan falls out of the driver's door and crawls forward, where he lies petrified under his personalised number plate: P177A 9.

'Not the Merc, lads, not the fucking Merc.'

A rain of missiles and the car's resale value depreciates rapidly in front of Pig Man's terrified greedy eyes.

'I'm one of you, for Christ's sake! I'm a good Catholic!'

Feet and weapons now as the mob surges forward, taking turns to smash and kick at this symbol of wealth.

'I'm just trying to get to my restaurant. Sure don't I always make you pizza, lads?'

'You always overcharge us for pizza, you greedy bastard.'

Turnip, his face wrapped in a red-and-white scarf, a brick in one hand and a petrol bomb in the other, crosses the road and stands before the petrified dough mogul. 'In light of the fact that our pizza money paid for this car, we are commandeering it on behalf of the Cornagrade Brigade.'

'Not the car, lads. Jesus, I'm only trying to get home.'

'Well, you took the wrong route tonight, Fat Boy.'

Turnip finds me in the crowd and waves me towards him. 'Volunteer, you will torch this car for God and for Ireland.'

I take the proffered petrol bomb and play with its weight in my hand. Someone else steps forward and offers me a green Clipper cigarette lighter. I can't look directly at Regan for fear that he'll recognise my eyes. It was only two nights ago that I stood directly in front of him, pouring beer over his decadent shoes. Exhilaration floods me. My hand shakes, but from adrenalin, not fear. A warm tingle spreads along my back and into my buttocks and groin as I step towards the car. How long do I count for? It won't matter in an enclosed space, will it? It's all gonna burn, baby, burn. I steal a cheeky glance at Pork Chops as I light the home-made fuse. A rumble begins deep in the belly of my audience. The sound of anticipation. The slow-building drone of opposition fans putting a player off at the penalty spot. The petrol-wet rag takes instantly, and I count to three, step forward, and smash the bomb through the open driver's door and onto the dashboard with all of my might. The crowd's crescendo peaks as the flames take hold, and we run for our lives away from the imminent explosion. As we watch from the safety of the slope a police snatch squad dashes forward from the hospital entrance. Three of them at speed behind two shields. They bundle Regan to the floor. 'I'm an innocent man' is heard above the cheers of the crowd, but the Queen's forces are taking no chances tonight. He squeals now, like the pig that he is, as he's grabbed under the arms and dragged towards the safety of an armoured paddy wagon.

The Mercedes explodes. We scream in delight. A bigger force ventures forward now. Six men with shields in a flying wedge formation, like a flock of black armoured geese. They veer sharply off the road on to the foot of our verge and when everyone runs uphill the boy with one knee can't and he is beaten mercilessly for all to see. The frustrations of an evening taken out on one fourteen-year-old boy by six grown men with sticks. We watch in silence as they guarantee his lifelong immobility.

He cries like the child he will no longer be and when he starts to scream out for his mummy we can take it no longer. Beneath a hail of stone and fire we charge, howling, at the bastards. They make the mistake of trying to manhandle the boy back to their own lines. If they had just dropped him and run they would have made it. There is a dull smashing sound as the line of rioters consumes the policemen. Men trained with truncheons lash out at youngsters wielding pipes ripped from under their mothers' sinks. We are too many. A cop goes down and as his helmet rolls away I momentarily see the life terror in his eyes before a broken brush handle is brought down heavily into his teeth. The police behind the burning Toyota scream like a pack of teenagers and rush forward to rescue their friends. The cops on the ground receive final boots and lashes, then we turn and run back towards the safety of our own burning car.

Something hits me on the right thigh and I fall hard onto my knee. I am hit again across the lower back and I know that it wasn't a plastic bullet. I roll away and turn to face my attacker. It is not a policeman wielding a baton but a rioter holding a hurley stick. He takes another swing at my head, and as I duck out of the way he runs on towards Regan's blazing Mercedes. Liverpool scarf, black jeans, denim jacket. I follow him through the smoke until I find Jonty crouched, catching his breath.

'Someone just hit me and it wasn't a fucking cop.'

'You're just confused in the madness.'

Behind him on the other side of the road a Liverpool-scarfed face waves a hurley stick at me. He runs his finger along his throat, then lets the scarf drop to reveal his swollen red face.

'Jonty. It's McGullion.'

'Your head's away with it.'

'He's standing behind you staring right at me, so don't look around.'

'How many of his boys are with him?'

'He's on his own, but they'll all be here somewhere.'

'They'll be too busy fighting the police to worry about Elephant Man.'

'What are you thinking?'

'Let's do him, Vinny, or it'll drag on for ever.'

'Do him in a Grant-and-Kyle kind of way?'

'Let's give the prick the hiding of his life in front of everyone and that'll be the end of it.'

'You and me?'

'We can take him, Vin, no bother.'

McGullion starts towards us brandishing his hurl like a scythe.

'You should probably turn around now, Jonty.'

He runs his finger along his throat again and my demon snaps.

'He's getting pretty close, isn't he, Vin?'

Who do you think you are?

'He's really close now, Vin. What's the plan here?'

Who do you fucking think you are?

'Vinny, seriously, what are we doing here, man?'

A bass line begins to pound inside my head.

'Vinny, snap out of it. Where the fuck is Turnip?'

Copper pipe now. Don't remember lifting it but it's in my hand.

'We could cut him in on the drugs money, Vin.'

Comforting weight to it, too. No one is gonna mess with Pipe Boy.

'Vinny, wake the fuck up!'

The drums kick in and join the bass line filling my head and chest.

'You familiar with the music of Rage Against the Machine, Jonty?'

'What?'

'They're a band from the States.'

'Jesus.'

'You love the States, don't you?'

'Yes.'

'I think you'd like them. Very angry music.'

As he closes in, the lead guitar and vocals complete the wall of sound inside me. As he meets me I drop to one knee and smash his left shin bone with my pipe. He collapses to join me and I stave in the left-hand side of his face with another blow. A sweet sharp note from his crushed cheekbone whistles along the hollow in my heavy copper pipe.

'It's like Mass down here, isn't it, McGullion? It hurts your fucking knees!'

He topples sideways as straight as a post and I am up quickly and on him. My feet find unprotected spots at will and I drive into his stomach and testicles again and again. I am grabbed from behind and lifted clean off my feet and he rolls away and is saved.

'Who do you think you are now, you cunt? Who do you fucking think you are now?'

I hear my pipe hit the ground as I swap it for the lit cigarette that Jonty is shoving in my face. The smoke taken deep makes my head spin and my legs buckle slightly as I exhale and watch McGullion twitching gently on the floor. He looks peaceful, rocking himself to sleep as the thick black blood spills liberally from his ripped mouth onto the tarmac and runs away towards the line of policemen.

'You all right?'

'Think so.'

'Pet Shop Boys?'

'Similar.'

'Is he dead, Turnip?'

'He would have been if I hadn't stopped Chuck fucking Norris here.'

We drag him to the grass verge where the rest of the wounded lie. The police will pick him up later and bring him to hospital before charging him with rioting and public order offences. It has not been McGullion's week. Sirens wail and we turn to face the wall of police. There is confusion as to where the noise is coming from, then shouts as our scouts come pelting back from the darkness towards the inferno.

'It's the Brits! The fucking Brits are coming!'

14

WE ARE TRAPPED, boxed in on the road between two burn-ing cars. The police we can handle but the British Army are different gravy. They are famous for firing more than plastic bullets into a crowd. The police cheer as youths panic and scramble up grass and over wood. Why they cheer is beyond me, as it clearly means they can't handle their own battles. They have been positively humbled by the youthful angry Irish fans of the English Premier League. Behind us there is a huge crash as the first army Saracen smashes through Pig Man's expensive German bonfire and into yielded territory. We stand at the top of the grassy hill and watch the carnage below. There are only two ways into this housing estate. The rest of it is ringed by the lough. We are fugitives now, trapped between the forces of law and nature.

'Where's Turnip?'

'He was here a minute ago.'

'Should we head for his house?'

'Look, they're moving!'

Buoyed by the arrival of their cousins from the mainland, the filth nose their vehicles towards us and begin to move into the estate. Word soon arrives that the Brits are doing the same thing on the road four hundred yards to our south, and as panic ensues, an army of masked individuals scatters at speed into a warren of alleys and gardens. The doors are all shut and the curtains are drawn tight. The narrow, empty little streets are a mess of broken bottles and ripped-up kerbstones. We sprint into an alleyway by the side of Turnip's house.

'Don't move! Stay where you fucking are!'

The London accent frightens the lives out of us and we turn on our heels and hare off again. I glance backwards and see three fully armed British soldiers giving chase. They are much bigger, but we are far faster. Past the sweet shop we sprint and over the railings into the primary school. Mrs Love's classroom rushes towards me and I stumble past it. I learned to read in there. Some fucking good it's doing me now. The tuck shop looms, then the bent rusted goal posts on the bad gravel football pitch with the slope in the middle.

'The roof. Head for the fucking roof!'

Jonty takes my foot in both hands and thrusts upwards as I pull myself skywards. I reach down and yank him to me, then we roll and roll until we are safely away from the edge. If I hold my breath any longer my heart will burst. I suck in a thin stream of warm summer air, barely opening my lips for fear of making a sound. The stars are very bright tonight. I can see them all clearly as I lie on my back looking up at the sky, while my heart bounces around desperately, trapped in a ribbed cage. I roll my face to the right to exhale and feel warm rough roofing felt on my cheek. Ten yards away from me lies a body. I stifle a cry as it moves. It pulls its scarf down, puts its fingers to its lips and winks at me.

When I raise myself slightly on one elbow I see them all. The roof is covered with fugitives. Every one of them went to this school and at some point climbed onto this roof to retrieve a badly aimed football. Every one of them has followed his instinct tonight, back to where he knows best. I try not to laugh out loud. Faces from the past visit me now as we keep our silent vigil. Brother John, Brother Nathan and Sister Pat Rooney. Master McConnell wandering the corridors with his ruler at the ready, and Mr Knox from the country with his Gaelic football obsession. Damien from Armagh, Gareth from Falkirk and Pat from Derry, with his endless collection of expensive *Star Wars* toys. Fred Atini from Nigeria. Did that really happen? His father was a doctor who came to work in the hospital, and poor Fred was left in here to study with the savages. We were only eight. He was the only black person we had ever seen. Nothing bad was ever said or done to Fred, but he must have gone home traumatised every day all the same. For the three months that he attended the school he stood at a rusty goal post every lunchtime eating his sandwiches, while the rest of us queued up to feel his hair. He was the first picked in every football team even though he couldn't hit a barn door. We thought he had to be good; he was black, after all. I shake with laughter and Jonty kicks me hard in the arse. Baldy, Boot, Minker, Moss, Hego, Hoppy, Fla, Santy, Cambo, Gilly, Doc. Not a Christian name amongst us. Not in this town, my friend. Your nickname is a badge of honour. Jonty kicks me again and I roll around to face him. He points down to the schoolyard below and touches his lips.

'They ran in here, a whole fucking gang of the little cunts.'

Collectively we stop breathing again. They are directly below us.

'Spread out, cross the pitch and we'll flush them out. There's no way they're scaling that wire on the far side.'

We watch them in our minds. A capable uniformed line moving stealthily across the schoolyard. When it comes the defiant roar is less assured than before. More of a question mark than a statement. The sounds of battle commence and we allow ourselves to look out over the edge. There are lads running from behind every prefab classroom. The army goes in hard. There is chaos at the post where Fred used to get his head rubbed. There are screams of agony as riot sticks bounce off flesh and bone. Another war cry now and the volunteers on our roof rise and hurl their stones at the backs of the English men. Half of the soldiers break ranks and come screaming back towards us. Frustrated trained killers who have been reduced to the role of policemen. Cooped up in barracks on foreign soil and itching for a fight.

'Fuck's sake, boys, I thought we were lying low up here. Let's move, Vinny, move.'

We run across the roof, skittling through our own men, and start to climb up onto the next level.

'Where are you two chickens going? Stay and fight.'

These two chickens ain't getting roasted by the British Army, mate. They have three hundred Es to sell at a rave on Friday night, where all the women have their tits out. There is no one else on the highest point of the roof so we run to its furthest edge, and then I freeze.

'I can't, Jonty!'

'We have to climb down that drainpipe and out of this school or we are dead men.'

'They won't search up this high. Let's just lie low up here until it's over.'

'Oi! You two!'

I slide down the drainpipe faster than I have ever run. I grip it tight with my fingers and most of their skin is left on the sandstone behind it by the time I hit the ground. Jonty is right behind me and then we are gone, across the car park and over the railings onto the road at the sweet shop. Another shout goes up to our left where the cops have established a checkpoint. They come after us now too, as we head downhill for the piers and the lough. We run along the path beside the water's edge and dart into the large adventure playground halfway around the loop. We can hear English voices to our right further along the path and we know that we are trapped again.

'Take your clothes off.'

'It's hardly the time or the place.'

'Take your clothes off. We're getting in the water.'

I'm already in my boxer shorts when he gets it. We stuff our clothes underneath the metal slide and pull our shoes back onto bare feet. We move quickly before the gap is closed. Shod but completely naked, we creep back across the path to the water's edge. As the voices get closer we push through the tough barrier of bulrushes and float out into the darkness.

We swim for what feels like an age, then tread water and peer back into the world that we have left behind. There are no lights on in any of the houses. The estate is a dark silhouette clinging to the top of the hill where it was built in the fifties. A pall of smoke hangs over the right-hand side of the picture where the two cars still burn behind the trees. The sound of baton rounds being discharged echoes through the concrete structures of the play park where we have hidden our clothes. Voices blurred by anger and distance float to us from where the riot still breathes, further and further away across the freezing dark water.

'I'm cold, Vinny.'

'It's just the shock of the water. You'll get used to it.'

'I'm not much of a swimmer, man.'

'Let's get to Portora School on the other side. It's not that far, and the swim will warm you up.'

We strike out for the opposing shoreline, and as the battle song recedes behind us, a new song reaches me from somewhere much closer. It comes in bursts at first, but grows in confidence as he masters keeping his nose and mouth above the water. It's not entirely in tune but I clearly recognise the first verse of 'Nightswimming' by REM. I have never heard Jonty singing before. He pauses for a second to float and rest, letting the piano and strings have their musical break. They play in my head, too, as I tread water beside him, and I smile to myself as he brings the lyric back in perfectly, never missing a beat.

We sit at the school boathouse and laugh at the world from which we have escaped. There is an outdoor swimming pool in the grounds above, where we can hide out until the fighting is over. The water heated by the endless summer soothes our freezing war-torn bodies. Cleansed and warm-blooded again, we sit on a diving board and pore over the adventures of our night. A caretaker from the school appears below us suddenly and tells us that we are trespassing on private property. Jonty hops down from our perch and stands before the man as naked as the day he was born, explaining to him politely the situation.

'We have just fought the pigs and the Brits in the same night, so if you think we're retreating from you, you need your fuckin' head examined.'

He leaves to phone the police, who, we know, have bigger fish to fry tonight than two shrivelled dicks in a private swimming pool. The sky is flecked with grey when we swim back to our clothes. There are still sounds of conflict on the morning air but they are further away now and far between. Turnip's back door is open and we hold each other in the kitchen in triumph.

'Look at the two gay boys back from the big riot!'

A cheer goes up when we enter the living room, which is packed tight with veterans and warmed through with marijuana smoke. In a hushed party atmosphere for the remaining hours of early morning we share joints and stories and beer.

'Did you see the Brit on the ground?'

'What about Regan's face when Vinny torched his wheels?'

'How many do you think were lying on the roof?'

'Jonesy is never going to walk again.'

The curtains are opened and we wave out at unmasked stragglers sauntering casually home from their war. Turnip enters from the kitchen with a mountain of bacon sandwiches that disappears in a starving scrum. When breakfast is over he sits beside me and lights a joint the size of an Orangeman's flute. 'Some buzz, man. Some buzz.'

'Yeah, Turnip. Some buzz, man.'

'Where did you two hide out, then?'

'In the water, Turnip. We hid out in the water.'

Ned's

1

SIX MEN IN a Vauxhall Nova is a very tight fit. When two of them are bodybuilders it's preposterous. Tucked into the back seat behind Mickey McCann, the pilot, I survey the scenery through the window against which my face is crushed. Long Jim rides shotgun while Fat Davy licks the other rear window behind Long Jim's head. Mickey's best friend Bingo McCaffery and Jonty are sandwiched between Schwarzenegger and myself. We blow town at eight, leaving time for a pint on the way in some village that I've never heard of. Like myself, Bingo McCaffery is a Ned's virgin. Unlike myself, he won't shut the fuck up about it.

'What time do we drop the pills, boys? Should we take them now, boys? Get the tunes on and get this party started, boys!' He's called Bingo as he has an incredibly irritating habit of asking you a question, then answering it himself, like a bingo-caller with his cheesy numbers and rhymes. Unused to a captive audience that can't escape the minute he opens his mouth, he makes hay, melting my brain as I strain against the door, desperate for the release of a quick but painful death.

Before leaving town we had sold eight of the pills to fund our evening's work. Expenses that can be deducted from our earnings in the morning. We need beer money, petrol money and entrance-to-the-club money. Turnip bought two, 'Just to have in-house for emergencies,' and our travelling companions purchased the rest. One for Mickey, one for Bingo and two each for Davy and Jim. Maybe the bigger you are the more ecstasy you need to find the love.

'You been before, Vinny? No, you haven't. You into the rave music, Vinny? No, you're not. What did you think of Cantona's goal the other night, Vinny? An absolute screamer!'

I'm granted a reprieve as Fat Davy shoves a joint in Bingo's mouth. Davy is a different man from the one I used to know. He used to be a big fat fucker. Now he's just a big fucker. His arms are like legs and his legs are like small independent countries.

'Not seen you for a while, Vinny.'

'Been a while all right, Davy. Think the last time I saw you was over my shoulder.'

He laughs. I don't. The fear is still almost palpable.

'We were young and stupid then, Vinny.'

'Speak for yourself, Davy. I was just young.'

He laughs again. It is warm and genuine and genuinely off-putting.

'Always the witty bastard, Vinny. You're a good man with the words.'

I wait for his colossal arm to sneak behind Jonty and Bingo and twist my head off my shoulders but it never comes.

'When did you get into the bodybuilding, then, Davy?'

'First time I went to Ned's was a watershed moment in my life, Vinny. When the love kicked in I stopped kicking heads in. I had an epiphany. I didn't hate anyone on that dance floor, not even the Catholics. When I stopped dancing and just stood there, mesmerised by the beauty of everyone around me, I realised in that very moment that I was a big fat bastard.'

'Fair enough.'

'The following Monday I joined the gym. Two months later I took my first course of steroids, and here I am a year after that, looking like a fucking legend!'

He roars his own approval and Long Jim joins in from the front. Bingo hands me the joint and starts fucking talking again. 'What weight are you now, Davy? Fifteen stone. Who are you training with, Davy? Long Jim, there.'

I take a few drags of the joint and pass it forward to the driver. With my right cheek pressed on the cold damp glass I close my eyes and try to drop off. For the umpteenth time Bingo asks for the tunes, and Jonty produces a cassette tape from his pocket and passes it forward to Jim.

Bang! Bang! Bang! Bang!

I guess I won't be sleeping then. I have to shout to be heard over the racket: 'Fuck me, Jonty, it sounds like a binmen's convention.'

'It's not Binman, it's X-ray.'

'There's actually a DJ called Binman?'

'He's class. He played Ned's last month.'

I close my eyes again and try to locate this tune that they speak of.

Bang! Bang! Bang! Bang!

It sounds like a Soviet tractor plant. Words now, but not sung, screamed at me by an irate Cockney man. They are not part of the tune: he is howling over the top of it like some old-time dance teacher off his tits on whatever Davy takes at the gym.

> *Ready for some harmony in the place?*
> *Are you fucking ready?*
> *Come on!*
> *Let me see those hands in the air!*
> *Let me hear ya now!*
> *To the beat now!*
> *To the beat, to the beat, to the beat now!*

'"Some harmony in the place"? It sounds like a gang rape!'

'It's what the night's called. It's run by a crowd called Harmony. Same tonight. Tonight's massive, man: X-ray and Carl Cox!'

I am aware, from the strange light in Jonty's eyes and the excess dribble coming from his mouth, that this is big news. It must be the rave equivalent of the Stone Roses and the Happy Mondays playing on the same bill. I close my eyes again, wishing they were my ears, and pretend to reserve judgement until we get there.

'Do you like a bit of X-ray then, Vinny? No, you don't.'

'It's a wee bit hectic, Bingo, but the lyrics are fucking amazing.'

The village is called Ballykelly. The pub is like any other, only the beer is flat. Jim buys the first round, then bends his back so that he can hand mine down to me.

'Why do they call you Long Jim? Because you're tall.'

'Yes, Bingo, because I'm tall.'

'How tall are you?'

'Six foot five last time I was measured, but I just keep growing.'

SKINTOWN

'Surely you're done now. You must be nearly twenty.'

'I'm twenty next month, Vinny, but I'll grow yet. I have a touch of giantism, so bits of me just keep stretching.'

'Giantism?'

'Look at the size of my face compared to Bingo's!' He sits on a seat and puts his arm around Bingo's ribcage, pulling him close until their faces almost touch. With him seated and Bingo standing, their heads are at roughly the same height. 'See?'

'Yeah, your face is much bigger than his, but is that not because all of you is much bigger than him?'

'No, Vinny. Look, I'm growing, I'm on the move. My hands are too big for my arms.' He reaches forward and grabs my left hand, which completely disappears inside his.

'You have big hands all right there, Jim, but again isn't that just the big-all-over thing as opposed to the bizarre-growing-syndrome thing?'

'I'm telling you, Vin, my arms and legs are abnormally long for my torso and my hands and feet are abnormally big for my arms and legs, thus rendering me completely abnormal.'

I marvel at his appendages as I stand beneath his seated frame. He could kick a hole in a man's chest. Right through the middle with a size-fourteen Nike. That's Jim's route home if you piss him off.

'What about your langer then, Jim? Like a baby's arm!'

I don't wait for the giant's reaction: I head for the bar. Hopefully he'll kick a hole in Bingo McCaffery, thus rendering him fucking quiet.

There is a woman serving behind the bar. She could be fifty or she could be thirty-five and desperately unhappy. There is neither eye contact nor smile as I order the pints. As I wait for them I bend my knees and rest my arse on the side of the pool table. There is no room in here for a pool table. The cues have all been cut in half to create the illusion of elbow room, but with the bar on one side and the wall on the other it's a pretty pointless exercise. I hand over the money and tell her to get one for herself. The change is returned ice cold and in full.

'Sure you don't want one in the keg for when you're finished?'

A till drawer slammed and the back of a promotional Guinness T-shirt answer my question. It is nine o'clock on a Friday night and we are the only customers. I resist the urge to point out the correlation between her being a morbid cunt and the lack of trade and retreat with my spoils to the security of the posse.

'Why the fuck do you stop at this kip every week?'

'It's sort of become tradition.'

'Is that grumpy bitch on the bar every time?'

'She's kinda why we come back.'

'That sour-faced witch?'

'Jim fancies her.'

'Sorry, Jim. She's gorgeous.'

'No, she isn't, Vinny.'

'Well, she has an inner beauty, man. I mean, for a woman of her age and everything.'

'No, she hasn't, Vinny.'

'Well, in a different way she does, Jim. I mean, she definitely has a quality about her you don't see every day.'

'No, she doesn't, Vinny.'

'All right. Well, why the fuck do you fancy her, then?'

'Because of her sadness.'

He drinks half his pint in a sip. The glass looks tiny in his hand. Maybe he's on to something here with this whole giant thing.

'I would love to make her smile, Vinny. That's all.'

'Have you ever talked to her?'

'We have all talked to her, Vinny. She just doesn't talk back.'

'I noticed all right. Is she married?'

'Don't think so. No ring.'

We nurse our drinks and watch the big man as he stares wistfully at the barren banshee standing across the room. Jonty catches my eye and winks. 'We didn't want to come back after the first night. I mean, it's a dump and the beer's shite and we're not welcome, but it has become part of Jim's routine.'

'Fair enough.'

'I would love to take her out for dinner and make her laugh. Remind her that it's not all bad out there. Her smile is hiding in there somewhere, Vinny. I'd like to be the man who makes it shine again.'

'Go up to the bar and slap your massive weapon out on it. That'll make her smile again!'

'Bingo, do you ever shut the fuck up?'

'Sorry, Mickey.'

'Unbelievable. I'm away for a shite.'

We drink slowly and quietly. Occasionally Jim's eyes wander from the bar back into our circle and I try not to make contact. The story of his mother's departure with a friend of his father when he was barely a year old comes back to me. She never came back to him. She was too busy up in Belfast, drinking vodka and getting nailed sideways. From the start he took abuse in playgrounds for it. He graduated to taking abuse about it in pubs too, but then he grew. Nobody takes the piss out of Long Jim's mummy now. Mickey appears from the bog and tosses me a roll of toilet paper. 'Share this out, Vinny.'

'What?'

The Oedipal tension explodes.

'What's so funny?'

'Your first pill tonight, Vincent! You're in for some buzz, ye boy, ye!'

'Nothing beats the first one, son!'

Davy lifts me in a cross-community bear hug and swings me around his head, a silverback playing with an Action Man. Everyone else takes turns to slap, tickle or pinch me before I am deposited back on the floor and jackets are donned.

'Seriously, what's with the toilet paper?'

'When you start coming up on your E you'll need a massive shite.'

'Don't take the piss, Jonty.'

'Swear to fuck, mate. When it starts to kick in and you're rushing your tits off you're going to need to empty your cage immediately.'

'Holy shit!'

'Precisely. In about two hours' time you'll be having the best shite of your life, my son.'

'That, Vincent, is why I nick the bog roll in here every week. You got a few thousand ravers coming up on pills and only a handful of cubicles? You can see the problem there, comrade.'

I've had a tension building in my stomach since leaving town, and the closer we get to our goal the closer it gets to my throat. Pills, Es, yokes, yingers, Donaghadees. Some are buzzy and some are trippy, some are bouncy and some are smacky, some people love it and some people die.

'Jonty, will we buy a few beers for the car?'

'The boys have beers in the boot. We buy water in here for the end of the journey. It's the last part of Jim's routine.'

As we squeeze past the pool table to the door, Jim approaches his caustic muse. He orders six bottles of fizzy Ballygowan mineral water. He pays for them with money and the biggest smile on the biggest face I have ever seen. In return he gets the biggest till slam and the coldest back. He looks genuinely heart-broken as he bounces towards us, the tiny glass bottles clutched across his chest with one ginormous giant's arm.

2

WE SWAP SEATS for the second half of the journey. The window is even colder on my left cheek and Bingo is even more annoying in my right ear. The coastline flashes by as the sun dives for the sea. I close my eyes as the canary-yellow Vauxhall Nova closes in on drug-induced death.

I might just overheat to more than a hundred degrees and my insides might cook, but it's a risk I'll have to take. Stop thinking and keep breathing. The percentages are minimal. The boys have never seen it happen, although Jonty did say that most weeks someone is so fucked up they're taken away in an ambulance.

'You know what you need to do, Vinny? Drink loads of water, man. Did you hear about the guy died at the rave in London, Vin? Drank too much water and he drowned.'

Jesus Christ, I have got to get out of this car.

'You dropping yours all in one go, mate? I reckon you should do it in halves.'

Bang! Bang! Bang! Bang!

The tunes are back. Maybe they'll drown out Bingo McCaffery.

> *Let me see those hands in the air!*
> *Come on now!*
> *Let me see ya now!*
> *To the beat now!*
> *To the beat, to the beat, to the beat now!*

Have these people never listened to actual music?

Eeee! Eeee! Eeee! Eeee! Eeee! Eeee!

Wait, I've heard this one before. No, that was in a hospital. A heart monitor screeching as someone flatlined. Someone who had taken ecstasy and was now dying to the beat, to the beat, to the beat now. The car stops and we spill into a clifftop car park for a cigarette and a stretch. It's a long way to the bottom. I can't hear the waves slamming into Ulster but I can hear the gulls crying halfway between me and the surf. A cocktail of salty air and smoke, and my breathing regulates. It'll be fine. You've taken shit before, it's just different shit. You won't worry for a second: you'll be high. I flick my fag end seawards and watch the sparks dancing down the cliff face.

'You worried?'

'A bit.'

'You'll be grand. It's all bollocks. Media talk to stop us enjoying ourselves.'

'I know, Jonty.'

'You're gonna have the night of your life!'

The gulls are laughing below me. Die, die, die, they cackle. Fly, fly, fly, I wonder. How long would it take to hit the water? Precious seconds of flight before giving in to the nothingness in the freezing-cold inky drink. The urge peaks as I light my second Silk Cut. I could throw the drugs instead of myself. Drop them over the side and watch the bag burst and the pills spray along the rock face and into the foam. The familiar itch starts, in the third vertebra of my lower back, though it won't be a parked car that explodes and kills me: it'll be my heart or my brain. The itch will find my blades in the end and drive me crazy if I don't walk away or chuck them now. Throw them and be done with it all. I drop my second fag butt into a vortex and we're pulling out of the car park by the time the ocean extinguishes it.

I've never seen Coleraine, and after we've navigated its buffet of roundabouts I gladly never will again. Ballycastle, Bushmills, Portstewart, Portrush. The jewels of the north Antrim coast. I have entered none of these towns before but their names have entered my consciousness through countless news reports of sectarian murders and careless off-duty policemen. Last week I watched a politician on television decrying American tourists who 'only visit the south of Ireland and never our stunning Antrim coastline'. I'm not surprised. Americans are big on service. Around here acrid women serve warm flat beer and bilious bigoted men serve cold hard death. Keith Moon is back on the stage. He picks up his tempo, filling my torso with anxiety as the miles race by and Ned's nightclub reaches for me through the night sky. The finest in the world, say some, the finest in Ireland, say all. Tonight I shall glide through the mother of all nightclubs on the father of all drugs. My bowels twitch in anticipation.

'Cops up ahead.'

'They're not stopping, are they?'

'Looks like they're searching every other one.'

'They're bound to stop six pricks in a shitty Nova.'

'Don't slag the Nova, Vinny.'

'I'm just saying, Mickey, they're looking for suspect people to search and we look like an omnibus of *The Bill* . . .'

'We look grand. Don't panic.'

'I'm carrying a very long jail sentence in my jeans, Jim.'

'And very little else.'

'We need to dump the gear.'

'We can't. They'll see you opening the door.'

'So we just wait and take a fifty-fifty gamble?'

'Yes, now calm down. The guiltier you look the more likely they are to search the car.'

I can't stare out of the window any longer; I've been staring out of it all night. I try to lose myself in 'the tunes' but the only place they will transport me to is a fucking mental institution.

'Do you not think we should at least turn that down and make an effort not to draw attention to ourselves?'

'OK, Vinny, I'm turning the music off. Now put a fucking sock in it.'

Someone is staring at me through the window. I can just make out a pale face under the peak of the dark green cap. I've seen too many policemen this week and all of them at very close quarters. We inch forward. Four men, two bodybuilders and three hundred ecstasy tablets in a battered yellow Vauxhall Nova. When the window is wound down the accent that greets us is Northern Irish but with a pinch of Scotland.

'Can I see your licence, sir?'

Why didn't I drop them down the cliff? Why didn't I stay at home? Why am I such a stupid cunt?

'Believe you had a bit of trouble up your neck of the woods the other night, lads?'

'From what I heard there was a bit of trouble everywhere, Officer.'

'Mind if I check your boot, Mr McCann?'

The rest of us stay in the car as Mickey accompanies him with the keys. You can't see the guns but you can feel them. You can't see tension either, but you know it's creeping into fingers resting on triggers. Total silence. There is nothing to be said. How many of them are out there in the darkness focusing on our car? It takes only one of them to panic. It takes only one of us to move. The door opens and Mickey slides back behind the wheel.

'So you're for Ned's, lads? Well, watch yourselves now. We don't want any of that country behaviour up here tonight.'

'No bother, Officer. Thank you.'

'You can thank me for not booking you for having six people in a Vauxhall fucking Nova. If there weren't twenty cars waiting you'd be coming with me, and your friends would be walking home to the bog they crawled out of.'

We're a mile down the road before anyone speaks. It's another mile before I'm satisfied that I haven't defecated in my trousers.

'They weren't looking for MDMA, lads, they were looking for RPG7s.'

Mickey turns the tunes up again and in unison we scream in euphoric relief. When I am finally hoarse I return to my window vigil and smile out into the night at the orange glow above nearby Portrush. Portrush weighs me up for a second or two, then winks and smiles right back at me through the balmy darkness of a summer's night.

3

NED'S CAR PARK is a zoo. I would go as far as safari. The animals are definitely exotic and dangerous, and although there are no signs up, it feels suicidal to be leaving the safety of the car. As we stretch and smoke beside our trusty little steed, we watch four girls peeing in a line next to a nearby bus. Two of them stare at us as they release with the bus at their backs, and two of them have their foreheads pressed against it for support. I ignore the two faces and admire the pair of pale arses pouting and pissing into the moonlight.

'Even outside the girls go in packs.'

'Put your tongue away, Vin. There's plenty more of that inside!'

At the boot of the Nova Jonty rips up the carpet that covers the spare wheel and we stash both bags of pills down in tight with the toolbox.

'Two pills for ourselves, for inside. I've wrapped them in a fiver to keep them dry. If they get sweaty they turn to mush, so be careful.'

'Keep an eye on me, Jonty.'

'Fuck's sake.'

'I'm just saying.'

'You don't need to say. It's what mates do.'

The deep boom of the speakers can just be heard through the walls of the club, and the beat creeps up through the tarmac into my feet. Every car stereo within a half-mile radius lays its own tune over this subterranean bass line as they patiently queue, within touching distance of their destination. There are people everywhere. Inside cars, around cars, on top of cars. A dozen coaches with number plates from far and wide eagerly spit ravers out into the car park at will. We move in single file into the madness. Halfway between our car and the doors of the club we stop with a group of lads who are swaying around a ghetto blaster. They openly smoke hash and manhandle a bottle of vodka. Before I can open my mouth to say hello I have a joint in it and the bottle in my hand.

'What about ye?'

'How's it going, hi?'

'Ah, the country boys are here.'

'Where are you from?'

'The New Lodge.'

'Where's that?'

'Belfast.'

'I don't know it.'

'Neither do I.'

He bends and twists the volume, and as the hash slaps me in the head, the tunes make it from my feet to my knees for the first time. Maybe this rave music isn't so bad when you're actually standing up. The Belfast boys are sparsely dressed in urban dancewear. Trainers, baggy jeans, then nothing up top but plastic fluorescent orange or yellow Department of the Environment waistcoats. The type that workmen wear on the roads for safety.

'Youse bumpkins up here every week? I'm sure I've seen you before, big man.'

Belfast hands his joint up to Long Jim, who sucks the life out of it then exhales a little grey cloud down onto the tops of our heads. 'You've seen me before, all right.'

'Here! It's yer man! It's the techno giant!'

'We watched you dancing for two hours one night, big man. We couldn't take our fucking eyes off ye!'

They marvel and paw at the dance-floor deity. Jim, Jim, the ravers' dream, the six-foot-seven-inch dancing queen. Behind our new friends from the north the doors of the club burst open and a techno tsunami smashes through the car park. Two men in black military-style bomber jackets appear, carrying a skinny, curly-haired unconscious youth. They lay him down gently twenty metres from the front of the club, and his friends rush through the doorway and gather around him on the concrete. The bouncers pull the doors closed behind them, damming the colossal tide of sound and leaving the group of friends to panic in peace over their annihilated number. The night is yet to fully begin and we have already encountered our first hospital case. His friends try to sit him up but he falls sideways again, like a drunken ragdoll, his head bouncing off the hard ground. People instinctively move towards the unfolding drama as Curly springs from his coma to his feet and turns to face the nightclub that has spat him out. With blood pouring down his right cheek he throws his arms to the heavens and screams his sermon into the night: 'Burn me! Burn me in the fires of Hell!'

The crowd that has gathered behind him cheers and takes up his call: 'Burn him! Burn him in the fires of Hell!'

He whips round and raises a fist to his new-found disciples, then stumbles off precariously towards the main road. One of his friends lunges for his waist but Curly Jesus shimmies side-ways, like George Best in his prime, and the friend hits the deck, like a broken skittle. He roars again, then he's gone, weaving through people like a winter hare, his imaginary per-secutors hard upon his heels. He pauses at the edge of the car park for a final bellow, then a huge roar of approval erupts as the chosen one disappears between two buses into the night.

Fat Davy, who had wandered off during the show, rejoins us with six cans of lager and a knowing look. 'Acid. Mad cunt dropped four strawberries and a penguin inside, then passed out.'

'Five trips? He's not coming down for a week!'

'Where did you get the tins, Davy? From those girls you were talking to?'

'No, Bingo, from the boot. Those girls are old friends of mine from Newry.'

The Belfast lads head off to put their stereo back in their car and neck their pills before entering the club, and we drink our beers in stoned silence as the madness unfolds around us. Davy checks his watch, then looks are exchanged and scrunched-up fivers are produced from pockets.

'How much should I take?'

'I'd take a half now and a half when it kicks in, Vinny. Here, I'll split this one with you and we can split another one inside.'

Davy nibbles on it gently and the pill comes apart in two perfect halves, a clean line right through the centre of the small dove emblem stamped on the top. There are many types with many emblems but ours are peaceful little white doves. My half looks tiny between Davy's dumbbell-swollen finger and thumb. How could that do any harm? A small white tablet to make you feel better. Don't all small white tablets make you feel better? He brings his finger towards my mouth and I'm back on the verge. A tiny white morsel on a huge brown finger. A tiny white speck that will melt my insides. I'm on the edge of the cliff again and it's far too late to jump.

'Chew it up and wash it down with your beer.'

Keith Moon's snare starts a death march as I hold my breath, close my eyes and bite down on for ever. It is hostile. Like nothing I have ever tasted. A corrosive synthetic black-hearted sourness that can only do harm. I swig and swallow, then gag and choke. I take more beer on board and swish like mad to wash the cruel lumps out of my teeth and onwards into my stomach. Jonty wraps his arm around my shoulders and holds me tight, like a proud parent after a poetry reading. It is done. What will be will be.

Behind us the biggest din of the night erupts and we turn to behold the resurrection. Curly Jesus is dancing on top of a bus as naked as the day he was born. He has stripped every stitch from himself but then been careful enough to put his Adidas trainers back on. He bounces on one spot, his arms whipping crazy circles in the air, like a broken windmill. Fists clenched, thrusting to the beat from his neck to his groin and back again. His hops get higher and higher as his cock bangs from one thigh onto the other, a fleshy white pendulum keeping time to the rhythm of his dance. It's too much for the crowd, and together we lose our minds, screaming and jumping for Curly Jesus and his dick and his shell-toe trainers that are kicking the shite out of the roof of the bus.

'*Come on! To the beat now! To the beat, to the beat now!*'

We leap around in circles, screaming back every word. As his tempo increases his rhymes improve, and his manhood attempts to detach itself from his body and fly away.

'Fee-fi-fo-fum,
I smell blow and I wanna get some,
But I can't get none cos it brings me down
And I wanna get high and jump around!
COME ON!'

Police appear amongst the dancers. I see the racing-green hats snaking through the sea of heads, their peaks pointed at our cosmic dancing stripper in the sky. Boos and cries of derision and the old familiar chant from the hospital road.

'SS RUC! SS RUC!'

More of them now, pouring in from all directions. They have a motorbike with them. It edges in from the far right, scattering people quicker than the foot soldiers ever will. A scuffle breaks out at the back of the bus as the first pigs climb for their quarry. Cans of beer arrive from every angle, smashing into policemen and ravers alike. A cop makes the roof via his comrade's shoulders but Curly is away again before his modesty can be restored by the law. He takes a step backwards and leaps onto the roof of a neighbouring bus. The nearest pig steps back, preparing to follow suit, but Curly takes flight once more, landing on his third roof of the night. The crowd erupts again and the police lose control of the situation. As the naked legend makes it to the roof of bus number four, and his pursuer nearly falls, landing on his second, Mickey pulls us together and shouts over the top of the performance: 'We need to move. If we're caught up in this we're never getting inside.'

We push through the rear of the crowd and retreat to the Nova to smoke a joint and watch the conclusion without being part of it. The police outrider, separated from his brethren, sits stock still on his bike as a dozen clubbers dance round its flashing light, singing 'I Fought The Law'.

On bus number four, naked, Curly Jesus salutes his audience one final time, then leaps off the roof and disappears into the darkness for the second time that night.

From the security of the queue we watch the protectors of the peace corralling and kicking a succession of dancing people into the paddy wagons that have arrived from the world. They experience limited success. Most people have made it to the line for the main event and the club seems keen to let us all in as quickly as possible.

'Surely they'll search us on the way in.'

'They might give you a quick frisk, but they couldn't give a fuck. Put your shit down your balls.'

'Why don't they care?'

'It's a rave, Vinny. It doesn't work if the punters have their drugs confiscated at the door. I reckon half the bouncers are dealing anyway.'

There's a team of them at the top of the queue. I recognise the pair who showed Curly Jesus the exit earlier. The clothing and the look are uniform. Bomber jacket, fat neck, Dr Martens, shaved head. The capability to inflict pain with minimum effort would appear to be a prerequisite for the job in hand. Every third person is given a token rub down and some girls' bags are glanced through. Unfrisked and stoned out of my tiny mind, I arrive at a glass window to pay. Twenty quid in and twenty quid for an E. It might be the best club in Ireland but, by Christ, you'll pay for the experience. The voices in the foyer boast an array of different melodies. I hear Belfast and Derry, Glasgow and Cork. The air is thick with smoke and perfume and anticipation. For these people life is about Friday, and only Friday is life. The other six days are a long, winding staircase that delivers one eventually to the front of Ned's. As we saunter towards the final set of double doors a twitch, not an itch, starts in my lower back. It doesn't tempt me to jump, though, and it doesn't need to be scratched. The twitch just wants to dance.

4

FIVE FLOORS WITH twelve individually themed bars and a restaurant. Tonight we turn our love on the four rooms that make up the 'Dance Depot'. The promotional posters promise a range of sounds from 'nosebleed techno to acid jazz'. I don't want a nosebleed and I've witnessed enough of acid's handiwork for one evening, thank you very much. The words aren't fixed to the paper properly. They swim, unsynchronised, and fight each other, trying to change the meanings of the sentences. As the doors swing open the bass drum kicks my guts. I clench my sphincter and hold back the torrent. Davy grabs me by the waist and carries me the last few feet into the club. Jim joins him and they elevate me to shoulder height so that I can stare at the heaving dance floor below.

'Welcome to the future, you Fenian fucker! Welcome to the best night of your life!'

I gaze down on the bouncing, sweating ritual below. The

crowd's faces are upturned as one as they worship the DJ on his altar at the far end of this massive musical church. To the left of his platform is a long bar with the husks of two old cars strung up on wires above it.

'Will we get a couple of vodkas to bring us up? A couple of vodkas, lads!'

'You'll come up anyway, Bingo, but, aye, let's get a couple of vodkas before X-ray comes on.'

We move down the staircase onto the floor and head for the bar. It's the smell that hits me first. Eucalyptus and sweat. The eucalyptus comes from the Vicks vapour inhalers that everyone seems to be sharing around. We pass two men naked from the waist up. They stand soaked in sweat, clasping each other's hands, their arms fully extended, forming an archway in the air. They each have a Vicks inhaler hanging from a nostril like a plastic stalactite. As I pass under their archway the duo inhale deeply, their eyes rolling into the backs of their heads.

'Jonty, what the fuck?'

'The Vicks is a good buzz when you're rushing, man. Your senses are heightened and it blows your mind.'

'Erases your fucking mind.'

'The ointment is good too, man. You rub it all over your balls. I have some in the car for later on.'

For once I say nothing. I just watch the biggest homophobe in Ireland mince off into the crowd, his T-shirt already discarded, his ball-rubbing tingle cream safely ensconced in the car for later on. When the strobe lights and lasers cut through the smoke, the faces burn vibrant for seconds before receding into the rave. Those not stripped to the waist wear garish coloured hooded tops or checked shirts. Bulging eyes peep out at me from under designer baseball caps or bandannas. In the midst of this chaos the girls as always have way more style than the boys. Classy cocktail dresses and intricate stacks of hair come and go through the flashing lights. We stop and watch two visions dancing. They are aware of nothing but each other. It's their skin that has floored us. Their beautiful brown sweating skin. They gyrate together, each clad identically in blue jeans and a black bra. A semi-clad feminine masterpiece. The world stops as they kiss. They are aware of nothing else as they chew tenderly on each other's lips. My jeans start to shrink as Davy takes me by the elbow and propels me onwards towards our goal.

The standard dance in the house tonight is a bounce or a hop. The feet flirt with one spot, like a boxer skipping, while the arms twist and swim, painting the air around the upper body. The faster you move your hands in a robotic mesmerising spider's web the better at 'raving' you appear to be. It's a competition on the dance floor to see whose arms can fly the swiftest. Some have mastered an impressive hypnotic futuristic pattern of movement. The majority, though, swat swarms of imaginary flies in front of their faces, or mime painting the ceiling and stacking some shelves. Many clutch glow sticks, fluorescent orange and green bolts slashing lines and tracers through the smoke and the mind. In the glare of the UV lights white becomes something else, a brilliant searing colour that has never been seen before. White T-shirts take on a heavenly shimmer and white-gloved hands chop and fly through the air like frantic phosphorus bats. I push on towards the bar, unable to make out my friends but confident that they're around me, a single unit floating in one direction. The music is drum-splittingly loud. The only thing that cuts through is the constant shriek of individual whistles from the ravers. They abound, around necks, on tapers and on strings, and they are blown at random over and above the wall of sound. I am almost under the two cars and I push through one final spring-heeled clique and step out into space to find Jonty, Davy and Jim standing at the bar.

'Where's Mickey and Bingo?'

'Bingo wandered off in the wrong direction and Mickey is looking for him.'

The vodka and Coke is ice cold. I nail it in one and take in my new surroundings. 'It was Bingo's idea to get a drink and he disappears?'

'Let's be honest, Vinny, it's a relief for a bit. He's like a broken parrot.'

The barman is a happier version of one of the bouncers. He talks and laughs to himself intermittently. Jonty leans into the bar beside me and gives me a hug.

'Fruit.'

'Now, now, that's your territory, Vincent. You feeling anything yet?'

'I don't know. I'm not sure what it is that I'm meant to be feeling. I can feel your hand on my arse.'

'You'll know it when it kicks in. Check out the barman!'

He is dancing on his own beneath the optics. Fists pumping, feet of fury pounding his spot behind the Harp tap. He smiles at us and his eyes roll over as his jaw spasms and begins to invade the rest of his face. He appears to be chewing a massive gobstopper that he will never defeat. 'He looks like a fucking retard!'

'That's exactly what you're gonna look like in approximately twenty minutes.'

Jonty's jaw tries some mild gymnastics now, and he smiles at me with sad wet eyes, like a big stupid dog.

'You look weird.'

'You look great, Vinny. I'm so glad we're in this together, man.'

He hugs me again, then holds on to the bar with both hands, eyes closed, head lost in the music. The DJ is building the tune, lifting everyone to a higher plane. As the drums and the electronic squeaks raise their game there is an almost palpable sense of journey in the room. Ravers go berserk, whistles fire short, staccato blasts, voices and spirits soar on this slow ascent to crescendo. Jonty lets go of the bar and grabs me for support, and I dance with him, tentatively finding my own hop. We dance faster now, faster and faster. The music builds and builds, dragging us with it to the top of the mountain. When we're about to scale its peak Ned's erupts as one in a cacophonous primal scream. Jonty punches the air and lets rip across from me, a demented, howling mess. I can't stop laughing. There is a smile stretched tight across my face that I'm not in control of. 'That shite's brewing, Jonty.'

'What?'

'I really need a shite.'

'You're coming up, man! I'm fuckin' wasted. Let's go for a dump.'

He turns and stumbles back into the crowd at the edge of the dance floor. I look behind me and Davy is following us. Jim has climbed over the bar and is pulling himself a pint beside the wasted dancing barman. He waves at me and flashes his massive smile as I disappear after Jonty into the eye of the storm.

There is a queue for the toilets. The smoke has thickened and my eyesight is blurred so I struggle to make anything out. I'm propped between Jonty and Davy as I wait patiently for my cubicle. Faces glide by, in focus for a mere second before they float back into the depths of the pea-souper. Jonty grabs my shoulder, points forward and to the right. There are people dancing everywhere. There must be something happening: the wee dick is doubled over in stitches. I watch him cracking up. He's two feet away but it feels like there's a film of something between us. An invisible screen that I watch him through, like a pervert at a peep show. Life on his side of the divide is normal, but life as I know it has stopped. My faculties wade slowly through deep sticky Sunday gravy. My hand, a sci-fi blur before my face, drips vapours, like a burning meteor blazing from the end of my arm.

'I saw Halley's Comet, you know.'

'Where?'

'Not in here. I saw it through a telescope up at Portora School.'

'What?'

'In 1986.'

'You all right?'

'Got a certificate and everything. It only comes back every seventy-five years.'

'You're freaking me out, Vin.'

'If I see it again in 2061 I fill in the other side of the certificate and I'm laughing.'

'Brilliant.'

'Not many people have seen it twice, Jonty. I'll be eighty-six, too!'

'Why will you be laughing?'

'What do you mean?'

'How do you know that when you see it again as an old man you'll be laughing?'

'It'll be amazing, man!'

'You don't know that. It could be shite. It could be the worst day of your life because it reminds you that you're eighty-six and you're fucked.'

'You're just jealous because you've never seen a comet.'

We explode together this time. Gripping each other tight we let rip from the depths. Hard, clean, ecstatic laughter. Davy and Jonty lift me above the bog queue and I let their shoulders take me, the king of space. With an arm around each of their necks I bounce as high as the stars and scream over the music and the whistles and the shouting.

'I think I'm coming up, Davy!'

'You think you're coming up? You should see the fucking state of yourself!'

'What were you pointing at, Jonty?' My own voice is distant and sounds like an older man's.

'The guy dancing in the wheelchair. Look!'

I follow his finger through the crowd and this time I find him. In the shadows against a large speaker, a man sits dancing in a wheelchair. He wears only white shorts and gloves and he's going for it like there is no tomorrow. Davy is watching him too and he shouts in my ear, 'That's the Wheels of Steel. He's here every week, he can't get enough of the buzz.'

'Does he need the wheelchair?'

'Of course he needs the wheelchair, Vinny. If he didn't need the wheelchair he'd be dancing standing up.'

'I know, but I thought maybe it was his thing.'

'His thing? An able-bodied person carrying a fucking wheelchair into a nightclub so they can dance sitting down?'

Jonty has heard enough. Prostrate at my feet, he sobs like a child or a girl or a fucking arsehole.

'He's UVF, mate. They stash all their gear in his wheelchair and no one goes near him.'

I watch a skinhead in a tracksuit take a bag of pills from the back of the wheelchair and pop one into its occupant's mouth. Two more geniuses appear and the Wheels of Steel squeals in delight as they soak him with water from plastic bottles to cool him down.

'Are they really UVF?'

'Fucking right they are. Your crowd deals from the speakers on the other side of the main bar.'

'I thought the RA were anti-drugs.'

'They're only anti-drugs if someone else is getting the profits. They won't be directly IRA but they'll be sending home a hefty cut and their backs will be well watched.'

The toilets are flooded. My desert boots are soaked through by the time I get a box to squat in. At least the water is coming from one of the sinks. Wading through shite would definitely kill the buzz. The release is intense.

Patrick Kelly takes it up the arse! Call 02220 567452 for hot bum fun

It's the other side of the country but the graffiti is the same. We clearly have an epidemic. What would a psychologist make of these findings? Why are Northern Irish vandals obsessed with sodomy? Do we find the same themes as commonly on English bathroom doors? Are these scrawlings the physical embodiment of the psychological reality that as a nation we've been fucked in the arse for the last twenty-five years? I need a fag. Not a hot bum fun fag, though, just one that you smoke.

'Jonty, have you got a light in there?'

'Aye, hold on. Fuck's sake.'

He appears above my head from the cubicle next door.

'How was it?'

'Emotional.'

'Here. Take your other half now and don't forget to wipe your hole.'

I watch the flame for an age before introducing it to the end of my Silk Cut purple. I let the smoke fill me up as I reread my green metal door. Hot bum fun. Does that mean the bum is hot or the fun is hot? It's confusing. I'm sure Patrick Kelly explains all if you take the time to call him. The other usual suspects are here too.

UDA.
Up the UFF.
Ulster says NO!
Ballymena Prods on tour!!

They haven't got very far – Ballymena's only up the fucking road. They make me feel at home, my little abbreviated friends. I must remember to call the plumber; this flood's really getting out of control.

'You got a bottle of water in there, Jonty?'

The plastic answer hits the side of my head, the side of the cubicle and the middle of the floor.

'Wanker!'

It tastes even worse the second time. My exaggerated senses scream as it burns craters into my tongue. I drain the bottle and fight to control my stomach, head between my skinny naked knees. Better now, much better. Head back to watch the patterns moving on the ceiling.

'Jonty! You can keep your jeans dry if you put your feet up on the door in front of you!'

Christ, I'm going all over again! Surely there can be no more left. Where's the paper? It's in your jeans, you bollocks, calm down. Another fag, that's what I'll have. Not a hot bum fun one, though, just one that you smoke. Already been here. Head's going round in circles. My mouth's as dry as Dave Allen. Is this the start of the dehydration? Stay calm, Vinny, and breathe. This is not death, this is life. This can never be bad because it feels so good. I lie back on the cistern, close my eyes and let the buzz wash over me. A steady tickle wherever I send it with my mind. My legs tingle, my face is tingling, my feet are soaking. There are real waves washing over my feet and ecstasy waves washing over my entire body. A woman sings now. At last, a tune within the tunes. 'I hope this night lasts for ever,' she coos at me. Shocking lyrics, but I love this woman's voice. Imagine what her fucking arse looks like. I hope this E lasts for ever.

'Vinny! You all right? You've been in there for half an hour.'

'I'm grand. I'm coming now.'

'You could have waited for a wank, man. Hurry up, X-ray's starting!'

5

IN THE BOSOM of the crowd our time has come. We vibrate, we hum, we beat to the drum. The angry Cockney man from the tape in the car is on the stage screaming at his mic. 'Are you ready for some harmony in the place? I said, are you ready? Noise crew? Whistle crew? Bounce crew? Let me hear it for Ireland's finest, Dee Jayyyy Eeex-raaaaay!'

A shower of sparks rains on the lips of the crowd. Thousands of burning golden fireflies spewed from the heavens above. A bright spotlight exposes a girl in a white bikini astride a speaker stack. The glitter stuck to her body fires small piercing beams of light back down on the fervent horde, who roar their approval at her appearance. She undulates seductively in her moment, tight flesh rippling on a wiry frame as she writhes and distorts her body to the whims of the DJ beneath her high-booted feet. A second beam, and another guardian is born above us. Her black Lycra body-glove struggles to hide the

contours of her secrets as she pulses and throbs above our gaping eyes and gobs. My posse is with me again, reunited for the
main event. Davy, Bingo, Mickey, Jonty and Vinny dancing in
a little circle in our own little world.

'Where's Long Jim?'

No one hears me through the drug. Bingo bounces over.
His eyes bulge and his tongue is fully extended as he rolls it
around his face trying to lick his own ears. He looks like a Jack
Russell with an overactive thyroid hanging out of the window
of a moving car. We gradually inch forward and are dancing
near the front of proceedings. The muscles and curves beneath
the Lycra make so much sense as they hover within a leap's
reach. There is a blast of light and a searing heat as a tongue of
fire shoots between the pair of elevated angels from somewhere
in the centre of the stage. The second bolt is close enough to
well-considered hairdos to have us scrabbling around on the
floor. I rise and watch this time as a painted man fills his mouth
with paraffin and prepares to blow his hat-trick. His hair is
shaved around the sides and pulled back tight in a ponytail up
top. Stripped to the waist and painted in neon colours, he
waves his wand in preparation. The third blast sails higher
than its predecessors and the rave is back on its feet, yelling its
communal approval. Slowly the music begins to build again.
The crowd senses another journey and the atmosphere con-
stricts. In a ritualistic cameo, Davy and Mickey take turns to
shed their T-shirts and tuck them into their belts. That leaves
only me and Bingo clad from our little school party, and maybe
Long Jim, wherever he is.

'Davy, have you seen Jim?'

'Don't worry 'bout Jim, Vin. You'll see him in a second.'

He gives me a knowing grin and produces a fat ready-rolled
joint from his pocket. Jonty sparks it for him and Davy puts the

lit end in his mouth and pulls me close. I put my lips around the roached end of the joint and Davy blows a steady stream of hot harsh hash smoke straight down into my soul. When I can inhale no more I stagger backwards and bend over, fighting to keep it inside for as long as possible. When I straighten and exhale, I wobble sideways and fall to the floor. My mouth hangs open and I have no power to close it as the marijuana floods through every cell, from my tongue tip to the back of my scrotum. My eyes slam shut and it takes a momentous effort to force them open again as vodka, ecstasy and Mary Jane gang up and pull me under. Jonty joins me on the floor, the smoke from his turn still spilling from his nose and mouth. We sit here for a bit grinning at each other amongst the dancing legs and bums and feet. My eyes keep closing by themselves and every time I beg them open he is still there grinning at me, like a fucked-up ventriloquist's dummy. Jonty the rave doll. Feed it pills and watch it shite itself. The louder you play your music, kids, the more he grins. The convulsions drop me further and I lie staring up at him, the cold wet dance floor against my cheek transporting me back to the car and the black north Antrim coastline. Not lain by the sea for so long. It's warm too. Lovely warm water soaking through my jeans and shoes. My hands feel good on my face so I rub them on my neck and chest. This feels even better so I rub them on my thighs and crotch. I can't see, but I can feel everything. Fuck, can I feel. I'm blind but I know that I'm not alone.

'He's smacking: lift him quick.'

Maybe you really could grow to like this music, you know, Vinny.

'He's laughing away to himself.'

Bingo drags me up by the pits and Jonty holds my lids open for Mickey to squirt water into my eyes.

'I'm all right, I'm all right.'

'You're smacking out, enjoy the buzz.'

'Came on like a ton of bricks there, Davy.'

'Oul blowbacks lift the lid clean off ye, lad.'

'My head's away with it, Davy!'

'Love ye, Vinny man! I love ye.'

I disappear into his massive sweaty naked chest. I can't breathe. I'm drowning in an iron bear-man love grip. I genuinely can't breathe. Beneath muffled proclamations of peace and love I twitch my last like a river-banked salmon. For three years this man stalked me through the streets of my hometown, nonplussed with my accident of religion, and now he will kill me in a misguided accidental outpouring of affection and brute strength. I slap his massive hams and he releases me.

'Mean it, Vinny man, I love ye. Now get ready for the show.'

'Is Carl Cox on already?'

'No, man, it's the big man!'

Long Jim really can dance. He has appeared beside us, resplendent upon a speaker, and I realise that this is why we are in this exact spot. This is what they were talking about in the car park. The people around us know this too. Long Jim is an event. He has no gimmicks, no paint or mask, he simply lets his dancing do the talking. Or maybe he is the gimmick, the dancing legend with a 'touch of giantism'. Unlike the masses, Jim's whole body engages with the music in the space. He's classic at first, his bottom half marking standard time while his top half creates the pictures. Bounce and paint, bounce and paint. Suddenly he chops across the music and cuts his speed in two, then three, then four. He is still in time with the DJ but he moves at a fraction of the speed of everything else in the room. It is electrifying to watch. This man mountain has channelled the elegant qualities of something else entirely. He is wind and fire, he is smoke and water. He is an element in his fucking element. He turns the revs back up now and we howl. He turns his arms and face to the sky and we shine. We dance beneath the techno giant, proud that he is ours. Most dance with us but some just stand there and stare. He moves through a fluid sequence of robotic stylings and surreal mimics, machine-gunning his people before resuming his trance-like elegance above the sea of enraptured eyes.

The music peaks and I am lost in a tunnel of sound. I see nothing but the pictures in my mind. I am part of the machine, I am part of the tune, I am part of something. I face the future and dance like it will be short-lived. Davy has one of my shoulders and Bingo the other, Jonty and Mickey complete the circle as we hold each other tight and dance through the intensity of the buzz. Our faces distort and stretch, our teeth grind, and our heads roll aimlessly on their stalks, like newborn babies trying to find the faces that own the voices that whisper in their ears. The circle moves and roars as one, and when the music can go no further Jim leaps into the air and lands with aplomb, smack-bang in its centre. We smash the ring and mob Gulliver, dragging him to the floor and pinning him beneath a tangled mass of limbs. A horizontal group hug ensues and I lie flat and close my eyes as they take turns to roll over me and grab their gentle giant.

My laughter is beginning to choke me when your strong hand takes mine and yanks me to my feet. I open my eyes as I climb, pushing upwards through my knees and thighs away from the shipwrecked bodies and back into the sea of music. Just a stare at first, then I manage a smile of thank-you, but when I try to speak you float away, smirking at me over your left shoulder. I stumble forward and grab an arm. Laughter now, but when I don't let go you shoot me some 'What the fuck are you doing?'

eyes. You have stopped, though, so I take your other hand and stare at you, a mad man incapacitated by beauty and class-A drugs. I want to speak but I have nothing to say.

Big brown eyes stare back at me, questioning and calculating and waiting for me to open my mouth. Ask her to dance. Tell her she is the most incredible-looking creature you have ever seen. Tell her you have been waiting your whole life for a woman who favours her left shoulder. There is a gentle hum all over my body. Up my legs and down my arms, a warm generous current flows. I can't move. I have been plugged into this spot on this floor and the very fabric of the earth is recharging my soul through my soles. I close my eyes and bite my bottom lip hard as a pleasure finger runs itself provocatively down the length of my spine. When I open them again you have taken the situation in hand and decided to lead the way. Svelte hips start to move through the beat and those big brown eyes look at me again and say, 'Dance with me for a minute if you want to then, you dick, but only for a minute, mind.'

We mirror at the start, keeping it simple, tuning in to the rhythm of each other's engines. I can't tear my eyes from your face. As your body undulates gracefully you glance at mine intermittently, those brown eyes a confident study of indifference. I shut mine again and concentrate on the music and myself. The DJ has slowed things right down in preparation for another crack at Kilimanjaro. I focus on the music instead of the girl and let it soak through my legs and into my groin and stomach. As I swell with confidence I feel my own lines and shapes extending from my body and reaching outwards into the tune. It is in me now and I am in it. When I look again you are standing still, watching me dance. A smirk has crept into your eyes and onto the corners of your mouth. I carefully try out my rubber mask and venture a small smile back. Your smirk spreads like a joy rash and your face lights up like Christmas. I step forward, knowing that if I don't kiss you right here and now I will spontaneously combust. Our lips touch momentarily, but you roll away and dance in a circle, arriving back in front of me but facing in the other direction. I put my arms round your waist and pull you into me, inhaling a deep chestful of hair and neck. We sway like this for ever, a single unit marking time together. When we finally break, the tempo has shifted upwards and we dance harder again skipping in front of each other a couple of feet apart. Our bodies travel wherever the music takes them but our eyes never move, their destinations having been determined the second that I rose from the floor. I scream at you without moving my lips.

You are fucking gorgeous.

Your almost-black pools reply to me over the whistles and the shouts and the drums and the madness: *You're not looking so bad yourself, boy.*

I want to kiss you, I need to kiss you.

I fucking dare you, boy.

I move towards you until our bodies are almost touching again. I lean in and put my lips on yours. We open our mouths together and for a split second I feel your tongue sneak inside my mouth and push itself under my own. Break again, but straight back this time, no dancing away. Both tongues so hungry to find each other. Sharp and raw at first, then hard lines soften and things curve and relax, and I know again for certain that I will explode. I put my hands on your back and pull you into my groin. You stay too, pushing tight against me. Your sweet breath fills me up as your hot wet mouth gives back as good as it gets. We relax now and play, a tongue thrust deeper here, a lip bitten there. Our faces locked together as our bodies keep time to the music. A bottle of water is thrust between our faces. Attached to it is the topless sweaty vision of my best friend.

'You guys having a good buzz?'

'Unreal, Jonty. Unreal, man. Thanks for the water.'

When he is out of your field of vision he leers and pumps one arm behind the other. I think he approves. The music bottoms out so I shake my cigarettes at you and you nod and lead me from the dance floor. We will share one, I think. Yes, let's share one: that feels more intimate. I caress the sides of your face as you take your time savouring the smoke as it pours inside you. You hand me the cigarette and the second your mouth is free mine is there again, on you, in you. I can't get enough of you. You push me up against the wall and our tongues fight once again. You rub my chest hard with one hand as the other tears at the front of my thigh through my jeans. Every touch, every movement is so vividly concentrated, like my senses are on fire. The music has left us and all I can hear are your moans. I smell nothing but your breath and your sweat and your skin. When your fingers touch my face a tremor shoots in a diagonal line backwards from my navel into my arse. You put your finger into my mouth, tentative and playful at first, then two fingers explore me in a solid filthy little invasion. As I bite down on your digits my erection screams and punches a wall of denim, and I think I'll finally give in and let go. Suddenly a searing burn between my fingers and I scream and shake the cigarette butt from where it has stuck to my flesh. I pull the lid off the water bottle with my teeth and douse my aching hand as we bend and crease in lust and laughter.

'I forgot about the bloody fag!'

'Can I have some water, please?'

I watch you drink. You have a voice now. I play the words

over and over in my head as the water bottle gently fucks your mouth and I try not to mess myself.

Can I have some water, please? Can I have some water, please? Can I have some water, please? Can I have some water, please? Your dark hair is cut into a sharp bob, one side lower than the other, *à la* Betty Boo. Your cheekbones are high and your nose is strong and direct, like the stare that questions me now.

'What's your name?'

'Who wants to know?'

'Vinny.'

'Why do you want to know, Vinny?'

'Because you're fucking beautiful!'

'Full of charm, you country boys.'

Another kiss. The bottle is dropped to the floor as we fall into the wall and back into our coma.

'I have to find my friends.'

'I'll come with you.'

'No, stay here.'

I run my hand between your legs and onwards to your breasts as you stare into my eyes and let me.

'Naughty boy. I'll see you later, Vinny.'

You are gone. I watch your back as it gets smaller in the melee, a sense of panic rising into my throat.

'Betty, you didn't tell me your name!'

Naughty boy. I'll see you later, Vinny. Naughty boy. I'll see you later, Vinny. Naughty boy. I'll see you later, Vinny.

Does that literally mean later, or if we bump into each other randomly in another lifetime? I am flooded with an overwhelming sense of loss. My knees buckle and I sit down on the floor and light a cigarette. Betty, Betty, Betty, Betty. I can still taste you in my mouth so I crush the cigarette in case it erases you. My eyes rest on the water bottle and I grab it and suck your saliva from its neck. Two hands on my shoulders, gentle. I spin where I sit, aching to see your brown eyes smirking down at me again.

'You all right, man? Where did Betty Boo go?'

'That's what I call her.'

'That's who she looks like, Vinny. Un-fuckin'-believable!'

'She has gone to find her friends. I don't know if she's coming back.'

'She'll be back. She was all over you like a cheap suit. Come on, we need to get out of here. It's nearly over.'

'But we haven't even heard Carl Cox!'

'Carl Cox is finished, Vinny. He's been playing for the last hour while you've been dry riding up against a wall for a non-paying audience.'

There are still people dancing, squeezing the last bit of marrow out of the night. Most, though, are gathering themselves and their people and their coats and getting ready to face whatever the outside world has to offer. We retrace the story of our evening, gradually picking up the various strings to our bow. We hit the toilets first, to piss out some of the water we've gorged ourselves on. My bladder feels fit to burst from the four litres I've put away, out of fear more than thirst. United we stand at the urinal, hosing for fun for what seems an eternity.

'I can't piss in pubs usually, Jonty man.'

'You've talked some skitter tonight, man. What was all that Patrick Moore shite about the comets?'

The laughter throws my head back then forward onto the wall and I lean there, comfortable, letting it and the endless stream pour freely from me. Back now across the rapidly emptying dance floor, and I feel the same sense of panic I felt when Betty left me as I watch our brave new world disintegrate. The rave is dying, replaced by a massive smoky vacant barn. Where there was life and more energy than I have ever seen before, now there are only empty bottles on a sticky floor. Mickey and Bingo are at the bar downing pints with the Belfast lads we met earlier in the car park. There is no sign of Jim and Davy yet. There is no sign of Betty either.

'Mate, I saw you with that wee brunette on the dance floor!'

'She was gorgeous, Vinny.'

'Unbelievable, mate.'

'You jammy bastard!'

'She's gone.'

'She'll be at the party, son!'

'She was all over you like the German measles.'

The car park is insanity itself. It takes us half an hour to get from the club to the Nova. Jim and Davy are sitting on the bonnet smoking a joint with two girls from Scotland. They want to come with us but we don't have the room. Arrangements are made to meet them at the party. I scan the car park for the umpteenth time but I still can't find you. How would I ever find you? There are a thousand minds exploding between here and wherever you are.

'She'll be at the party, Vin.'

'I don't know, Jonty. She never mentioned it.'

'Where was she from?'

'I never asked her.'

'What is her name?'

'She never said.'

'You don't know much, do you? Don't worry, she'll be there. Everybody will.'

We crack cans of beer at the boot and glug them down, like babies on the bottle. The bubbles are good. I've missed you, my fizzy little friends. I've been drinking water all night and it's just not the same. It may have prolonged my life but beer is still my saviour. There are a good thirty cans in the boot so I drain mine and crack another.

'We're well stocked up for the party, Vin.'

'So I see, Mickey. Are you fit to drive?'

'I only had that beer on the way up and one just now so I'm grand. I'll stick to the drugs.'

'So where is this famous party everyone's talking about?'

'At the White Rocks, Vin. The party's at the White Rocks.'

6

I'M BACK AT my window. Its coolness on my cheek is helping to hold the panic in my stomach at bay as the little yellow Nova carries us back to the future. The White Rocks. It has a majestic, mystical, important ring to it. I can imagine you at the White Rocks, dancing by a bonfire or just sitting smoking on your own somewhere in the moonlight. I can imagine you anywhere, at any time, wearing nothing but that smirk. The music from the car stereo is drowned by your voice as I stare at the oil-black sea and wonder where you are.

What's your name?

Who wants to know?

Vinny.

Why do you want to know, Vinny?

Because you're fucking beautiful!

Full of charm, you country boys.

It feels like I've never left this window or this coastline, with its occasional lights flashing out at sea. Have I been here all night, imagining the entire thing as the life slowly drains from my veins and your face is slowly erased from my brain? Has any of it been real? Were we really in that club? Did I really see all those people doing all of those mental things? My bottom lip trembles uncontrollably though my emotions are in check. When I close my mouth all is well but when I separate my lips it's off on its own, like a spastic rabbit. The tremor deepens and grips my bottom jaw in its entirety. Separated from the rest of my face, it hangs and flaps loosely as if the hinge that keeps it fixed to my skull has snapped. My eyes crash shut again and I'm back on the floor of the club with Jonty grinning over me, the smoke from the blowback spilling from the corners of his mouth. I can't force them open but I can still see you, Jonty. I want to call out to you and tell you about my eyes but I have no control over my mouth. My jaw stops twitching but it locks in place and won't move at all.

Everything is locked. I can't move. I'm buried alive inside my own dead body. I try to shake my arms but nothing works. I attempt to sit up off the seat but only manage to topple sideways into the car door. It holds me suspended precariously above the speeding black tarmac. I imagine the impact on my face and shoulder if I hit *terra firma* at the speed at which we're travelling. I would die for certain, but not before my face was ripped off on the cold hard road. I sink deeper into my seat and further into the recesses of my mind. My arse is so close now, almost touching the earth as I fly along this road in total blackness. The car door gives eventually and I fall out into the night. I don't hit the road, though, I plunge over the edge and down the cliff face towards the sea and the rocks below. I pass my cigarette from earlier on the way down. Still lit, it is caught in a thermal and it bounces around the sides of the cliff face, winking down at me as I plummet past it towards a watery grave. I really should make more of an effort to quit, you know. The facts are irrefutable.

As I'm pondering the colour of my lungs I'm lifted on a warm current and carried horizontally along the shoreline. I was seconds from the huge cruel stones below but now I fly above them, like a gaunt Irish genie on an invisible magic carpet. There is something bright over to my right. I think it's the headlights of the Nova as the boys make their way to the party without me. I try to call out to the little canary car but I have forgotten that my mouth doesn't work. They wouldn't hear me anyway over the noise of the engine and those infernal tunes blaring from the stereo. I wonder where I'm headed then, if it's not to the party. I don't care. The wind that has lifted me up is pleasant and warm, and now that my vision has returned I can see for miles and miles along the coastline. If I keep flying in this direction I can land in Belfast in no time. I can fly around the entire rim of Northern Ireland and take a right after Larne into Belfast lough where the ferries dock. What will I do there? Is Betty really the girl from my dream? I sense something above me and there you are, smirking down on my comatose self.

Betty, I can't move.

My name's not Betty, boy.

You never told me your name.

I don't date paraplegics as a rule, Vinny.

Your face changes. Your smirk widens and you morph into the grumpy barmaid from the pub in Ballykelly. She floats towards me, and the closer she gets the wider her smile becomes, until she's sitting on the end of my carpet, laughing hysterically.

'Hey! You never laugh! Have you seen Long Jim? He loves you, you know. He would love to see you happy.'

She stops laughing and hits me hard across the right-hand side of my face. Realising that I can't defend myself, the bitch hits me a second time and something deep inside me kicks for life. I shout and cough and manage to claw my eyes open again. Bingo is there right in front of me, his face almost touching mine.

'I think he's back.'

He hits me hard again on my left ear, then leans in even closer. I can smell his smoky, beery breath now as he moves within kissing range.

'How are you doing, Vin? You're off your face.'

'Jesus, I thought I was dead, man. I was in a coma and I thought I was dead.'

He hits me again.

'For fuck's sake, Bingo!'

'Sorry, man, but you're in a coma.'

'I *was* in a coma. I'm not in one any more. I just fucking told you about it, didn't I?'

'Well, there's no need to shout. What was I doing hitting you, Vinny? Well, I was only saving your life.'

We're in another car park, looking down at the sea. I have vomited twice and feel more like myself. The other five smoke nervously around me as I sit at a picnic table drinking a can of beer. A couple of cars pull in behind us and spill revellers out into the night. My posse moves off to gather the gossip, except for my best friend who perches beside me just in case.

'I'm sorry, mate, I couldn't move. It wasn't good.'

'It's all right, you were smacking out badly. I think your second half kicked in a bit later than mine.'

'I'm grand now. We need to stay focused and remember why we're here.'

'The sooner we get these things sold the sooner we can relax and enjoy the night.'

'Was she real, Jonty?'

'Oh, she was real all right, Vincent. Particularly her tits. They were very fucking real.'

Our table is enveloped by the ensemble cast of our moonlit adventure, and a circle of chewing, twisted faces discuss our options for the remainder of the night. I am handed gum by a man from Stoke-on-Trent and the chewing action instantly releases my jaw from its chains. The White Rocks is off. Two or three miles further along our route the police have put a road block in place and have been searching and arresting people trying to get to the party. Joints and rumours are passed solemnly amongst the disparate nocturnal band. I thank Stoke-on-Trent for my chewing gum and Jonty and myself pass beers from our boot to our new selection box of friends. As well as the guy from Stoke, there is a girl from Durham, three blokes from Wexford and two girls from Glasgow. I don't even ask. I get it now. People come from all over for this rave. People from all over are gathering everywhere for raves. Tonight I have met university students and bricklayers, lawyers and the unemployed. I have listened to Scotsmen and Englishmen, the north of Ireland and the south. I have no doubts I will smoke a joint with someone Welsh before the night is over. It's the concept of these gatherings that has the forces of order blocking roads and making arrests a couple of miles to the north. Davy apologises to our new English friends on behalf of our medieval police force.

'They've already stopped us on the way here. It's a joke, mate, and you coming over here from a civilised country for a good night out.'

'This isn't about Northern Ireland, Davy. It's the same all over. If I was bringing you to an outside party in Manchester tonight it would be the same shit, mate. It's this fucking Criminal Justice Bill.'

'They're frightened. The Man is fuckin' frightened.'

'Too right, Jonty. "We're all just working for the Man."'

An actual bill drawn up to curtail groupings like our very own. No gathering on land in the open air of twenty or more people at which amplified music is played during the night.

'I'm working for the Man?'

'Too right you are, Bingo!'

'"Twenty-six dollars in my hand".'

'That's Lou Reed, Bingo.'

'So?'

'That's "Waiting For The Man", written by Lou Reed, performed by the Velvet Underground. "Working For The Man" is by Roy Orbison.'

'Well, it's the same thing, isn't it?'

'No, Bingo, it is not the same thing. The man in Lou Reed's song is a heroin dealer that Lou is standing waiting for, hence the twenty-six dollars in his hand.'

'Lou Reed can get heroin for twenty-six dollars?'

'The man in Roy Orbison's song is the Man he busts his balls working for every day.'

'Where can he buy heroin for twenty-six dollars?'

'In 1967, mate.'

I would love to have been a fly on the wall in the Home Secretary's office as he and his cabal of middle-aged, middle-class, middle-of-the-road cronies came up with the vagaries of this new law to stop us dancing in the moonlight.

'It's like *Footloose*!'

'*Footloose*, Jim?'

'You know, where they live in that wee American town and John Lithgow has banned dancing in case you get the horn and ride his daughter.'

'Yeah, Jim, it's like *Footloose*, only on a nationwide scale where the entire country is banned from dancing.'

'Well, we're not banned from dancing, though, are we? We're just banned from dancing outside. At night. In big groups.'

A car is coming towards us at speed from the direction of the abandoned party. Fearing the law we ditch joints and scatter to the four corners of the car park. It isn't the cops, though, unless they're driving around undercover in souped-up Toyota twin-cams. We appear from the shadows to be informed by the skin-headed driver that the party is at the Ballintoy caves. By all accounts it always has been. The White Rocks was merely a decoy for the filth.

As we drive off, buoyed by this revelation, towards our new destination, I think of D-Day and the lengths that the Allies went to ensure Hitler's Panzers were as far as possible from the actual landings. I return to my window vigil and smile, excited at being part of something this big. We pull off the main road and follow the Toyota downhill towards the sea. I search in vain for signs of revelry, my eyes straining to pick out anything in the blacker ink that drenches everything beyond the beaten track. We hear it first. Windows have been opened and the stereo abandoned, and it reaches in to us from the distance through the dark. A low, steady, sonic boom. It could just be the waves of high tide crashing into the Ballintoy caves. We sit in silence, ears pricked and pupils dilated, as it draws us towards it. As we round each winding corner the decibels increase and the repetitive industrial nature of the noise confirms to us that we're not listening to the ocean. Butterflies in my stomach and

Keith Moon in my chest. The combination was overwhelming an hour ago but I find solace in it now as I rub my hands over my torso and remind myself who I am.

The final corner is turned and the music fills the car with sound as we pull into our fourth car park of the night. We hold a council of war at the back end of the little lemon pack pony. Mickey deploys tins of beer and Bingo rolls another joint. Davy and Jim watch Jonty retrieve the bags of pills from under the wheel, and I head into the darkness to empty my bowels again. They promise to wait and I stumble into the night and onto the corner of the small hill that separates the car park from the party. When I'm finished I move away from my deposit and sit on my own in my night. This is my night. There are many others like it but this one is mine. I laugh to myself, then hold my breath for thirty seconds to get the purest clarity of sound. You can only really hear at night when you're not breathing. I could hear the party and the music and the fire, but now I can distinguish it from the sea and the lads in the car park. I gorge my lungs once more, wolfing in the clean black air, then stretch out my legs and curl back into the slope. Hold, hold, hold. I can hear my heart, I can hear the grass, I can hear the bats above me in the Coca-Cola sky. Even with the music and flames beyond the hill I can hear them squeak when they dip low, and I can sense their strange frenetic changes in direction. I blot all else out and focus solely on the winged ones. Alone, I search the night as they swoop and sweep above me, desperately hoovering up insects, before dinner is sucked over the hillside into the smoke and the flames beyond.

'Vinny, you all right?'

'Yeah, I'll only be a minute. I'm just lying down here.'

'You fucked again?'

'No, I'm grand. It's nice here. I'll be over in a minute.'

'It's your turn on this smoke.'

'Finish it, Jonty. I'm all right till the next one.'

I roll onto my stomach and let the grass do whatever it wants to my face. I grind into it and let the smell of the earth fill me up from the boots to the balls to the ears. Another flip and I watch the stars. I'm aware that I have never watched them before. Not like I watch them now. I have seen nothing like I see it now, smelt nothing like I smell it now and heard nothing like I hear it right now. Boots. Moving downhill through the grass towards me. Stock still I lie, with my ears focused on the music of their footsteps. A body hits the ground to my right and another slightly lower down to my left.

'You all right, "Skintown"?'

'I'm fine, "Newlodge". Just enjoying the night.'

'You on the hippie buzz, big lad?'

'I think so. I've been watching the stars. How was Ned's?'

'Mental. After we left you in the car park we went on a mad one. Had trouble getting in because Franco was totally spannered. So we left him round the side, paid in, then sneaked him in a back door half an hour after.'

'Genius.'

'How was your first time? I'd give me left ball to do me first Ned's again!'

'It was unreal, mate. Unreal. Took my first E and everything.'

'You took your first pill? Holy fuck, I'd give me right ball to take me first pill again! How do you feel?'

'Amazing, man. I took a bad turn in the car on the way here. Smacked out and thought I was dead, but I'm fine now. I'm not fine, I'm amazing. I'm buzzing, man.'

'Good lad! The wee country boy on his first pill!'

'What's the party like up there?'

'Insane, man, but there are no drugs about, so enjoy your buzz while it lasts. The cops busted two dealers on their way here. Hundreds of Es in the car and apparently a couple of handguns.'

'There's a party but no pills?'

'I know, man, it's a fucking disaster. Place will start coming down in an hour.'

'We'll have to see about that then, my Belfast friend. As the man said, for every problem, there is only a solution.'

7

WE KEEP THE plan simple. The Belfast boys buy what they need for themselves and head back to the party to gently spread the word. Davy gives them strict instructions not to go shouting mad about it or we'll be mobbed as soon as we hit the brow of the hill. We opt for the selling speed of splitting up combined with safety in numbers and plump for two groups of three. I will be the seller in one group and Jonty the other, with a pair of bodyguards apiece. As payment we give the lads another pill each for free and it's decided that no one takes any more until business is complete. There will be a lot of money to be sorted, and security issues, and whatever wits we have left should be kept firmly about us. It turns out that Davy and Jim know Kyle and Grant pretty well.

'Do they mean it?'

'Yes.'

'They wouldn't kill us, though, would they?'

'Why take the risk, Vinny? Anyway, second prize is a kicking you'll never recover from. Does that whet your appetite?'

'How well do you know them?'

'We were in that marching band with them since we were kids. You might have bonded during your car crash but, believe me, these guys neither trust nor like Catholics. They haven't been here. They haven't realised we're all the same. They haven't been anywhere outside their tiny fucking angry minds.'

'That was extremely philosophical, Jim.'

'Poetic, I would say.'

'Be I a philosopher or a poet, lads, it's the case, so let's get this done and the money safely locked back in the boot of the car. Then we can find Vinny's new girlfriend, forget about everything else and get totally fucking melted.'

We haven't seen the fire that lives beyond the hill but we know that it's there. It surges and roars, filling a lull in the music as we reach the crest of the hill and take in the carnage below. Hundreds of people shimmer beneath us in various states of undress, moving at different speeds to the beat of the same drug. The blaze rages in a hollow, surrounded on three sides by slopes. The fourth wall is a little rustic harbour, complete with an old stone pier jutting out into the sea. As I take all of this in, I catch intermittent details of the boats framed for a second in an orange glow as they swing to and fro in the current on their mooring ropes. Some folk dance around the flames in circles, like ancient worshippers before some pagan fire deity, but most get down on the hillsides, throwing shapes and angles onto the ritual below.

'Right, lads?'

'Right, Davy.'

'Jim and Bingo, stick with Jonty. Head right from here, and when you get down to the harbour start edging your way into the crowd beside the fire. Ask a few people if they want any pills. Once you sell a few, chill. Don't start shouting about it and don't move around too fast. Sit for a while and let them come to you. They'll be like flies round shite. Jonty, do the talking. You two, watch him like hawks but don't scare people away. Every ten sales or so, give the money to Jim so you aren't trying to handle pills and cash. And, Bingo, keep your fucking mouth shut.'

'What do we do when they ask if the pills are duds?'

'Point at Bingo's face and explain that he's only had a half.'

'Do I look that bad? Don't be freaking me out!'

'We'll do exactly the same thing on this side and we'll meet in the middle in an hour, directly opposite here by those bushes on that hill. Got it?'

'Yes, Major.'

'What if something goes wrong?'

'Nothing will go wrong, Mickey.'

'How do you know that, Jim?'

'It's a rave, Vinny. Everybody is in love with everybody else. Adolf Hitler could walk through here right now, handing out signed copies of *Mein Kampf*, and people would tell him not to worry about anything any more as everyone has a strained relationship with their mother at some stage.'

It's not even business. We're doing people a favour for twenty quid. I don't have to ask the first lot if they want anything, they ask me if I have anything. The pattern continues as we wander gently through the evening towards the bushes. At this rate it won't take long to shift three hundred little dancing beans. Most buy more than one or two. I sell a girl from Derry ten pills and she hands me two hundred quid as if it's the most normal thing in the world. She is beautiful too, in her cocky twenty-something I'm-just-buying-some-fucking-drugs kinda way. We watch her half walk half dance back to her little group of friends lying around on the grass. She turns and smiles at me as her friends jump up and cheer the arrival of the purveyor of class As. Where are you, Betty? Are you here somewhere, sitting on the grass with your confident sexy friends? Come and find me and I'll sell you all some drugs. You can have yours for free, though. I can afford that. I am the dealer, after all. The big dealer man. This dealing lark is piss easy. I just walk around looking cool and people come and buy my shit. They give me the money and they smile at me as they walk away.

'Snap out of it, son. How many are left?'

'I think we've sold about fifty. Count the money and see. That's safer than me standing here poking through a big bag of pills.'

The faces come and go. They smile and gurn and twist and churn. People are kissing everywhere. A trembling mess of shimmering oblivious people. There are a lot of bodies on the ground, massaging and mauling each other. Our friend from Belfast reappears and takes another twenty for later. I don't even speak as I hand him his dessert. I smile and he winks and smiles right back. There is a huge whoosh below us as the great fire yells and shoots up into the night sky. Someone must have doused it with petrol. Even here, halfway up the hillside, I can feel its heat on my face. Davy points up and left, and we move towards a large clutch of people dancing at the top of the hill. Twenty pills lighter, we move on again, skirting the ridge and watching for clients below. A cigarette break and some basic mathematics tell us we have fifty-one tablets left to sell. I wonder if Jonty is doing as well. He has the patter. The wee bastard probably sold the lot to the first person he met.

Tomorrow will be beautiful. As long as we get some sleep. Or maybe not: who needs sleep? We can go straight to the pub back home and get stuck into the pints. Two men my father's age approach and ask me if I have any gear to sell. I stare dumbly at two moustaches. One small, well-trimmed and black, the other ginger, bushy and neurotic. Davy bounces lithely forward and takes control of proceedings.

'Does he look like a dealer?'

'I don't know. What should a dealer look like?'

'I don't know either, mate. What should the DS look like?'

'The what?'

'You're walking round a party in cords and a waxed jacket asking for drugs.'

'Pardon?'

'You're clearly Drug Squad, mate. Now fuck off.'

'We really are not the Drug Squad. Look.' He takes a ready-rolled joint from his pocket and holds it out to Davy.

'All that proves is you've already confiscated someone's hash tonight.'

Ginger takes a lighter from his pocket and holds a flame in front of Black's face. Black sucks deeply on the joint to get it going, then offers it to Mickey. Why do Northern Irish men over forty all have moustaches? I sway slightly and scour my memory for a clean-shaven uncle.

'Yeah, right, mate. The minute I accept that you'll have me cuffed.'

'We are not the Drug Squad, lads. We're just out for a good night. We have money.'

'Of course you have money, you're on a government wage.'

'I'm smoking the bloody thing! How could I be in the Drug Squad?'

'I've seen *Serpico*, mate. You fuckers can do whatever you want when you're undercover.'

'That was in America.'

'So you admit it?'

'No, I'm just saying that was in America. Stuff like that doesn't happen here.'

'This is Northern Ireland, man. We have teams of under-cover soldiers going round shooting innocent people.'

'We are not in the Drug Squad and we are not undercover.'

'The two things are mutually inclusive.'

'Excuse me?'

'If you're not in the Drug Squad it goes without saying you're not undercover.'

'What?'

'What would you be undercover for?'

'If they are undercover, Davy, they're pretty shite. They look like the royal family on a fishing holiday.'

'We are not undercover, we're teachers!'

'Well, then, you should be undercover.'

'And you're still on a government wage.'

We sell them two Es. Their first, apparently. I vow to find them later and watch their moustaches dancing on their twitching, grinning, extracurricular faces. By the time we reach the bushes I have twenty-seven ecstasy tablets left in my bag. I lie beside the resplendent Jonty and look back at my stars in the night sky. I don't need to ask him: his face wears the relaxed smile that only empty pockets bring. There is no need to move again. The world knows where we are. We keep four of my remaining pills, two for tonight and two for a celebration tomorrow. The remaining twenty-three are gone in no time, as people come and get them. The world knows who we are. When all is said and done, it was easy. Minus the four freebies we gave the boys and the six for ourselves, we have sold them all. When we present the two day-release patients with their five grand we will still have eight hundred quid between us for one night's work. Not bad for a couple of budding Pablo Escobars. Jonty, Davy and Long Jim escort the cash to the safety of the Nova's boot while the rest of us stretch out and wait.

I'm getting used to the acrid taste now. Third time lucky. Jonty drops his all in one go but I opt for another half. After my little jolly along the coastline I think it's best to take things easy. One more beer to let the tummy settle, then the big boys are up and dancing again. We sit and admire Davy's steroid-ripped frame skipping around the flesh totem pole we call Long Jim. He is incredibly neat on his feet for a big man. Precise and compact, almost dainty. Fred West meets Fred Astaire. The sheer size of the pair starts to attract attention, and when Jim gets into his repertoire the punters flock to join in.

'What was it you said earlier, Davy? Like flies round shite?'

He laughs and throws his empty beer can at my head. Bingo and Mickey announce that they're getting into the thick of the action at the fire to chat to birds, so Jonty and I opt for a wander. At the very top of the hill, at the very back of the crowd, there is a void. A black wall between here and there. A stark, silent no man's land between the party, the people, our states of mind and we know not what. We turn our backs on the unknown and watch the masses dance. Behind us the entire world is in darkness. I run my eyes slowly from my feet along the ground up into the people and the party before us. Before us the world is on fire. Before us the people explode. So many stars, shimmering at the very peaks of their existence. As my eyes pass over them in a long and loving inspection, I bask in their perfection, proud to have been here when their potential was finally fulfilled. When my eyes eventually reach the people at the back the darkness returns and the penny drops. This is the light and the light only shines here. In here we burn brightly, but out there no one really knows. Here I stand on the edge, teetering on the brink between reality and the lie called civilisation. I have seen the light. I have seen the light and I have danced and basked in its rays and nothing will ever be the same again.

'Jonty, my head is completely melted.'

'Me too. I'm thinking about some scary shit here, man.'

'Is it about light and dark and the point of your existence?'

'No, it's about my sister's friend catching me wanking on the kitchen table.'

'Fuck up.'

'Seriously. I rubbed a load of Vicks on me balls a couple of weeks ago and I was lying back on the table, welting away, and she was just there staring in the window in shock.'

'You were jerking off in the kitchen?'

'What's wrong with that?'

'What's wrong with your bedroom?'

'That's typical of you, Vinny.'

'Me?'

'Anyone else would have pointed out that wanking on a table was strange.'

'What?'

'But for you it's all about which room the table is in.'

'Who wanks anywhere outside their own bedroom?'

'Plenty of people.'

'How do you know? Are you in a wankers' therapy group or something?'

'You don't need therapy for masturbation, Vincent. It's perfectly normal.'

'It's perfectly normal in private, not in your mother's kitchen on a fucking table.'

'Do you think Betty Boo's here?'

I look at the wee bastard for an eternity. There will always be more to Jonty than meets the eye. He lights two fags at once and hands me one. After a couple of drags we swivel 180 degrees and prepare to face our demons.

'If she's here she'll find me.'

'Too right, man. What's for you won't go by you.'

I reach my arm down and put it around his shoulders, pulling him close. 'Some night's craic, Jonty man. Some night's craic.'

He reaches up and wraps his arm around my waist, and as one we step out into the darkness.

The second the light evaporates the sound goes with it. As the music recedes behind us we are drawn forward by the song of the sea. Downhill at first we tread, careful and slow, two blind explorers reading the braille of the earth with the soles of our feet. The ground beneath us begins to change and we start to bounce gently along, like two stoned astronauts on the dark side of the moon. We stop and hold each other, confused by this sponge beneath us. I fall gingerly to my knees and let my hands do the seeing. It's the grass that has changed. It's that big soft springy clown grass that only grows near the sea. We push forward again and the comedy grass begins to recede, replaced by sand. I can hear it, the sand, as hundreds and thousands of particles are scattered in front of me, displaced and disregarded by the giant rubber soles of my battered brown desert boots. My eyes begin to adjust and I stare upwards at the silhouette of another hill standing in our path. It looms ominously above us, a small black mountain, proud and solid and in our way. Silently we run at the dune and attack it together. It fights back hard, sucking at our feet and legs as we thrust down and deep, determined to punch through its defences and make the summit above.

The moon sits somewhere behind our goal. We can't see him yet, but his smile reaches upwards, lighting the crest of the massive sand dune and showing us soldiers the way. Nearly there now, lads. Just keep those legs powering down and forward. As the acid in my thighs begins to burn, Jonty begins to yell and laugh at the same time, as his energy drains from him and he lunges desperately for the finishing line. I join in with a blood-curdling scream as we dig deep, clawing and kicking for the top. We fall over it in the end, rolling nearly halfway down the other side before motion and laughter finally stop and we lie in silence, staring at the moonlit waves that break on the deserted beach below us. There is nothing to say. This was here before us and will be here long after words have become a thing of the past.

'Is her chat good?'

'I don't know, man. As I said, we didn't do much talking.'

'I noticed.'

'She seems smart.'

'What does that mean?'

'She had a vibe about her.'

'That's what you want her to be like.'

'What's what I want her to be like?'

'Sexy and clever. It's very rare.'

'Thanks for that, Don Juan.'

'I'm telling you, man.'

'You're telling me what?'

'Nobody has it all.'

'All what?'

'Nobody has it all.'

'I heard what you said, but what does it mean?'

'Some people get a lot of one thing but little or none of another.'

'No shit, Obi-Wan.'

'You either look good or you sound good.'

'Jesus Christ.'

'He had it all. One of the exceptions.'

'What are you talking about?'

'Jesus was attractive and intelligent and people wanted to hang out with him.'

'He didn't exist.'

'Yes, he did.'

'A bloke called Jesus Christ may have existed, but he couldn't cure lepers or turn water into wine, and he didn't look like Kurt fucking Cobain.'

'He was probably more Paul Simon, to be fair.'

'You don't believe in God.'

'I know.'

'So what are you banging on about?'

'You're right, and it proves my point. If there had been a Son of God walking the earth, spreading genius to the masses, it's more likely he would have been a very intelligent, very ugly man.'

'There are exceptions to the rule.'

'Who?'

'There are always exceptions to the rule.'

'Bollocks. Politicians and lawyers are brainy and say what people want to hear, but they are ugly bastards. Actors and models are beautiful and look how people want to look, but they are stupid bastards.'

'Robert De Niro.'

'Smart, yes, but chicks don't find him attractive.'

'Women don't fancy Robert De Niro?'

'Blokes find him attractive because in his movies he's who we want to be, but women want Tom Cruise and his big shiny teeth.'

'Tom Cruise is pretty smart.'

'He believes in aliens.'

'Brad Pitt!'

'Stupid.'

'Johnny Depp?'

'Creepy.'

'Daniel Day-Lewis!'

'Acquired taste.'

'Exactly! Attraction is not a science.'

'Look at this year's films. The intelligent movies win the Oscars, right?'

'Generally.'

'*Schindler's List*. A genius film full of ugly clever bastards: Ralph Fiennes, Liam Neeson and Gandhi.'

'Who got Best Actor?'

'Tom Hanks, playing a homo with AIDS. Again, not what the ladies want to see.'

'Un-fucking-believable.'

'Now *The Fugitive*, there's a different story. Harrison Ford and Tommy Lee Jones. Two sexual dynamos with the brains of children. Film made a fuckin' fortune.'

'*Mrs. Doubtfire* made a fucking fortune.'

'But Robin Williams fits into neither category. He's just an annoying cunt.'

'Can you see that ship coming towards the beach?'

He stares with me into the night beyond the waves.

'There. To the left of that flashing light.'

'Oh, my God, yes!'

It appears to be coming right at us out of the deep, but we both know that it isn't really there.

'Look at the purple bits of sea behind it, man!'

As soon as he says it I see it, a bright purple oil slick surrounding the ship that is a figment of my imagination.

'Are those people in the water?'

'Hundreds of them.'

We can't make out their faces but I can hear their voices in my head, calling out for no one to save them.

'The ship is getting smaller.'

'It's sinking! It's sinking fast!'

'That's a submarine surfacing over there! It must have been the one that took them.'

I can just about make out a conning tower over the tops of the waves.

'Germans, Jonty. They must be Germans.'

We continue like this for an age. Whatever I see he sees it too, and whatever he describes immediately appears inside my head. There is the faintest tinge of grey now beginning to stain the horizon behind the drug-fuelled battlefield of our imaginations.

'Do you hear it?'

'Yeah.'

'Laughter?'

'Maybe.'

'Is it real or inside our heads?'

'I don't know.'

As we listen the sound gets louder, coming along the beach from the direction of the harbour.

'Girls?'

'I think so.'

My eyes are drawn towards the gentle tinkle of their voices and I see two tiny orange lights that keep vanishing and reappearing a few hundred metres along the beach.

'Look, Jonty, over there. They're smoking.'

Inspired, we light two cigarettes ourselves and stumble downhill towards the strangers below. It is beginning to get lighter but it is still impossible to make out anything more than a few yards in front of your feet. Acoustic orientation will have to suffice. We pin their voices in the middle of our compass, and smoke and mumble our way down the beach to the water's edge. When we reach the waves I can still hear them in front of me, and I begin to doubt their realness after all.

'They're out there, in the sea.'

'Right, so a couple of mermaids popped up on shore for a Marlboro fuckin' Light then?'

'I don't know. It sounds like they're out there.'

'Look over here.'

Two perfectly neat little piles of women's clothes sit about twenty metres up the beach. Shoes at the bottom, jeans folded on top of shoes, T-shirts and bras on top of jeans, and two little pairs of black lace knickers perched on top like two black cherries adorning two tantalising cakes. We sit beside a pile each and listen to their mysterious owners as we finish our cigarettes. Eventually two figures emerge from the sea. They are mere silhouettes in this dark grey morning light, and as they begin to move up the beach I jump up in panic, realising that two strange men sitting in the dark beside their underwear might just scare the shite out of them.

'Hi, girls. How are you?'

They turn and run back to the sea where they plunge in,

covering their naked selves, leaving only two floating heads staring intently up the beach.

'Are you going through our things?'

'Fuck, no. We were walking past and we heard you laughing so we stopped for a smoke and a listen.'

Silence. It eats into me the longer it goes on. Maybe we should leave.

'You'd better get in, then.'

'What do you mean?'

'Well, we're not going to walk up to you in our finest, are we? And it's starting to get cold, so the obvious thing is for you two to take your clothes off and get into the sea too.'

When she's finished talking all I can hear is her friend giggling behind her and the pounding of my heart. I have my T-shirt off and my jeans around my knees before Jonty can put his tongue back in.

'What are you doing?'

'Exactly what she says.'

'Seriously?'

'There are two naked girls in the sea asking us to join them: it's not rocket science, Jonty. Now get your fucking jeans off.'

'But you know my swimming is shit. I barely made it across to Portora.'

'I'm hoping you won't be doing much swimming.'

'Well, we won't be doing much else. Our dicks will turn into maggots with the cold.'

His voice is behind me, though. By the time he decides he'd better join me I am ankle deep in the North Channel. Jesus, that's cold. I give a little shout as I go in over my knees and the two girls begin to laugh again.

'It's fuckin' freezing.'

'It's all right once you're in. Go on, get your head under, you pussy.'

I take a deep breath and fall forward. The girls aren't very far out but it is deep enough to hide my modesty as I wade over to them and introduce myself. The one who does all the talking is waist-deep with her arms folded across her chest. She is a big girl with platinum-blonde hair cropped close to her scalp. Her friend is hiding behind her, submerged up to the neck.

'I'm Vinny.'

'Skinny Vinny, eh? I saw you in the club all right. I'm Tanya. I believe you've met my friend.'

'Hey there, country boy.'

You don't show your face. You stand behind your friend, then seductively stretch a leg out to the side, like Anne Bancroft on the poster for *The Graduate*.

'Hey, Betty.'

'Who the fuck's Betty?'

'That's just what my friends call you, because of your hair.'

'Is your wee mate getting in or what?'

You float towards me. When you've made the distance you stand up tall and kiss me on the mouth. Your breath fills me up again, and I can feel your nipples pressing on my chest. The maggot factor isn't going to be an issue.

There is a loud splash behind us, followed by more sporadic thrashing and the sounds of someone drowning. When he appears beside me he looks genuinely frightened, and I can't work out if it's the sea or the females that have him in a panic.

'It's fuckin' freezing.'

'Girls, this is Jonty. Jonty, this is Tanya and . . .'

'Mia.'

'Hi, Tanya. Hi, Mia. We call you Betty, cos of your hair.'

'I heard.'

Tanya dives forward, disappearing completely into the water. A moment later Jonty vanishes too, as she pulls his legs from under him and drags him to the bottom. You take my hand and we swim off together as Jonty resurfaces and starts to shout. 'What the fuck did you do that for?'

Tanya is nowhere to be seen, though, and his second question is cut short as she grabs him again and pulls him down. When he surfaces for the second time it's laughter we hear, and I sense that he has met his match.

'How long have you been in the sea?'

'How long have you been watching us?'

My lips are numb with the cold but when you press yours onto them a warm glow spreads throughout my entire body. I run my hand down your back onto your tight arse and pull you into me. You roll your head back and I run my face from your neck down to your breasts, licking the salty water from your skin and gently taking one of your nipples in my mouth. You moan quietly as I move between your breasts. When I bite down you moan louder, then grab me roughly by the hair, lifting my head and bringing our mouths together again. My bottom lip is nipped sharply in revenge, and I am the one moaning now as sharp nails puncture the skin of my right buttock.

'Let's get warm and dry, country boy. I'll race ya!'

I swim after you, grabbing at your legs to slow you down, and we laugh our way up onto the beach towards our clothes. You have your knickers on in an instant and you slap my arm away when I try to rip them down again. I pull my T-shirt over my head to ward off the shivers, and we fall onto the rest of our clothes, rolling around through cotton and denim and sand. I drop my hand again and this time there is no rebuke. Thigh and hip muscles relax and legs open just a little to invite me in.

There is a gust of wind along the beach and my back twitches as my fingers arrive in soft hot velvet.

'Are you two riding up there?'

'No, Tanya, we're just getting warm.'

You raise my hand from your crotch and kiss my fingers, and we pull each other close while the wind coats us with sand and our friends move towards us from the sea.

'You'd better put your shorts on, Vinny. That thing sticking in my leg might just frighten our Tanya.'

8

CLOTHED BUT DAMP, we float along the beach towards the harbour. You and Tanya have a bottle of wine in your car and announce that we farmers are worthy of a share. After no deliberation we gallantly agree to drink with the two of you, and defrost by the epic fire back at the party. They have two friends somewhere amid the madness, and if we all stay in one spot we will be found eventually by our respective clans. You lie back between my legs, your head resting in the perfect spot bridging my chest and shoulder that evolution has hollowed out specifically for girls to rest their heads in. I hold beauty, tightly soaking it up through my skin as the drugged blood bubbles and races through my veins. I am happy. I am ecstatic. I am a pig in shite. I take the last half-pill from my pocket and show it to you. You take it from me and bite half of it off, then wink at me and put the remainder into my mouth. We wash it down with the end of the wine and our kissing builds until it is totally out of control.

'Let's go for a walk, Vinny.'

Around the fire the world burns slower now, as the infant sun prepares to paint the embers of the party a cold stark morning grey. There are no more spires of flame, no angry bursts of heat blasting up the surrounding hillsides. People cling to each other for some warmth. The music has changed to suit the mood. Less banging, less harsh, it has a subtle ambience to it that has been absent throughout the night. As you lead me by the hand I smile at Tanya, who is waving at me from where she dances with Jonty. I say dancing: they sway together by the dregs of the fire, his arms around her waist and his head shoved firmly between her tits. She sucks on a cigarette, her elbow resting on the top of his head between drags.

'Wait a minute, this is the best song yet.'

A simple electronic loop is building gradually with no real discernible beat. Eventually a rhythm cuts through and takes the lead, and our bodies begin to sway gently, taken by the power of the music. There is a new noise now, played on an instrument that I have never heard before, pitching hypnotically between two notes from low to high and back again. An organ joins the ranks, and some sort of keyboard choral effect swells and fills out the tune with layer after layer of tone and colour. Suddenly the drums stop stone dead and leave us floating and melting in the middle of a sheer orgasmic cacophony of sound.

Follow me, follow me, follow me, follow me

I look at you but your lips aren't moving, and as an intense rush of pleasure rips through my back and legs, I realise that the voice is inside the music.

Follow me, follow me, follow me, follow me

'I'll follow you anywhere, mate. This tune is fucking amazing.'

We hold each other and let the music wash over and through us until it is finished, and then we stumble off towards the shore. I see Bingo and Mickey hugging each other over to my left, and then out of nowhere big Davy appears and throws his arms around me.

'Love ya, Vinny. I love ya, baby!'

'I love you too, big man. This is Mia.'

'Nice to meet ya, love. You look after him for us now. This kid's the dog's bollocks.'

As he releases his grip on me he grabs my hand and slides something into it. When our journey resumes I open my fist and a condom is winking up at me in its perfect little square silver wrapper. I smile from my balls to the tops of my ears and shout backwards as loudly as I can, 'I really do love you, you know, you big ugly Protestant bastard!'

We make love in the tall grass behind the harbour wall. I have never made love. As I lie beneath you, staring into your bourbon eyes, I feel cheated. Cheated by the times that came before. I lost my virginity in the disabled toilets in a public park. I sat on the big high porcelain bowl with my pants down, holding onto the little metal safety rail as Jenny Armstrong rode me sideways, her eyes rolling in the back of her head, a woman possessed. As I clung on for dear life I imagined that I was a fairground ride she had put 50p into and that she had to get her money's worth before we came full circle and the music stopped. Physically I felt nothing. Emotionally I suffered waves of panic and fear at the prospect of her actually breaking my cock off at the root. Eyes closed and knuckles white, I tried not to laugh out loud as the gypsy fairground man in my mind urged her onwards to oblivion. Scream if you wanna go faster!

We are one, though, Mia. There are no thoughts, no planned moves, no moments of doubt. I kiss you for the love of kissing you and for the fear of no second chance. I run my hands all over you, my rough fingers fascinated by the subtle soft finish of your skin. Our bodies instinctively find what they need to. Eyes wander occasionally to take in a pornographic angle, a union, a gentle entry, but they always come back to the beginning. Back to the moment when they locked together as I reached up from the dance floor and climbed inside you. When you are on top of me with your face an inch from mine, we come together. You take my head at the crook of my neck and force your mouth hard onto mine, stifling two sets of moans with the deepest kiss of them all. Afterwards I know that there will be only before this and afterwards. As we lie in each other's arms, my leg wrapped over the small of your back, I know that this is it. This is the one. I nuzzle down behind your ear and wolf you deep inside me. High on your scent, I close my eyes as the drums build in my head, and John Squire's guitar confirms that part of me will stay here in this field for ever.

You are up on one elbow, staring at me, when I wake. A brown-eyed naked stare in the hot buttered dawn sunlight. I glower intently until your smirk reappears and you offer your lips up for breakfast. We are buck naked in a little nest amongst the tall grass, our discarded clothes dragged on top of us for modesty and insulation. There is only us. Only we exist in this silent morning world. I roll onto my back so that you can put your head on my chest, and I catch the tail end of some movement in the pale blue sky. Small fast birds swoop and soar acres above us. Swallows or swifts, I think. Before, it was the bats.

The night-time keepers of the sky. Now up in the baby blue the last vestiges of darkness are swept away by the soaring little birds of light. When I try to talk you put your finger on my lips. When I try again you climb on top of me and silence me with your mouth. You take me in your hand and my blood rushes to meet you, then you whisper, 'Don't worry, darlin',' as you guide me inside you. Without the layer of rubber to keep us apart your silken wet warmth is almost too much to bear. I panic, but you read it in me and you smile and mouth, 'Don't worry, darlin',' again, then you ride me hard but slow with your hands on my chest and your eyes lost in mine, until I can stand it no longer and I lose all of myself inside you. When we sleep again you stay with me in my dream. We are drinking pints on top of a London bus as you tell me all about your days at school. I sit in silence, surfing your voice, and as we cross the river and pass Waterloo station, I realise that, whatever happens in the real world, you will be locked in here with me in my dreams for ever.

Their voices wake us. Far away but getting closer. They are making their way towards us, beating the grass, seeking out the pair of love-struck fugitive pheasants. At first it is only Tanya, a soft feminine voice carried easily on the breeze as she gently coos us home.

'Viiiinny! Miiiiiia!'

Then Jonty joins in and our bubble is finally well and truly burst.

'Vinny! Vinny, you stupid prick, we're gonna fuckin' leave without you!'

To the soundtrack of my animated little friend, the four of us wander back to the car park. The girls laugh warmly at him as he fights to get all of his words out at once. It is a tale of discovery and joy, a story of unparalleled wonder, of nature and friendship and ecstasy. It is a monologue of Shakespearean magnitude delivered by a man of Napoleonic proportions.

'We were pure out of our heads in the dark, and I just followed Vinny, holding on to his sleeve cos he's taller than me, and everything looked purple and mental, like we were in an episode of *Tales of the Unexpected*, and then there was a big mental sand mountain in front of us, so we ran up the bastard, and when we burst over the top the moon was shining down on you two in the sea in the nude and you looked like a pair of mad mermaid angels, so we freaked out and got the horn and ran down the hill, like a couple of lunatics, and we sat by your knickers as you swam about naked and didn't even know we were there, and then Vinny made me get me jocks off and I shit meself cos I didn't want to get me cock out, but then I did get me cock out and it ended up being the best night of me life. Will we go somewhere for a pint or two after, just the four of us?'

The car park is nearly empty. Four cars and a small gathering of smoking, chewing, smiling people are all that remain. The boys are there, Mickey, Davy, Bingo and Jim. They are drinking beers at the Nova with your mates, Deborah and Zoë.

As we approach, hugs and kisses abound, and you and I get a warm, jealous, sarcastic round of applause as Davy hands out tins of lager from the breakfast buffet.

'Did you pass the teachers on your way over?'

'Who?'

'Remember the two teachers we sold the pills to last night? They're over there on the hill getting stuck into each other for all the world to see!'

We approach them cautiously, like a team of twitchers not wanting to frighten the exotic birds that have landed on our humble shores for the very first time. Sure enough, halfway up the grassy knoll the two gentlemen teachers lie in each other's arms, kissing tenderly but with tongues. Enraptured, they sense not our approach. They are oblivious to the world. Enthralled and captured by each other's moustaches they care not for the rising sun or their possible discovery by pupils or neighbours. They are both partially naked, their waxed jackets and shirts having been scattered liberally around the surrounding area with, dare I say, gay abandon.

'How has he done that?'

'Done what, Bingo?'

'Well, that guy has his jeans on with no shoes, right?'

'Correct.'

'But that one is in his underpants and still has his shoes and socks on.'

'And?'

'And how the fuck do you get your jeans off without taking your shoes off?'

It's a veritable homoerotic ship in a bottle. We stare for an age in confused admiration.

'He obviously had the shoes and socks off, then decided to put them back on at some point.'

'Yeah, but why, Jonty?'

'I don't know, Mickey. Maybe he had to go for a shite in the night and didn't want to hurt his feet.'

'But you would just pull your shoes on. You wouldn't take the time to put your fucking socks on too!'

'Nothing makes sense when the Es kick in.'

'Amen, big Davy.'

'We are talking here about two semi-naked married men in their forties making out on a hill.'

'How do you know they're married?'

'They both have wedding rings on. I gave them a good once-over earlier when I still thought they were cops.'

The girls slide their wheels in beside ours, dwarfing the Nova, which cowers in the shadow of their brand-new Range Rover. Bose speakers bounce creamy house music at us off leather seats as we sit in a semicircle at the arse end of this civilian Panzer. The tunes are tight and perky and create the canvas onto which the morning's bullshit can be sprayed.

'Who owns the four-by-four?'

'Mia's da.'

'Mia's a Prod?'

'None of us are Prods.'

'Really?'

'Really, Jonty.'

'What does he do?'

'He's a solicitor.'

'A Catholic solicitor?'

'They do exist, you know.'

'Maybe in Belfast, Zoë, but not where we come from.'

'There are Catholic solicitors at home, you bollocks. What about yer man Nolan and that prick Gleason?'

'They're not real Catholics, Bingo. They drink gin and tonic and play golf.'

The beer is good and the company is better. When I awoke I thought the drugs had worn off, but as I lie here with my head in your lap I know that my blood is not yet my own.

'Did you all sleep?'

It's a spontaneous group reaction and the laughter lasts for a long time.

'No, Vincent, only you lovebirds slept. The rest of us danced the night away.'

'Smoked the night away, man. We've nearly finished all the gear.'

'We'll get some more when we hit town, which will have to be soon enough, lads, as it's nearly eight o'clock.'

You rise, take my hand and lead me off to say goodbye. No insults traipse behind us. We are followed only by the reverential silence of friends who recognise the imminent arrival of heartache. We lie in the lee of the Range Rover at the foot of the hill where I discovered my bats the night before. Hidden from the world by thirty thousand pounds' worth of unnecessary British engineering, we claw and clutch and cling to our ending.

'When will I see you again?'

'Whenever you get your arse up to the city, Vinny.'

'I'm coming soon. We have the money now from the pills, so next week I'm going to head up and get a job sorted and somewhere to live. I'll get a piece of paper and take your number.'

'I don't have a number. We're students, the last thing we can afford is a phone.'

There is a loud crunching noise from inside the Range Rover and the music stops. I roll onto my back to look at the beast, half expecting a face full of expensive hot metal. Instead the music kicks back in and I get an earful of expansive American jazz trumpet.

'It's just the CD changer.'

'Your car has a CD changer?'

'My dad's car has a CD changer.'

'What is a CD changer?'

'It revolves sixteen CDs inside the stereo system.'

'Right.'

'I take it your dad doesn't have a CD changer, then?'

'My dad doesn't have a CD. Are you very rich?'

'No, Vinny. I'm an English student.'

'How will I find you?'

'I know you think it's the Big Smoke, Vinny, but it's only Belfast. I live in the Holylands. Three hundred and thirty-four Fitzroy Avenue. Failing that, the girls and I are in Lavery's bar nearly every night of the week.'

Returning, I can barely see the Antrim coastline. I stare blindly at it but all I can see is you. The most beautiful stretch of coastline in Ireland, they say. With eyes like those I won't disagree. The angry rave tape has been swapped for something better suited to the time of day. Primal Scream seem to appreciate the point of the morning glow, so we agree to let Bobby Gillespie and Andrew Innes drive us most of the way home. We pull in at Dunluce Castle to ceremonially smoke the last of the gear while we look down on the medieval ruins. With the final bit of life sucked from the scorching roach, Davy, Jim and I lie on our bellies at the edge of the road and look down on our three companions, who run like children through the magical sunburst ruins at the top of the cliff below.

'Was that really the last joint, Long James?'

'That, Large David, really was the last joint of an astonishing fucking evening.'

'Sensational, I would say, James.'

'You in love then, Vincent my son?'

'I wasn't the only one getting a bit, Jim.'

'Yeah, you were. The big girl let the wee man play with her tits while she whacked him off, but that was as far as he got.'

'It's far enough.'

'It certainly is.'

'Great tits, too.'

'Impeccable.'

I float to the car and turn up the stereo as my favourite track from the album weighs in.

'This pansy music is all right, you know, Vin.'

'It's good smoking music, that's for sure.'

'This one's the best. "Higher Than The Sun". Wait till the sax kicks in.'

We dance gently at the side of the road. The three of us just swaying through the morning. Cars slow down to watch us and some beep their horns as they round the bend but we care not. When the saxophone finally ejaculates, we grab each other and howl like banshees at the ghosts of Ireland's past, who dance through the castle below us. From within its walls our boys howl back, Mickey and Bingo and Jonty. We did it. We did it all. We are a team. We are the boys. We are fucking legends.

9

CHALKY IS ON so we have no bother getting served, despite looking like patients from the local asylum whose escape route has taken in the well-stocked pharmaceutical dispensary. We hide at the table under the jukebox and nurse golden bubbling chalices, like cats who hate cream and prefer to stay up all night drinking pints and taking drugs. The Bramble doesn't do meals, so we won't be disturbed by real people who eat food. If you're really desperate Chalky will make you a cheese and ham toastie. If you can't stand the thought of food, even though your body is crying out for it, get through your second pint as quickly as possible and all will be forgiven. With that in mind I hand Jonty two quid for the jukebox and prepare to hit the bar for round two.

'Put the whole of *Dark Side of the Moon* on.'

'Really?'

'Really.'

'*Dark Side of the Moon?*'

'Pink Floyd, Jim. Perfect from start to finish.'

'I know who it is, Vinny, I'm just worried there aren't enough toilet cubicles in here for us all to hang ourselves in.'

'I've never been in here before.'

'I'm not surprised, Davy. Your former hobby was trying to castrate most of the clientele.'

Chalky is lighting the fire across the lounge so I sit at the bar and stare at the TV. The BBC news is starting. It's lunchtime, so it's fucking Witchell as usual.

'What's happening, Nick, you dick?'

'The People's Republic of China and Russia have agreed to de-target their nuclear weapons against each other as of today . . .'

'Remarkable, Nicholas, you copper chopper.'

'. . . ending more than thirty years of tension between the nations that became known as the Sino-Soviet split.'

'But surely these two were big Commie besties, Nick the prick?'

'The worsening of political and ideological relations between the world's two largest Communist nations in the fifties eventually led to a split with decades of tension, and ultimately a nuclear standoff ensued.'

'I didn't know that. Are the 'RA still finished?'

'Reports from Belfast indicate that the Provisional Irish Republican Army ceasefire has now successfully entered its fourth day.'

'Thanks, Nick. Maybe if the war's over and the Communists are all making friends I should at least give you another chance.'

'That's all from me. We'll be back at six for the evening news.'

'Fuck you, Witchell! Don't ignore the hand of peace when it's offered. And stay away from Moira, you ginger bastard!'

The news finishes and the BBC meanders apologetically to coverage of an international athletics meeting at Crystal Palace. Chunky Romanian girls are limbering up and preparing to put their weight behind large orbs of metal.

'Same again?'

'Always, Chalky.'

'No football today. I'll be bored off me balls for this shift.'

'See the war is still over, Chalk?'

'I was thinking the war must be well and truly buried when you walked in here with those two.'

'Davy and Jim are grand, Chalky. Jesus, we had the best night's craic!'

'Well, Davy and Jim used to be grand at kicking the shite out of Catholics, and a leopard never changes his spots, Vin, especially if his spots are red, white and blue.'

'The times they are a-changing, Chalky. Couple of nights in Ned's and you'd soon see the difference.'

'That's just drugs. When the novelty and the MDMA wear off we'll be back to what we know best: mistrust, murder and terrorist-sponsored cheap diesel.'

The front doors swing open and the alcoholic substitute teacher strolls in, like John Wayne on a diet. He surveys all before him, sniffs the air cautiously and joins us at the bar.

'Pink Floyd, Vinny?'

'Yeah, Pink Floyd.'

'Good choice.'

'How do you know I chose it?'

'Well, I know it wasn't that small chap you hang around with – he has no taste – and it was neither of the apes he's sitting with, who frankly quantify what I have just said about his taste.'

'How do you know my name?'

'It's a small town, son. Everybody knows your name.'

'Would you like a whiskey?'

'It's a bit early, even for me.'

'Pint then?'

'No, I'll have the whiskey.'

Mickey and Bingo had dropped us at the door of the bar earlier, then headed on home. It was sad when they left. The team finally broken up after its finest hour. I don't want it to end. I'm frightened about what comes next. I know if I keep drinking, though, all will be well. Just keep the party going, Vincent. Keep the party going, my son.

'Will you join us under the jukebox?'

'I think I'll just dance over by the fire, son, but thanks for asking.'

'No bother.'

Eight minutes later and we're all dancing by the fire. 'Time' is belting out of that old jukebox like tomorrow may never arrive. We sing in unison as Chalky shakes his head, gives in and pours himself his first of the day.

Four men and one alcoholic substitute teacher. Ten eyes closed, twenty fingers bending Dave Gilmour's sweet solo, note for bitter note. As the piano immorally tricks us into 'The Great Gig In The Sky', together we mouth the immortal words of the Abbey Studio's Irish doorman whilst separately acknowledging our own mortality.

I keep my eyes shut tight for the upcoming journey. I know there is no turning back because I've been on this trip before. Nothing human could create such a sound. I will never accept that this is the voice of a woman. It must surely be the song of an angel. Our lives as men will be a constant search for this melody. An eternal, frustrated, pointless quest to hear the throat of a woman fulfilling her dreams and desires and achieving her fundamental basic goal of satisfaction.

'That answers one question, then.'

'What's that, Da?'

'Who nicked my Pink Floyd tape?'

I have no idea how long he's been standing in front of me, but he has a beer in his hand so he's been here for a while.

'Here's another question, Vincent.'

'Fire away there, Da.'

'Why are you in the pub slow dancing alone with your eyes closed on a Saturday afternoon?'

My team have abandoned me and are sniggering from the bar. So many snake-eyed yellow-bellied funny fuckers.

'It's a brilliant song, Da.'

'You look like shite.'

'Thanks, Da.'

'Do you want a pint?'

'Yes, Da.'

'Right. I'm buying you arseholes one pint and that's it.'

I hit the jacks to compose myself. I have no need to deposit but I drop my bags anyway and find some comfort from a draught on my naked shins. There must be a hole in the bottom of the wall somewhere. Nothing has come out of my arse since the after-party. Though I shat enough last night to do me for a couple of weeks. Nothing has gone into my stomach either. Nothing but pills and booze and smoke. I haven't eaten since . . . Jesus! When did I last eat? I haven't eaten for fucking days. My stomach cramps and spasms as I visualise the empty puce cavern inside me. I kneel down, put my face where my arse was and try to let go, but there is nothing to give up. It hurts like fuckery as the cogs grind down and bite into each other. Milk, I need milk to oil the machine. The lager and bile are too skinny: they're just running away to the sides. I hope Jonty hasn't told him we have money. He'll smell a rat. A big fat pungent drug-dealing rat with a pending criminal record. The oul boy's pretty tolerant, all things considered, but if he thinks we're dealing drugs in a country where drug dealers get shot in the legs he'll cut loose and wreck the shop. Mother of God, that's sore. That is so fucking green. A watery lime soup from the depths of my stomach is running off my chin and dripping into the toilet. As another wave of pain racks me I watch, fascinated, as the thicker human liquid explodes in the toilet water in little emerald clouds, like when we washed the paintbrushes in the sink in primary school after badly painting pictures of chestnut trees. The quicker I re-enter the fray the better. Jonty's mouth is capable of summoning the mother of all shitestorms well before you add sleep deprivation, love drugs, alcohol and marijuana to the mix.

They're all sat back underneath the jukebox, and Dad is slap-bang in the middle, holding court.

'Are you all right, son?'

'Yeah. Why wouldn't I be?'

'You've been in the toilet for a week.'

'Da, this is Davy and Jim.'

'I know. I've been chatting to them here while you slept on the toilet.'

'I wasn't asleep. I didn't feel well.'

'I wonder why.'

'What do you mean?'

'Well, you've been on the rip for days. The only time I see you is in a pub.'

'The only time I ever see *you* is in a pub.'

'Come on, boys. Isn't it great? You're in the boozer together. I never get to sit in a bar with my father.'

Situation defused by the wee man. As soon as Dad isn't looking I wink my thanks to Jonty. He smiles back. He's in control. I needn't have been worrying about his mouth. Davy and Jim are leaving. Everyone is leaving me. Mia, Bingo, Mickey, Davy and Jim.

'It was lovely to meet you, Mr Duffy.'

'You too, Jim. Take her easy.'

Dad takes his leave for a piss, and we embrace for the final time.

'Remember, you're meeting those balloons at three for the drop, so get your heads together and slow down on the pints.'

'All right, Davy.'

'Now stick to the plan. You keep five hundred each and explain that it's a few quid light as you had to cover expenses, like getting into the club and shit. They'll only be a ton or two short of five grand, and they'll be happy to get out of there with that. Just keep them talking. Then you'll have all night to celebrate.'

'Goodbye, Jim. See you later, Davy.'

'There is no such thing as goodbye, Vincent.'

'Hopefully you'll have that wee Betty doll with you next time, cub!'

'Course he will, Jim. She was all over him like scabies.'

When they are gone we sit content, smiling at each other for a while.

'That was the night we'll be talking about when we're fifty.'

'You reckon?'

'Totally, Vin. The night we'll never tell our kids about.'

'I hope so.'

'It'll be hard to beat.'

'What about Tanya, then?'

'What about her?'

'You know what I mean.'

'I do?'

'Yes.'

'Who the fuck am I – Uri Geller?'

'What's he got to do with it?'

'He's a mind reader.'

'He's not a mind reader, he's a spoon bender.'

'But he bends them with his mind.'

'So?'

'So he has a powerful mind.'

'And?'

'And if it's powerful enough to bend spoons it's powerful enough to read minds.'

'What are you fucking talking about?'

'Uri Geller.'

'Why?'

'Because you accused me of being a mind reader.'

'I didn't accuse you of anything.'

'How do I know what Tanya's thinking?'

'What?'

'Who knows what any woman is thinking?'

'I didn't ask you what she was thinking.'

'You said, "So what about Tanya?"'

'That's me asking you what *you* were thinking!'

'You're not making any sense, mate. You're blocked.'

'I am not blocked. I've only had two pints!'

'You've had two Es, fifteen cans of lager, half a bottle of vodka, and you've smoked the gross national product of Morocco.'

'Fuck you!'

'Fuck me?'

'And he doesn't bend spoons with his mind.'

'Yes, he does. I've seen him doing it live on the telly.'

'He bends them with his fingers, then tells idiots like you that he bent them with his mind.'

'You're so cynical.'

'I'm cynical?'

'It's all science with you, isn't it?'

'What the fuck are you on about?'

'It's OK to believe in something, Vinny.'

'It's OK to believe in Uri Geller?'

'You shouldn't be ashamed of being spiritual.'

'Jesus fucking Christ.'

'It doesn't have to be him either. We can break away from the formal religious boundaries dictated by modern society.'

'Shut the fuck up.'

'We just have to try.'

'What are you two shouting about?'

'You know what your son's like after a drink. He'd argue shite was chocolate.'

He watches us for a bit. The moustache is gently sucked but I can't gauge where the mood is going. 'It's nearly over.'

'You think it will hold, Da?'

'There's been ceasefires before, Mr Duffy.'

'Dark side of the moon, boys.'

'We're coming back to the light side, man.'

'Now that the hatred and the evil have passed over!'

'The album. *Dark Side of the Moon*. Which has been playing since I arrived. Is nearly fucking over.'

'Oh, right.'

'What are you two on?'

'Nothing, Da. Just the couple of pints.'

I start to laugh.

'You're stoned!'

'I'm not, Dad, I swear. I'm just a bit pissed. We've hardly slept.'

'Where were you last night?'

'At a party in Mingin McGrath's house.'

'Who the fuck is Mingin McGrath?'

Jonty starts laughing now. It's infectious. So infectious that he falls off his seat.

'Get a grip, you two. It's the middle of the afternoon, for Christ's sake.'

'Mingin McGrath is the lead singer of Fudgegrinder.'

'I heard they were shite in the Mirage the other night.'

'That'll be them.'

'Have you spent one night in the house this week?'

'They were pretty good, actually. They can certainly handle the aggressive tracks quite well.' The alcoholic substitute teacher has a tray of drinks with him. He passes round pints, then sits and toasts the table with a very large whiskey.

'You were there?'

'Does a hobby horse have a wooden cock?'

Jonty buckles again. He falls the other way this time and hits his head on the bottom of the jukebox.

'You shouldn't have gone and bought a big round.'

'I didn't, lads. These are from Chalky.'

Chalky joins us for his second pint of the day. He sits between me and my dad, facing the door so that he can keep an eye on the bar.

'Well, Kevvie, did you see United the other night?'

'I did indeed, Chalky. We're looking good.'

'This Giggs lad is on fire. If he keeps that up he'll be around for years.'

'He's good all right, but Cantona is something else.'

'Eric is the king.'

We silently raise our glasses to the contrary French footballer who has lit up our lives. I wonder if Eric likes Pink Floyd. I bet he does. He is a man of taste.

'So what did you all hear about the riot?'

My laughter dies. 'Heard fuck all, Da.'

'Apparently it was bad, son. They pretty much wrecked the estate.'

I raise my new pint, the fourth, and suck deeply, wearing it like a mask while I remind my face how to play dumb.

'Finbar Regan got a hammering from the cops while the rioters torched his Merc.'

'Burned it out?'

'Total write-off.'

'I drove past the hospital yesterday morning and there were two blackened cars pulled up on the verge.'

'The one furthest up the hill is his. The only thing still recognisable is the personalised number plate on the back.'

'He deserved it.' I hadn't spoken for a reason.

'He deserved it, son?'

'You know what I mean.'

'Have you learned nothing? That's this country's ills in a microcosm. "He deserved it." Is he a prick? Yes. Is he a money-hungry bastard? Yes. Is he a moral vacuum who thinks he's better than everyone else because he cornered the rural market in pepperoni? Maybe. Did he deserve to have his fancy car set on fire by a crowd of wee hoods, who haven't a clue what they're rioting for or the gravity of what they're doing or the history of their people's struggle or just how far they're sending their own community backwards in the eyes of the world, on his way home from work? No, he fucking well didn't. Unemployed, disenfranchised, threatened by sectarian bands and ignored by the government, so we wreck our own housing estates? Where's the logic in that? If you have to wreck somewhere make sure it isn't where your mother and your granny live. A quarter of a century of blowing up our own town centres because it might cost the British government a few quid? Well, that may or may not have made Denis Healey, Nigel Lawson and Kenneth Clarke think a smidgen harder about a fraction of their budgets, but it made damn sure Uncle Denis and Cousin Nigel and your mate big Ken shat their pants every time they left the house for a loaf of bread or a tin of beans in case they got their fucking legs blown off. The Prods will self-destruct. All we have to do is give them enough rope and they'll hang themselves. Let them march around all summer like children in fancy dress, peddling hatred and calling it culture. That's the point. It's triumphalism. It only works off a reaction. When no one blinks they lose. That's how you beat it. Every person in every Catholic housing estate that they want to march through should open their doors and give out tea and buns and paint their faces and their arses red, white and blue. Let's all get on board for the big Orange win because then they'll have lost. Mark my words, it's hard to be triumphalist when you're defeated. If we had the brains to ignore the bait, their so-called "culture" would be gone long before Ryan Joseph Giggs hangs his fucking boots up.'

'You know, he captained England Schoolboys but then changed his mind to play for Wales.'

'It's a myth, son.'

'How do you mean?'

'He played for England Schoolboys because the school he went to was in Salford.'

'I heard he was angry with his father, who was English, because he'd dumped his ma, who was Welsh.'

'That's bollocks. For a start, his dad was Welsh too.'

'So he doesn't hate England?'

'Not everyone hates England, Vincent, and not everyone makes life-changing decisions to spite one of their parents.'

We sip for a bit and let the concept of peace wash over us. There is a strange noise inside my head. I concentrate on it and a sadness is triggered. There is no music. The album has finished but no one has refreshed the jukebox. My dad has finished talking, and no one can top him. There are no words. I'm back in the field by the harbour and your head is on my chest. That was the last time I heard this noise, this silence. The saddening starts to swell in my chest so I nail my pint and make our excuses before it becomes something that bursts.

It is hot outside on the street. We squint at our feet and shuffle up the town, like a couple of hungry vampires who forgot to drink any blood and have now failed in the race against light. A spate river of sweat has burst its banks and is racing down the middle of my back before we are halfway to the Vintage bar. My feet feel wet and sticky in my desert boots, like I'm wading through lasagne.

'I don't feel good, Jonty.'

'When we get this shit done we should go somewhere and eat.'

'I don't feel good in my head.'

'What do you mean?'

'Something bad is going to happen.'

'No, it's not.'

'I'm never going to see her again, am I?'

'If you want to see her again you will see her again.'

'Where did you get that logic from?'

'Common sense.'

'What if these two kick the shite out of us and keep all the money?'

'They can't do anything in a public bar, man.'

'They can do whatever they want in a public bar, man.'

'Give me your money.'

'Why?'

'They can't take what we don't have. I'll nip into the Market bar and get Turnip to hold it for us. Now go and sit in the Triangle for five minutes and get your fuckin' head together.'

I take my constantly counted and lovingly rolled-up wedge of notes out of my pocket and pass it to him. Kyle and Grant's money we have split into two, wrapped tightly in a couple of Wellworths bags and shoved down the front of our jeans. We look like the front row of a Status Quo concert.

'I'm too wrecked to sit up there in the open. You never know who will walk past.'

'Vinny. There is nothing wrong. Nothing bad is going to happen. You are coming down, that is all. Now get your head together until we seal the deal. Then we can get wankered again and you will stop feeling and behaving like a total arsehole.'

10

ELECTRONIC MUSIC IS coming from the speaker mounted on the door of Island Discs record shop. I sit on the bench nearby and try not to look too suspicious. The lost and found parade past me in their finery as I smoke and watch them from the front row of the stalls. I know them all. I have seen them all many times. I know what school they went to and which ones their kids are at now. I know what bars they drink in and where they buy their shoes. I know what football teams they support and I know what side of the fence they sunbathe on. I know what kind of cars they drive and I know whose minds are smaller than others', shrunken from years of bitterness and giving a fuck about sides of a fence. Look at you all, floating by on your Saturday business. Shopping, drinking, going to the bookie's. Is it any different from any other day? You have to listen to the kids for its entirety. You have to feed the wee bastards three times instead of two. You have to look at the wife for longer than is healthy, and there is no sign of the bit of fluff from work who wears those skirts that ride up her hole a bit too far when she bends over the photocopier.

The fear ignites inside me again. Please don't leave me here. If you leave me here, as sure as hell I will die here. I have been dying here for eighteen years already. Whoever you are that controls this thing, hear my prayer. I am young and I have a lot of love to give. So please get me out of here. It's really not too much to ask. I don't want to know everyone. I don't want to know anyone. We shall party tonight, we shall fall apart on Sunday, and on Monday morning I swear to fuck, and all that is holy, I'll do it. Clothes in a bag, call the sister, hop on the Belfast bus. I am gone if you please, please, please, let me get what I want this time. Whoever is working in the record shop is a Smiths fan. There is a God, and he is probably from Manchester. I light a second cigarette and listen to Morrissey's haunting lyrics as Jonty walks towards me across the street.

'You feeling any better?'

'No.'

'Not surprised, listening to that shite.'

Kyle and Grant are at the same table where we sat with them a few days before. It's comforting to think of them sitting there ever since, laughing and singing and interacting with the other punters as life rolls merrily by. Unfortunately, though, when we left here the other day they left too. Then, after sharing some fried food and a family-size bag of wine gums, they probably spent the rest of the week bullying and intimidating people and generally behaving like a pair of cunts. There are no marching-band uniforms today, which is a disappointment. In jeans, trainers and sweatshirts Kyle and Grant have lost their historical edge. We sit in silence for a bit, smiling at each other over beers like two nervous couples about to throw the keys in the hat.

'So, boys? How was your night at the big disco?'

'Emotional, Grant. Vinny got his hole. Have you got a bag or something? There's a bit too much cash here for the old coat-on-the-chair trick.'

'You serious?'

'Yeah. He banged this wee brunette doll. She was scorching too!'

'About the money.'

'Serious as Nicholas Witchell, Kyle.'

'You sold them all, Vincent?'

'Piece of piss, Grant.'

'How?'

'Well, we stuck to the basic rules of commerce, Kyle. Ask someone if they want your product, then take some of their money for it in return.'

He allows a scrawny smile to tread carefully on his anaemic lips. Grant is beaming down at me like a white rhino with a dildo up its arse. Something is wrong here. This is far too easy.

'We like you, Vinny son. Always the funny fucker. Even in the immediate aftermath of an unfortunate but unavoidable car crash.'

'I do my best, Kyle. And you could have braked.'

'I think a celebratory drink's in order, boys. Don't you?'

'Sure we have our pints. We're grand.'

'I mean a fancy drink, Jonty. A special-occasion drink.'

'Like a Christmas Eve drink, Kyle?'

'Straight after midnight service, Grant!'

'Will I get four gin and tonics, Kyle?'

'You sucked the words right out of my mouth, Grant.'

The image keeps us company while he heads to the bar, like a massive wet shit in the middle of the table.

'So you had no trouble at all?'

'You mean did anyone ask us where we got all the pills, Kyle?'

'I mean did you encounter any opposition to your selling of them, Vincent?'

'Same thing, surely.'

'Not necessarily.'

'Why don't you tell us who you stole them from, Kyle?'

'You don't need to worry about that, Jonty.'

'I will, if the original owners come looking for the two culchies who were selling them on Friday night.'

'The buck stops with us, lads, so don't you worry about that.'

'We got lucky, Kyle, that's all that happened. We got fucking lucky.'

'You're an all-round good-luck charm this week, Vinny. Surviving car crashes, successful drug dealing, the whole nine yards.'

Grant arrives back with a tray full of gin and tonics. I nail mine in one. I'm so desperate to get it out of my hand and back on the table before they can see me shaking.

'So how did you pull it off?'

'The dealers that were heading for the after-party got lifted by the cops. We just stepped into the void.'

'Lifted by the cops with more than a load of pills, too. Couple of handguns by all accounts.'

They look at each other for a beat now. Of course they do. Someone somewhere in this little province is wondering where all their ecstasy tablets went, and the only people who can automatically access that many ecstasy tablets can also access automatic weapons for shooting the knees off whoever automatically springs to mind.

'How can we be sure that the buck stops with you, then?'

'You'll just have to trust us, Vincent. A bit of solidarity in this brave new world of peace and prosperity. Cheers.'

'Cheers.'

'Now where's our money?'

We rise together and allow Grant and Kyle to ogle our bulging crotches. They look impressed.

'We'll give it to you out the back after we finish our drinks.'

'Judging by the size of that thing, Jonty, if you give it to me out the back I won't walk right for the rest of the week.'

Kyle thinks it's the funniest thing he has ever heard. Grant knows it's the funniest thing he's ever said.

'It's a bit short.'

'It doesn't look it!'

I give them ten seconds to appreciate their own comedic dexterity.

'The money is a bit short.'

That's done it. Stone fucking dead, too. Both of them. Tumbleweed, the works.

'How short, Vincent?'

'Only a ton and a half, Kyle. Expenses. It was twenty quid in, and we had to give lads petrol money and buy a few drinks to look the part.'

'You had to buy some brunette a few drinks, you mean?'

'It's an expensive night out. We couldn't have sold anything for you without spending some cash.'

'Let's take the ton and a half out of your wages, then, Vinny. That's what anyone else would do.'

Jonty is up off his seat before Kyle's sentence is finished.

'Yeah, but you're not anyone, are you?'

I grab at him but he shrugs me off and slams his glass down hard on the table. 'Don't speak to Vinny like that. Have you any idea what he's done for you? This whole thing only started by accident because a car crash stopped you two kicking the shite out of him, and now after we've headed off like a couple of idiots to the other end of the fucking country, where we could have been shot for selling drugs, to bring you back thousands of fucking pounds, you're going to short-change us on the few hundred quid you fucking promised us?'

'Sit down, man. The barman is looking over.'

'Fuck you.'

'You should sit down, mate.'

'Fuck you too, Vinny.'

Jonty sits, his black rage staring through me, and I know that he's gone. When he finds no answers he whips back around again and glares at his twin tormentors. 'We've more than pulled our weight. You two are having a fucking laugh. Sending a couple of eighteen-year-olds to Port-fucking-rush to sell your stolen fucking gear? You need us and you fucking know it.'

'Why would we need you, Jonty?'

'You need our fucking silence, Kyle!'

'You have an awful mouth on you, son.'

'Sorry about that, Grant. I think he has a mild form of Tourette's. It seems to really peak when someone's trying to fuck him over.'

'Why should we do anything other than take you out the back and kick seven shades of shite out of you?'

'What was it you said there, Kyle? A bit of trust and solidarity in this brave new world of peace and prosperity? It's our secret. We'll never discuss where we were or what we were doing and neither will you. We've made good money out of it and you've made a shitload of money out of it, so no one is short-changing anyone and no one is letting the cat out of the bag.'

'A hundred and fifty quid isn't the end of the world when we're getting nearly five grand anyway, Kyle.'

'Maybe not but it's the principle of the thing I'm concerned about, Grant.'

'The principle? You are about to accept thousands of pounds from the sale of illegal class-A drugs that you nicked from someone else in the first place!'

'Amen, Vinny. A-fucking-men.'

By the time I get my mitt on the second gin and tonic the tremor in my arm has stabilised somewhat. I take my time with this one, savouring the bitter assault of the gin on my swollen tongue. The inside of my mouth is raw and sore from where I've been chewing on it all night, and there is a deep ache in my jawbone and right up into the sides of my skull.

'So what are you two going to do with your money? A future dealing drugs, is it? You're a proper little pair of Tony Montanas.'

'Vinny is moving to Belfast.'

It's the first time I've heard someone else say it out loud. So matter-of-fact. So final. I look into his eyes but they are still too black to tell me anything.

'Belfast, is it? They don't mess around up there, Vin.'

'It's just another place, Grant.'

'I don't know, son. The people are mental.'

'The people here are mental!'

'But we're all pretty nice down here, really, son. Belfast is very sectarian.'

We give them the money in their car, and even though he has reminded us twenty times that he knows where we live, Kyle insists on counting it twice. When he is satisfied, we step out of the vehicle and smoke a final cigarette together. This is a small town but I have a feeling I won't see these two again for a while.

'Oh, yeah, Vinny. We saw your mate McGullion again.'

'You didn't "sort him out", did you?'

'Someone had beaten us to it: he's in a wheelchair.'

'Last time we saw him he had a head like a bull's ball bag, and now he's a proper cripple.'

'Where did you see him?'

'Trying to wheel himself through the town. Looked like hard work, too. He's clearly the kind of guy that birds shite on.'

Turnip has two pints of Guinness half pulled before we get our arses on the stools.

'We don't drink Guinness, man.'

'You've been on the go all night with no food. You need calories, and a pint of black is a pint of Christmas dinner.'

Christ, it's good. Thick luscious milky alcoholic ice cream sliding down my throat and covering hell's acidic inferno with a fire blanket of freezing-cold velvet.

'Have you heard about McGullion?'

'How bad?'

'Bad.'

'Will he walk again?'

'Like John Mills in *Ryan's Daughter*.'

Three goes for a Guinness, my dad always says. The second the pint's settled right you take a long, slow pull on her, but not so much that the taste overpowers the sensation of it sitting in your mouth. You leave it for a few minutes then and admire the look of it. On a good pint the glass will never go clear. The legs of the Guinness should always hang around, reluctant to be dragged to the bottom as you greedily dispense with it, already hard for the next one. The second mouthful is a different beast. At least half of what's left sluiced straight down an open gullet and into the stomach, with all thoughts of taste discarded in a desperate greedy onslaught. After the penultimate gulp the barman gets a wink, and he starts working on your next pint. When that's half cooked and settling nicely, the third and final quaff combines gluttony with taste sensation as you stagger the delivery slightly, drizzling the stout into the belly over the tongue, and savouring every subtly burned creamy black centilitre.

'The cops will never know who it was.'

'McGullion knows who it was.'

'I know who it was.'

I haven't thought about it since. Something has been tickling the arse of my psyche but it has never managed to cut through the drink and the drugs and the sex. I see him now in the mirror behind the bar. I watch his swollen burgundy face as he jumps on the boy's head. The Coke can crunches and crumples in my ears as he smiles, and the boy's eyes flood with panic as they're forced slowly forward out of their sockets. He steps out of the mirror and stands before me with his hurley in his hands and his Liverpool scarf pulled tight across his mouth. I fucking hate Liverpool. I close my eyes and feel my rage become a tangible force as it travels through my body and down through my arm and onwards into my pipe. I feel nothing when it bites mercilessly into his shin, crippling the cunt for ever. That's for all the boys on all the floors. That's for your mother's guilt at bringing you into this world. That's for my mother's heartache at the cards she was dealt. That's for my sister, whom I haven't even spoken to since she ran away from all the shouting. That's for my grandfather, whom I didn't visit for three months and then he died before I could get the distance. That's for all of them and all of their hurts, and I hope it really truly does hurt McGullion.

'Fuck him.'

'Is right.'

'He was asking for it.'

'For years.'

The second pint goes down a treat. As my stomach fills, a warm glow spreads through me. Saturday afternoon with our pockets full of gold and the world is our oyster.

'You're a hardy boy when you need to be, Vinny!'

'I have a bad temper, Turnip, but I still have a lot of love to give.'

'You worried about him coming for you?'

'Sure he'll never be able to catch me.'

'What you two doing tonight to celebrate the biggest drug deal in the town's history?'

'I don't know, man. What do you fancy, Jonty?'

'I've never tasted champagne.'

'We don't sell any.'

'I don't mean now, Turnip. I mean generally speaking.'

'I've never tasted it either.'

'There you go. You have cash in your pockets and neither of you has ever tasted champagne.'

'I'd like to go somewhere really plush, just the two of us, and drink a bottle or three.'

'Very romantic. Where had you in mind, darling?'

'The Killmoran Hotel, Vincent. Let's get a table by the window overlooking the lough and have posh wankers turn their noses up at us, and camp waiters bring us champagne on silver trays!'

'That is simply the best idea you've ever had, old boy.'

'Sure treat yourselves to a taxi now that you're flush.'

'Nah, Turnip. I think we'll walk. Sure it's a lovely day out, right, Vinny poppet?'

'You're rarely wrong, Jonty dearest. You're rarely fucking wrong, my son.'

11

HE'S NOT THE MESSIAH
HE'S A VERY NAUGHTY BOY

'WHAT DOES IT mean, Vin?'

'It's a quote from *Life of Brian*.'

'Brian who?'

'It's a Monty Python film.'

'Is he one of them old black-and-white dudes?'

'It's the name of a comedy group from the sixties and seventies.'

'I can't watch black-and-white. Subtitles are worse. I want to watch a film, not read a fuckin' book.'

'There are no subtitles and it's not in black-and-white.'

'I watched a film at me granny's one time and it was black-and-white and had subtitles.'

'Why did you watch it then?'

'It sort of sucked me in and trapped me. I literally couldn't move off the sofa, even though I hated every second of it. I nearly shat myself.'

'What was it about?'

'I don't know. It was in French.'

We sit across the road from the cinema, looking up at the sign while we smoke. Jonty produces the last two Es and opens the can of Harp that Turnip has given him.

'Down in one or halves?'

'Half now and a half later. Could be a long night.'

'Good plan. Bottoms up.'

I like the taste now. There is comfort in its appalling bitterness. If it didn't taste so bad it wouldn't fuck you up, and we want to be fucked up.

'I like him, Jonty.'

'So you agree that it couldn't be a woman?'

'It could be a woman, but I know it's a man.'

'How do you know?'

'It's just a feeling.'

'What's *Life of Brian* about?'

'The ridiculousness of religion.'

'Is he messing about or making a point?'

'Hard to tell. In this country you can't help making a point even when you're only messing about.'

A brisk half-hour walk sees us at the gates of the hotel. We are greeted at the imposing reproduction neo-classical doorway by an employee with an imposing reproduction smile. Resplendent in *faux*-antique finery complete with black top hat, he looks more bell-end than bell-boy.

'You gentlemen here to meet someone?'

'No.'

'Are you staying with us this evening?'

'Maybe, if we meet someone.'

'But you weren't meeting anyone.'

'Exactly.'

'What is the purpose of your visit?'

'What is the purpose of your hat?'

'Excuse me?'

'We're here for lunch.'

'Lunch is finished now, gentlemen. The hotel will be serving high tea.'

'Great. We'll have tea then, and I can assure you that it will be high.'

We commandeer two fat armchairs at a small table at the far end of the lounge by a huge window that overlooks the lake. A short but appetising waitress approaches us cautiously, armed with a genuine smile and an A4 jotter.

'That's a big notepad.'

'I know, sir. I lost my usual one so I've been using this all day.'

'You don't have to call me "sir", we're the same age.'

'Of course.'

'My name is Vinny and this is Jonty.'

'My name's Melissa.'

'Jesus, Melissa. That's a brilliant name.'

'Thanks, Vinny.'

'Can I ask you a question, Melissa?'

'Of course, Jonty.'

'What the fuck is high tea?'

'A selection of sandwiches and pastries and a pot of tea of your choice, Jonty.'

'A pot of tea of my choice, no less! And what are my choices, Melissa?'

'Breakfast tea, Darjeeling tea, Earl Grey tea, Lady Grey tea or green tea.'

'OK, here's the craic, Melissa. We'll have high tea for two, but instead of tea we'll have a bottle of champagne.'

'Which kind of champagne would you like, Vinny?'

'Which kind would you recommend, Melissa?'

'Most people go for the Moët and Chandon.'

'How much is a bottle of that, Melissa?'

'Thirty-one pounds, Vinny.'

'Perfect. We'll have one of those. In one of those icy-bucket scenarios.'

'I have one final question, Melissa.'

'Of course, Jonty.'

'Do the sandwiches have crusts?'

'That is entirely up to you.'

'You mean the chef will dispose of the crusts upon request?'

'Certainly.'

'Then off with their heads, Melissa.'

'Hang on, I like the crusts.'

'Vinny, I have dreamed for years of being served small sandwiches with zero crusts.'

'It's not a problem. We can do half with and half without.'

We stare fondly at her arse as she saunters off to have the staff personalise our bread.

'Nice girl.'

'Yeah, Vinny.'

'What does "Yeah, Vinny" mean?'

'You should hear yourself.'

'You should see yourself.'

'"Jesus, Melissa. That's a brilliant name."'

'I'm just being friendly.'

'You're just being a wanker.'

'I was being nice.'

'You think you're Keanu Reeves after last night.'

'Keanu Reeves is a dick.'

'Exactly.'

'What about you?'

'What about me?'

'What about last night?'

'What about last night?'

'Tanya?'

'Nice girl.'

'Did you ride her?'

'Don't cheapen it.'

'Do you like her?'

'Get a grip.'

I know he does. It's why he can't talk about her. He daren't go there in case something is released that he has no control over.

'You're emotionally stunted.'

'I'm just short.'

'You are emotionally crippled.'

'Here comes the champagne.'

'Retarded, even.'

'Sandwiches look good.'

'Pathetic.'

'Melissa, you're back already. Let me give you a hand there, love. Vinny was just saying how much you remind him of Sally Gunnell.'

'The runner?'

'Yeah, won the hurdles in Barcelona. I can't see it myself but he thinks you're her ringer.'

'But she has blonde hair.'

'And a massive nose but there's no telling him. He's convinced!'

'I'll just get your glasses.'

It's a different kind of fizzy. The intensity of the indignant bee-hive in my mouth is like nothing I've ever experienced. I take a little too much in the second mouthful and it goes up my nose and almost comes out of my eyes. It has a sharp, unhappy taste, which I notice has engendered a visceral response from my partner in crime who is doubled over in his armchair opposite me.

'You all right?'

'It's mental.'

'Thirty-one quid too.'

By the fourth mouthful we have mastered sitting up straight and swallowing at the same time. By the sixth we have stopped pulling the faces of men whose mouths have just been pissed in.

'It's like white wine with bubbles in it!'

'It is white wine with bubbles in it.'

In fifteen minutes we have finished the bottle and are gorging on cucumber sandwiches to kill the sickly taste in our mouths.

'It's mingin'.'

'But it gets you really hammered.'

'Will we order another?'

'Melissa!'

We take our time with the second bottle. Our surroundings need drinking in as much as the plonk, and of all the evenings this one must be caressed and savoured the most. Melissa hates me so much that she has assigned us another waitress and retreated to the bathroom to study her face from various angles in multiple mirrors.

'So is Betty the one?'

'You don't get to ask me questions about Betty if you won't talk about Tanya.'

'Good sandwiches.'

'You seemed to get on well.'

'No crusts makes all the difference.'

'She had great tits.'

'Watch your mouth, Vinny.'

'Bet you tried getting all of them in your mouth too.'

'I'm warning you, man.'

'Probably tried to get your jangler between them.'

'All right, I fucking like her. OK?'

'OK.'

'Now fuck up.'

'Wasn't hard, was it?'

'Was when I was shoving it between her tits.'

The tables beside us begin to fill with the great and the good of the town, as the sun, perfectly framed in the window behind us, begins its lazy evening flop towards the lough. He has offered something up at last so, as always in our age-old game of chess, I must offer him something in return.

'Betty is not the girl from the dream.'

He opens his mouth to discharge the customary violation, but something in his eyes changes and he kicks the gates shut again.

'You sure?'

'Positive.'

'But you never see the girl in the dream.'

'I know.'

'So how do you know it's not her?'

'I just know.'

He watches me carefully for a second or two in an

uncharacteristic pique of silence. He leans forward and fills both of our glasses to the brim, then stands up and raises his in front of his face. 'I propose a toast.'

'Sit down, everyone's looking over.'

'To all the girls.'

'All right, to all the girls. Now park your arse.'

He sits again and resumes his peculiar wistful stare. The old couple at the next table are looking over and whispering, so I fix them with a big smile and flip them a wave and they soon fuck off back to their brandies with ginger.

'There is no girl from the dream, Vinny.'

'There is, Jonty.'

'There isn't, Vinny.'

'There has to be, Jonty.'

'There doesn't, Vinny.'

'It has to mean something!'

'Oh, but it does.'

'Well, fucking spit it out then, Yoda.'

'They are "all" the girl from the dream.'

'All the girls in the world?'

'No, all the girls that you like.'

It's my turn to slam the brakes on an insult and stare at the other in a baffled inquisitive fashion. I down the champagne in my glass in a oner, and he begins to blur slightly in front of me. He smiles at me knowingly, and a very faint but discernible glow appears around his head and shoulders.

'You have a halo.'

'You too, man. Yours is purple.'

'Nice.'

'Do you know what I mean?'

'I know what purple looks like.'

'About the girls.'

'I think so.'

'When you have a girl in your life that you're mad about, then she is the girl in the dream.'

'Right.'

'When you don't have anyone in your life then the girl in the dream is the next one you just haven't met yet.'

'Yes!'

'Yes?'

'Yes!'

'Are you coming up on that pill?'

'Like a motherfucker.'

By the third bottle of champagne the taste has been well and truly acquired.

'So I had no one, then I dreamed of Betty, then I met Betty and she stopped being the one I dreamed about even though she was?'

'She is.'

'But she isn't.'

'But she was.'

'My brain hurts.'

'You'll never be happy.'

'I am happy.'

'No, you're not.'

'Yes, I am.'

'You think you're happy.'

'I'm really happy!'

'You're ecstatic.'

'I can't win.'

'Every time you meet a woman you like she will be super-seded and out-manoeuvred by an imaginary dream woman you have never even met.'

'Oh, my God. You're right.'

'You will spend your entire adult life in a constant state of limbo where you never commit emotionally to anyone, as you will always think there is something better around the corner.'

'Isn't that what everyone thinks?'

'Up to a point.'

'So what are you saying?'

'I'm saying that your own inflated notions of yourself and of womanhood taken literally from your dreams are going to ultimately leave you single and lonely and probably childless.'

'But I really like Betty.'

'I know you do, but you may as well forget about her as you'll only fuck her about and let her down the minute you start dreaming about some other faceless imaginary chick with a better arse.'

'Thanks.'

'Don't mention it.'

'Will I order another bottle?'

'Fuck that, we've blown ninety quid already. Let's get a couple of pints.'

'Can you hear that?'

'What?'

'I don't know, it sounds like a piano.'

'It is a piano.'

'How do you know?'

'Because I can hear it.'

'But how do you know it's a piano?'

'Because it's not a banjo.'

'What?'

'Vinny, it's a fuckin' piano. There's a guy over by the bar playing it and he's been doing so ever since we sat down.'

'Really?'

'Yes, really. Do you want to go over and see?'

'I don't know what will happen if I stand up.'

'I know how you feel but let's give it a go.'

The piano man begins a rendition of 'Summertime' and we float along the notes through the lounge towards the bar. When he starts to sing, his deep baritone is a workman laying steps for us along the musical stave towards himself and that piano. It's only a hundred-odd yards back through the foyer to the bar but it seems to take for ever. Everyone stops what they're doing or saying and watches us intently as we pass. My face is fixed in an absurd manic grin and I have my hand on Jonty's shoulder to steady my walk or my float or my swim or whatever the fuck it is that I'm doing.

I can see him now. To the far right-hand corner of the bar. A large back and a small head with a baseball cap perched on top. He sits on a tiny stool before a massive grand piano, which seems somehow offended by his working-class American headwear.

'My sister plays the piano, you know, Jonty.'

'I know.'

'How do you know?'

'Because she's your sister and I'm your mate.'

'I don't know what your sister does in her spare time.'

'Well, if you asked me instead of making up your own fantasies about what she does in her spare time you'd know.'

We get to the bar with no discernible controversy. Melissa is behind it but when I ask her for two pints she ignores me and asks Jonty what he would like. She has no problem giving him the two pints, even though she knows one of them is for me. I can't stop staring at her. She'll think it's because of Sally Gunnell's nose but truthfully it's because she is gorgeous and real and I would love to talk to her about what she does in her spare time.

An old man is approaching us from beyond the grand piano. He could in theory be approaching the bar from beyond the grand piano, but when I look into his eyes and assess the tension in his shoulders, even from a distance I know that it is us who are being approached.

'Young man, you're drunk.'

'Excuse me?'

'You heard perfectly well what I said.'

'We're not doing any harm. We're just listening to the music.'

'It's not that kind of establishment.'

'Why do they have a piano, then?'

'Don't take that tone with me.'

'Which tone?'

'How did you even get in here?'

'Through those rather decadent double doors.'

'Girl, could you call the management?'

'Her name is not "girl". Her name is Melissa.'

I can sense her thaw even though she refuses to look at me. She lifts the phone but stops herself dead and places it back in its cradle. 'They really were only having a quiet drink, Colonel.'

I love you, Melissa. I fucking love you. Who do you think you are, deciding who should be allowed into a public bar? Jonty appears on my shoulder and I feel an extra cushion of air in my sails as I face the man down. 'There really was no problem until you came over and created one.'

'Do you know who I am?'

'What does that matter?'

'Pardon?'

'Who you are has no bearing whatsoever on this situation.'

'Everyone knows me.'

'Evidently not.'

'I am Colonel Sanderson.'

'And what is the secret of your recipe, Colonel?'

'Pardon me?'

'Pardon you from what, Colonel?'

'I've had enough of you.'

'Few years past playing soldiers, aren't you, Grandpa?'

'How dare you?'

'Why don't you saunter off back to your evening, Colonel, before you get so excited you piss in your cords?'

'That's it. Call the police!'

Melissa lifts the phone and dramatically clicks the cradle a few times to turn it on and off. As she's doing so she looks me square in the eyes to say, *Not if our race depended on it*, which I know actually means she wants to bang my brains out just to prove to herself that she doesn't have a big nose.

'I can't get an outside line, Colonel. Go on back over to your wife and I'll have these two escorted off the premises.'

She winks at Jonty subtly to inform us she will do no such thing if we just wise up and stop making nuisances of ourselves, and the colonel turns on his polished heel and harrumphs off back to the retirement home beyond the grand piano.

'Lads, finish your pints round the corner in the foyer and keep a low profile, please.' She disappears through a door at the back of the bar and leaves us to our pints and our devices.

'She fancies me, mate.'

He doesn't answer me, just laughs.

'She totally fancies me, mate.'

He's laughing so much now that the piano man has stopped voicing whatever tune he was abusing and is watching us while he tinkles.

'There is definitely a vibe, Jonty. I'm telling you, man.'

'She thinks you're a total prick, mate.'

'She was raping me with her eyes, man.'

'She was hating you with her eyes, man.'

'Bollocks.'

'You're off your face, Vin. If the colonel's wife comes over now you'll think *she's* after your wand.'

'Right. Enough of this kip, Jonty. I'm taking a shite, then we're grabbing a taxi back to civilisation.'

There is something missing in here. Even with my trousers around my ankles I feel somewhat out of place. Granted, it's the finest throne I've perched on for a while, but it's just not right. I draw the string and bend the bow and shoot my mind back to my cousin's wedding a few years ago in that big hotel down south. I place the photograph of the memory over the reality of the here and now and it's almost a perfect match. In the photo the tiles on the floor are smarter and the lock on the door is more substantial, but in the here and now I'm completely off my tits on ecstasy. So the here and now wins by a first-round knockout. The drugs alone should ensure pants down that this is the premier toilet experience in the entirety of my eighteen years two months and six days.

So what's missing? I lean back on the cistern and demand some answers from my well-finished minimalistic chamber. The music has stopped playing. The piano, one of the fractions that made up the complete sum of the last hour, has dropped out of the sound sphere and now the equation is incomplete. I slump forward on the bowl and search desperately for a replacement that will redress the balance in my eardrums. The outer door swings open and the piano man comes in for a slash. I know it's him instinctively. I don't even have to look. It explains why the algebra has stopped adding up and why there is a total

lack of music in my life right now. I picture him sliding his baseball cap back on his crown in a vain attempt to improve his
view of what happens beneath his stomach. Old Mr Piano Man
has not seen Mr Bojangles for many a starry starry night.

'You're sounding great out there tonight, man.'

I know he'll think for a minute before answering a complete
stranger who is behind a toilet door, so I take the opportunity
to pull up my jeans.

'Excuse me?'

'I'm just saying that you're sounding fluent in all you do
tonight.'

'Thank you.'

'Do you ever get bored playing the same covers to the same
people in the same venues every night? Wouldn't you rather be
playing your own stuff?'

'I don't write my own stuff.'

'Fair enough. Well, your covers are excellent.'

'Thanks. Again.'

'Do you do requests?'

'What would you like?'

'Know any Sinatra?'

'Is Gerry Adams a Catholic?'

'What about "Something Stupid"?'

'Kind of pointless without a female vocalist.'

'Fair point. "Strangers In The Night"?'

'Who shall I dedicate it to?'

'Betty.'

'Where is she sitting?'

'Inside my chest.'

'Consider it done.'

As the door slams behind him there is a flash of lightning
behind one of my eyes and I am practically knocked

unconscious by a week's wages' worth of pennies dropping. They bounce off my head and bite the tops of my ears, then scatter and clatter all over the floor of my cell-shaped epiphany. I have no reading material! This plush lush high-spec toilet cubicle is completely devoid of abbreviations. Graffiti has a class system. Posh people have no desire to express themselves illegally on other people's property. I suppose they have nothing to be angry about. Or that's what they would have us believe. I wonder, if they did take to daubing their fears and frustrations, their rages and loyalties around the place, would they stick to the tried-and-tested format or would they extend my beloved abbreviations, drawing them out to the elongated glory of their former full-length selves? Would greater vocabularies gleaned from years of isolated well-paid-for educations add wit and verve to the walls and doors of our nation's water closets or complicate and confuse the issues even further?

I stare at the door and imagine a well-structured and balanced essay in favour of a united Ireland. Fuck that. Up the 'RA!

As I leave the inner sanctum and float through the foyer I hear the first strains of 'Strangers In The Night' calling me back to the bar. Good old piano man. As good as his word. My smile bursts on my face and laughter sprinkles from my eyes, flooding my cheeks until it's a choking, soaking, raging torrent of happiness.

'What do you think of this, Betty? Me and oul Jonty banging pills with the snooties up in the big hotel! This one's for us, darlin': "Strangers In The Night"!'

'Sir, could you please stop shouting in the hotel? The other guests have already complained.'

'Oh, fuck them, Melissa. And I told you not to call me "sir".'

'Please, Vinny, keep it down for two minutes. Jonty has already ordered your taxi.'

Before her sentence is finished I find him behind her in the middle distance. He is propping up the bar with a grin on his face, like a cat from a shit part of England where footballers buy real estate.

'All right, my son?'

'Yeah, mate. Cane this pint, our taxi's coming.'

'Your halo's massive. I can actually see it from over here.' I stare at it proudly, knowing that I have one of my own. It bristles and burns, a red-and-yellow tantrum protecting the back of his head.

'Your one is red and yellow. Is mine still purple? Is it as big as yours?'

I attempt the words but something sucks them from my chest before there is time to fire them properly in my mouth. I try again to call out to my friend, and as he opens his mouth to reply his halo erupts, filling the entire frame with a searing white light and engulfing everything and everyone in the bar.

12

WHATEVER IT WAS that stole my words punches me sharply in the guts. As I snap forward in a perfect right angle from my midriff it kicks me hard in the chin, sending me skyward in a backwards tumble. Amongst chaos and fire I rise, surfing the crest of the inferno's wave. I am joined momentarily by the colonel, who tumbles past me at speed, his trademark scowl fixed perfectly on one side of his face, the other side slapped with a boyish question mark. Reality bites hard into my right arm and the pain is like nothing I have ever felt before. It burns and scalds like the fires of Hell. As I scream in pure silence my lungs are filled with dust and smoke and I begin to panic and die. As the last gasps of air spill from me I complete my final revolution and begin my descent into the mouth of the volcano. I burst through the film of light towards the blackness, and as I land flat on my back the last thing I see is Jonty above me, flying at speed towards the big revolving doors that we entered through in triumph only a matter of hours before.

I wake on my left side. There is a pain in the back of my head that makes it difficult at first to open my eyes. Melissa lies opposite me, staring through the dust at nothing in particular. I say hello but I can't hear my voice. Her face is relaxed and beautiful now that the pressure of her shift is over. We are lying on the floor in the foyer of the hotel. I recognise the carpet, and when I roll my eyes towards the back of my head and over to the left I can just make out the toilet door hanging off its hinges. When I bring them back towards Melissa there are feet standing between us. Big black practical boots obscuring her face from my view.

Get out of the way. I'm trying to talk to Melissa.

I still can't hear my own words, but I figure they must be cutting into the big thick shaved skull that sits on the shoulders above the legs that carry the boots. He turns on his heel and steps towards me.

Fuck off, mate. I'm warning you, don't come near me.

He crouches down and looks in at me. His face looms through the smoke, obscured behind some sort of white mask, and he holds his fingers up in front of my eyes. I twitch and try to get away but I can't move a muscle, and his hands disappear and he is pulling at my clothes and pressing something cold into my chest.

I can't hear you, man. You're wasting your time. I can't even hear myself. Now piss away off so I can look at the girl.

He is gone as quickly as he appeared. A ghost disappearing into the void beyond my peripheral vision. Her expression hasn't changed and she still won't look at me, and I know I have a lot of ground to make up.

Melissa, I'm sorry about earlier. I'm not normally like that.

She doesn't reply but she doesn't get up either, and that's encouraging in any man's book.

I'd like to make it up to you and show you who I really am.

She smiles the tiniest of smiles and I beam back at her across our carpeted strip of no man's land.

I saw that! You smiled! I saw it! You couldn't help yourself!

The smile dies as quickly as it lived, and a small trickle of blood starts to come from her left nostril. The boots return. He shoves his face really close to Melissa's now, and his arse really close to mine.

Get away from her, man. I fucking mean it.

He opens her blouse and begins to massage her chest.

Get your hands off her, you dirty bastard.

He seems to lose interest in her breasts now and his fingers paw at her throat, ready for the final kill.

Get your hands off her neck, man. I mean it, I'll kill you, you fucker! I'm going to kill you!

He rises and looks back down on me and then he starts to leave, and I can tell from the eyes above the mask that I have him worried.

What about dinner, Melissa? My treat. Somewhere really nice, not just one of Regan's shitty pizzas.

There is a steady stream from both nostrils now. I manage to lift my head a little and look across the carpet to where the front desk is. One of the bar stools is sticking through the middle of it at a perfect right angle, and the big glass mirror behind it has been completely smashed. There is someone lying sleeping halfway between it and Melissa's back. I start to laugh. It hurts like fuck but, Jesus, it's funny. There was the mother of all parties in here tonight. Those pills were electric. I barely remember a thing. I rest my head on the floor again and focus on Melissa. Beautiful, ethereal, unobtainable Melissa. You could be the girl in my dream. Why not? Maybe I've broken the cycle and met the girl from the dream before I've actually had it. I smile and wink over at her, and as I look for the flicker in the corners, the middles swell dark black-blue, and blood begins to seep freely from both of Melissa's eyes.

Belfast

1

FEARGAL IS INSPECTING the stitches in a long slice on my right forearm. It is not a straightforward wound. It springs below the elbow joint and meanders south towards the wrist, slowing in the middle in a series of savage bends. If it were a river, that's where I would fish. There will always be something hiding under the bank in those big deep dark turn holes. He is taking his time. He had put the stitches in there himself when I was first brought in. I had watched him work in spells as I swam in and out of consciousness. There was love in his fingers. It flowed through his needle and into my flesh. It was not a love for me alone but a love for all of humankind. He is an artist whose work will be judged for ever on the canvas of my body, and I had found solace in his heartfelt delicate technique.

'Your hands aren't shaking.'

'They don't when I work, Vinny.'

'Have you been drinking?'

'No. They just never shake when I'm needed.' He smiles at me, his eyes two polluted blue pools swamped in the wrinkles of his heartache. 'Your mother's still here. She knows about the drugs.'

'I'm sure she always has.'

'You're going to love the stuff we have you hooked up to in here, kid. It's free, too.'

He stops what he's doing so that I can raise myself just enough to check on my mother, who snores gently from the camp bed they have made up for her just inside the door.

'She's been here from the second they carried you in. Won't leave. We even have to bring her food.'

'I couldn't see or hear her for the first couple of days but I still knew she was here.'

'She was the only person with you when you finally came out of it.'

'She sings to me every morning.'

'I've heard her, when I'm on my rounds.'

'When I wake she's sitting beside the bed with a cup of hot tea stuck between her knees singing away. I don't open my eyes until she's finished. I'm worried that if she knows I'm awake she'll be embarrassed and never sing to me again.'

'I told you she was an angel.'

'I know, but I honestly don't think I can handle any more Neil fucking Diamond.'

He slides my sleeve back down with a theatrical flourish and checks the intravenous needle in my wrist. 'Does your arm hurt?'

'My dreams hurt.'

'Yes. I'm afraid they're going to.'

When he gets to the door he turns to me once more. 'I'll get one of the nurses to put a fresh dressing over that. One of the cute nurses, just for you, Vinny.'

'Feargal?'

'Yes, Vinny?'

'Is the girl dead?'

'Yes, son. I'm afraid that she is.'

When I sleep there is only darkness and when I wake the light is a dream. The bed doesn't always hold me. Sometimes when I bend my thoughts I can rise above it and look down on the broken bodies that litter the ward below. I know that the colonel or what's left of him is in here somewhere. I haven't seen him but a young woman visits most days and pushes his wife around in her wheelchair. This morning they stopped directly beneath me and held each other while they wept. The piano man might be here too but I've heard my gut whisper that if the blast came from his corner he may already have been a small casket at his own farewell. When I hover high enough above the bed I can just make out the television on the distant back wall. There has been little to watch. There is a prick called Alan who comes on in the afternoon to teach us how to grow watercress, followed by an arsehole in a cheap suit who coaches fat fuckers on benefits to stop fighting and start eating together again, and there is the news. I haven't watched the news yet. Whenever it has been on I've been floating in the darkness or orbiting the country on my magic carpet.

It's coming on now, though. I can hear the music beginning. That warning staccato of electronic beeps and bleeps designed to slap you into a state of awareness so that you can process and accept all the badness that will follow. As the drums finish, Big Ben tolls and I know that it's six o'clock *post meridiem* on the first evening of the rest of my life. My heart soars as we cross-fade from the big old clock to the big old hair of one Moira Clare Ruby Stuart. Resplendent in a wine-red blouse under a cream suit jacket, she looks positively regal. The volume of her hair is supported by the acute angle in her shoulder pads. She looks like she's been shopping with Janet Jackson.

Hey, Moira!

Hello, Vinny.

You look amazing, Moira. Chalky's tongue will be sunburned.

Well, that is sweet, Vinny, but I can't say the same about you.

I know, Moira. I've been in the wars.

You certainly have.

My arm's messed up and there's something wrong inside my head.

You're actually a statistic in one of my reports today, Vinny.

I'm hardly special, Moira. Northern Ireland's human statistics are ten a fucking penny.

I'd better kick on here, Vinny. There are fifty million shopkeepers waiting to hear the weather.

Of course, Moira. Fire away there, love!

I hear nothing when she speaks. I watch her beam out at the United Kingdom as they collectively soak up the last bit of egg yolk with the penultimate chip. *Sans* audio, her show is still most impressive. I watch her lips move, knowing that she is gently bathing the nation in the chocolate current of her voice as the requisite amount of pathos is released through the sad windows of her eyes. Three minutes into her report Moira pauses and, with an almost imperceptible flicker of her eyes, looks through the nation directly at me, and I know that my statistic is upon us. As she opens her lips to continue, Jonty's angry acid halo appears behind her head and there is a bright white flash from the television that fills the entire hospital ward, and I'm back in the big hotel foyer lying on the floor by the reception desk.

'The death toll from Saturday's hotel bomb in Northern

Ireland has risen to four. Colonel John Sanderson, a retired British army officer, died this morning from injuries sustained in the blast. He was seventy-six years old.'

I see him near the ceiling above me. The scowl on one side of his face gone, the question mark still firmly in place on the other. The scowl has been replaced by nothing. When it left it took his right eye, all of the skin and most of the flesh with it. I can clearly see the colonel's skull on the right side of his head: cheekbone, teeth, eye socket, the works. I shout out to him as he flies past me, but I'm sure he has more pressing things on his mind.

'The young woman who died in the bombing has been named as eighteen-year-old Melissa Quinn from the nearby village of Tamlaght. She was working as a waitress in the cocktail bar.'

When I met you! She can barely hear me singing but I belt out the Human League's classic hit for her anyway. The blood coming from her ear tells me that her drums were perforated in the blast. She smirks at me, though, to let me know that she loves those iconic lyrics too, so I raise my voice and belt out the *Don't you want me baby?*s for all I'm worth.

As my rendition comes to a close I know that her life is leaving her. I watch it running away as quickly as it can. Out of her nose and eyes it runs, across her cheeks and onto the expensive carpet without so much as a thank-you or goodbye.

'The piano player from the hotel who died has been named as Dermot Rooney. He was a forty-three-year-old local resident. The fourth victim will not be formally identified until relatives have been informed. Thirty-seven people were injured in the blast. Four of them have been described as critical.'

There it is. My moment of fame. My own statistic and I had to share it with thirty-six other fuckers.

'Police are working on the theory that the bomb was left inside the piano. No one has claimed responsibility for the atrocity, though it is thought to be the work of a Republican splinter group, possibly the Continuity IRA.'

The colonel, Melissa and the foyer disappear in an instant, and I am very much back on the ward staring at the television.

The 'Continuity' IRA, Moira?

Yes, Vinny.

As in the verb 'to continue'?

The very one.

As in 'continuing'?

Bingo, Vinny.

Like simply 'keeping going'?

Don't get yourself in a state now.

That's all they could come up with?

I suppose they were thinking of the unbroken and consistent existence of something over a period of time.

Yes, Moira, of course they fucking were.

Please, Vinny, you need to rest.

But the war was over, Moira!

There is always someone in Ireland who wants a war, Vinny.

It would appear so, Moira.

At least the Provisionals don't exist any more.

They're just on holidays, Moira.

All-inclusive?

I wouldn't think so in Donegal.

The 'We're still here, you know' IRA.

Quality, Moira.

The 'more of the same' army.

Not so good, Moira.

Sorry, Vinny, it's been a long day. I'd better finish the news.

Moira, is this actually real?

Yes, son. I'm afraid that it is.

Can I ask you a personal question, Moira?

Anything, Vinny.

Are you 'seeing' Nicholas Witchell?

Of course not, Vinny. He's ginger!

I always knew you were a woman of taste.

Vinny?

Yes, Moira?

I'm so sorry about your friend.

2

I DREAD THE night. Sweat fear. Fear sweat. At first the dreams are varied but gradually the choice of channels diminishes and I am left with a single movie on an endless loop.

I wake in the lough. I can't feel my feet and I can't tread water for ever, so quietly I strike for shore. The lights of the estate are extinguished but I can just make out the top of the hill in the glow of the various fires that burn low now around it. The battle sounds have been quelled but the odd pocket of resistance can still be heard in the distance. My numb fingers grip the end of the pier and I try to find the energy to resurrect myself from this cold wet tomb. Voices. English. I slide back into the drink. Soldiers. Two of them, sauntering along the shoreline without a care in the world. The battle has been won, then.

I find my clothes in the concrete play park and wrangle them roughly over wet skin. My copper pipe is here too, and I massage its length, taking confidence from its strength and weight. The path skirts the bottom of the hill before opening into a rectangular field that finishes at the road's edge. Maybe two hundred yards across, maybe two hundred and a half. Clear this, then the road, and I'm in the safety of the hospital grounds. Before making the road I will have the Island Barracks on the opposite bank on my right and a row of friendly houses on my left, flanking the field and willing me on.

There will be ten minutes until the next patrol so it's now or never. On hands and knees I sprint to the base of the hill. On my back I stare at the stars and wait for the pins and needles to subside, the burning, biting, boring little bastards. Which of them has the belt? Orion or Sirius? Isn't Sirius a dog? The Dog Star, or a canine constellation? How could one individual star look like a dog? The frying pan. There it is, the only famous discernible pattern in the entire celestial sphere that I can ever find, and it's a fucking frying pan. The pins and needles have finished their show so I flip over and go. The fear prevents the air from reaching the depth of lung that I'm accustomed to. Before thirty metres are up, my chest and legs are in a play-off to see who can let me down first. At fifty metres someone shouts encouragement from the row of houses on the left, alerting the barracks on the right, and my route is perfectly dissected by a high-powered searchlight. I rip into a frenzied zigzag and my body screams murder at me. Like Ricky Villa, I slash one way then the other as the pale blue light bites at my heels, desperate to prevent any shot at City's goal.

I hear them before I see them. A pair of the Queen's Cockney finest coming at me through the night. One is faster than the other and he greets me on his own. As the searchlight catches us plumb in the centre of its beam I swing my pipe, catching him plumb in the centre of his jawbone. I'm aware of his fall, though I never look back, my focus on number two, who has emerged from his friend's shadow and dropped to one knee, his weapon raised to his shoulder.

Why have I stopped? In the clear cold crystal air I hear nothing. As I stare down the barrel of his SA80 assault rifle I hear nothing. I swing my arm and launch my pipe. He ducks easily out of the way and retakes aim at my head. He has a thin green scarf pulled tight around his mouth, and I can just make out his eyes between it and the lip of his helmet. The short space between us visibly fills with breath as we pump it out at an industrial rate. We stare into each other's terrified eyes, gasping to refill our rapidly depleting tanks. His thumb comes away from the plastic pistol grip and flicks off the safety catch. I see a calm resignation flooding his eyes and I know that he's going to shoot me.

'Who do you support, mate? You Chelsea scum or Arsenal? I'm a United man myself. Cantona's some player, eh?'

He drops the barrel a couple of inches so that it's pointing at the larger target mass of my chest, and pulls the trigger. Click. He pulls it again. Click. Click. Clickety clickety fucking click. Misfire, like so many before it in the Gulf War. The Brits really should have listened to sense and splashed out on some American hardware. I rush him, screaming death at the slit between his scarf and his bastard Anglo-Saxon helmet.

'You tried to shoot me, you cunt! You tried to shoot me!'

Like a pair of stags we meet head on. He swings wildly with his weapon but I duck beneath its arc and let my momentum take him off his feet by the waist. His helmet spills away and I sit on his belly lashing punch after punch into the sides of his head. His left hand appears in front of my face with a dagger in it and he slams it down, burying it in my right forearm, dragging it backwards towards him along the bone. I howl and roll and he is out from under me, raining kicks into my back and head. I catch his foot and pull myself up and sink my teeth through his army bags, deep into the soft flesh of his inner thigh. This sound I have never heard before. A tortured animal screaming in pain and rage and indignation. I punch him hard in the testicles and stumble away before he has time to wield his blade again. His blood is in my mouth. It tastes of cutlery. Those cheap school-dinner spoons, whose sharp metal tang always cut through the sugary pink custard.

He catches me at the water's edge. I parry his first blow from the inside out, keeping the metal away from my vital organs. His second attack comes from low, and as he tries to pull the blade up and into my stomach, I thrust down and grab the top of his arm. We wrestle, a good clean honest battle of strength and will, as he tries to shake his arm free from my grasp and slash at me again. We are so close that I can smell the shampoo from his soft hair as I rest my chin on the top of his head. I push down with all my might as he bucks and writhes for all he is worth. He pulls backwards and his arm pops free, and as he straightens his back and looks at me in triumph I pull him to me with his other arm and stove my head into his mouth, my forehead destroying both of his lips on his teeth. I hear his blade hit the ground, then his knees buckle and he sits gently on the grass before me. I kneel down and pick up his knife in my left hand.

'I know you.'

The voice comes from the blood-red mess that soaks through the scarf where his mouth was.

'I know you.'

I lash out and sink the cold hard Sheffield steel into the soft warm flesh of his throat. We watch each other in shocked silence as he gropes with both hands at the gaping neck wound. His eyes beg me for answers as his life begins to abandon him, a blood-red waterfall that cascades through fingers and over elbows, staining the grass below. I stare at the burgundy pool between his legs, and as it swells and bursts its banks, I know that it is over and I throw the knife into the heart of the lough.

'Is it bad?'

I stare at the wet red rag.

'Is it really bad?'

'Are you Irish?'

'I'm dying. Does it matter?'

I start to convulse as he tips over and lies on his left side, staring up at me. He breathes only through the wound now. The breath bubbling and gurgling like a baby as it escapes through the hole I have made in his throat.

'I know you.'

'What do you want me to do?'

'I know you.'

'Stop fucking saying that!'

His eyes implore me. I look away. I want to run but I can't move my legs. If I could only move my legs I would leave, I would leave him here to die on his own.

'Vinny?'

I shove my fists in my ears but still I can hear him.

'Vinny!'

I scream to drown him out but still he calls my name.

'Vinny. Vinny.'

In a ball at his feet I claw and scratch and bury myself in the earth, but still I can hear his voice.

'Vinny, Vinny. For fuck's sake, Vinny.'

I give in and lie in front of him. I reach out and press my hand firmly over the wound. The blood is warm and sticky, pumping through my fingers. Warm and soft and soothing. We lie like this just breathing for a while. When our breaths settle and are as one I smile in at him and he winks back out at me twice.

'I know you too.'

'Use my scarf.'

I manoeuvre myself behind him and slide his shoulders up onto my knees. I lift his head gently so that I can remove the scarf from the lower part of his face, then I ball it up tight and hold it hard into his butchered throat.

'I'm sorry, Jonty.'

'Wasn't your fault.'

'It was.'

'No, it was theirs.'

'Jesus, Jonty.'

'That has a ring to it.'

'I don't know what to do.'

'Don't do anything, mate.'

'Your mouth's an awful mess.'

'You should see my throat.'

We sit like this for an age. I rock him gently in my lap as I listen to the sirens and the shouting and the laughter up in the estate. Hours later I accept his passing. Not because he is quiet or because I can no longer feel his breath in his body, but because the blood soaking through his scarf onto my hand is cold. Soon we will go. Before they find us we will leave. I will hide you from them. I will drag you through the rushes to the water's edge and set you free in the deep black depths of the lough.

3

THE SKY IS lower here, much closer to one's head than in the west. Maybe that will change when the sun comes out. The rest of the country is bathed in late-September gold, but it has yet to cut through the heavy coal-sodden clouds of Belfast. Heaven's granite blinds rolled down tight to meet the wet slate roofs of the frightened little houses in an endless canvas of bloody grey. I scaled Cavehill this morning. Took the bus up the Antrim Road and climbed through the grounds of Belfast Castle to the top of the mountain. I say mountain, it's more of a hill, but by the time I had rolled and smoked my breakfast and let my imagination fill in the lives of the people below, I was definitely king of a mountain. Beneath me the city stirred and scratched its balls and thought about crawling out from under the green-and-orange patchwork quilt that is smothering it. There is no discernible pattern. There is a lot of orange to the east and the west is mostly green, and there are parts that need constant repairing where a small square of one has been acci-dentally sewn into a larger section of the other. I'd figured that if I climbed to the top it would bring me closer to the sun, but as I chewed over the collage of anger and blind faith dangling between my feet I realised it had brought me closer to leaving.

Fuck it, I'm having another pint. I'm not working tonight. Three nights in a row in that kitchen is enough. I wink at the barman and he puts me on another Guinness.

'What have you been up to today, Vin?'

'I've been up Cavehill today, Freddie.'

'Nice?'

'Same shite, different angle.'

'Lived here me whole life and I've never been up it.'

'I'd consider leaving it for another life.'

The pints are good. Lavery's bottom bar is famous for its stout, and for the eclectic greatest hits that sit inside all day drinking it. I feel at home with my jar, though I sit alone at the bar. There is snooker on the box on the wall above me and the vivid colours, the soft clink of the balls and the sparse clichéd snippets of commentary are soothing.

'Higgins was in yesterday.'

'Alex?'

'The very boy.'

'He lives round the corner, doesn't he?'

'In a flat on Sandy Row.'

'Still drinking?'

'Walking skeleton.'

'Jesus.'

'Even he can't help him now.'

'You serve him?'

'He comes in and stands about until he's recognised, then someone always buys the legend a drink.'

'Poor oul bastard.'

'It was odd yesterday, though. John Higgins was on the telly and Alex stood underneath it staring for fifteen minutes while John built a big break. Just kept staring, never moved a muscle. I think he was fixated on the name Higgins at the bottom of the screen and the score getting bigger and bigger.'

'Surreal.'

'Life must be so empty when you've been to the top and there's nowhere to go but down.'

'Completely.'

'Another pint?'

'Complete me.'

The kitchen is hard work but it's good craic. My sister's housemate's boyfriend told me about it when I was buying Es off him the day after we met. He used to sell them out of an ice-cream van around the housing estates on the north Antrim coast, and now he knocks them out around the Holylands and the bars of student-riddled south Belfast. Sinéad has no space in her place, so after a week on a tiny sofa in a living room with a broken window and a life-threatening breeze I splashed out. There was three hundred and fifty quid left from my five hundred (you can't really spend a lot in hospital), so I took a room in a house full of students from Derry. The whiny accent is hard to live with, but they're decent lads, and it's only ninety quid a month, so I laid down a month's deposit, then caned what was left over three days, in an attempt to re-program my brain. The ice-cream man's cousin works in the bar of a posh restaurant, and after some cajoling he talked me into the kitchen as a porter. I wash stuff. Dishes, pots, knives, floors. Washing the floor after a hard night's service is the worst job in any kitchen, but I relish it. The tougher the stains, the harder I try. I don't see the grease or the soup or the gravy. I see Melissa's black clotting blood destroying the expensive carpet of the hotel foyer and I have to get it out before it dries in. The ice-cream man's Es are good. Not Ebenezer good, but fucking good. The first night I tried them I sat in a dingy bedsit on University Avenue with some chefs and waitresses from work and talked shite. Eight people in a small room chewing their faces off while extolling the virtues of this brave new peaceful Utopia that we have just inherited. I freaked out and left. I thought the drug would help me escape, but it channelled the bad stuff along an empty motorway directly to the middle of my heart. Outside the party I got lost in the history of our future.

The apricot hue from the street lamps of the Holylands takes the darkness and changes its colour but it doesn't actually make it light. Aimlessly I stumbled along bleak, empty copper streets that I didn't want to be on but didn't know how to get off. On Agincourt Avenue I turned left and walked downhill, stopping and wondering at the exotic names of every cross street on every intersection. Jerusalem Street, Damascus Street, Cairo Street, Carmel Street. When I got to the bottom and burst out of the orange bubble I'd been trapped in and stepped onto the glare of the Ormeau Road, I was faced with another name I recognised. Sean Graham Bookmakers. I sat directly opposite, smoking, while the film played out inside my head. Enhanced by the drug, the cameras of my mind shot it, cut it and projected it crystal clear onto the walls and the road in front of me where it had all actually happened.

The two UDA gunmen in their boiler-suits and ski masks casually walk towards the bookie's from University Avenue on my left, where they have parked their blue Ford Escort. Seconds after they enter the shop, the roar of the Czech VZ58 rifle on full automatic drowns the crack of the smaller, though still deadly at close range, British Browning automatic pistol. As they exit and split, there is a second of silence before the horror of the screaming begins, and I snap my eyes shut so that I can see the inside of the shop on the inside of my lids. The bodies of the innocents are barely visible, lying beneath the cloud of cordite that fills the tiny room. Four are already dead and nine are injured. One critically, a fifteen-year-old boy. Like shooting frightened rabbits trapped in a small dark box.

After crossing the road I stopped for a minute outside the shop and tried to feel some sense of the men whose journeys were abruptly terminated there. Perhaps some spiritual residue of what they might have been or become.

Finding nothing I wandered onward to the off-licence at the back of the Hatfield bar. The rust cloud cloaked and comforted me at the second time of asking. I took a long fizzy swig of Olde English cider followed by Rugby Avenue, and found myself at the back of the main Queen's University campus. When I had made it through the myriad prefabricated classrooms thrown out to the edge of the road, I arrived at the heart of an impressive nineteenth-century building. Under a small tree I sat in a lush green garden surrounded on three sides by red-brick archways, stained-glass windows and the ghosts of a million first love stories. Here, sporadically, I lost, re-found, then lost the fear again. I cried and sang to myself and for my crippled heart, and gradually Dr Cider's prescription kicked in and the virgin sunlight refracted through the hued glass, freckling my face purple and green, and as the new day dawned on me, I remembered who I was supposed to be.

'What's the story tonight?'

'Get a carry-out, find a party.'

'There are plenty of those now the students are back.'

'You showing the United game?'

'Champions League. Place will be rammed.'

'Galatasaray won't be easy.'

'They're unfurling a big banner that says *Welcome to Hell.*'

'Giggs will tear them apart. Stick me on another Guinness there.'

As he turns and reaches for a fresh glass, I see her at the corner table under the television. She is sitting with a guy and a girlfriend. Or a guy and his girlfriend. I neither know nor give a fuck. The first time I looked for her I did. I gave a lot of fucks. For hours I sat drinking at this bar, knowing it was ridiculous, the chance of meeting her in a pub she had once mentioned. It was her laugh that did it. I'd been scanning the bar in front of me for hours but I'd never thought to turn around. Like a wave it swept across the floor and crashed into the legs of my stool, splashing up my back and chest and into my ears. I didn't move. I couldn't. I should have turned around but something in me wouldn't.

For an hour I sat watching the clock above me on the opposite wall as her audible delight ripped me apart. Not wanting to draw attention to myself I didn't even order another. I just sipped what I had while the mother of all battles raged inside me. Turn around and say hello. Walk over and join the company. Play it cool and be yourself. So what if she's with another fella? She's not. She is. She's fucking not. She fucking is. There's sex in that laughter. I can see him behind her. His eyes rolling in his bastard face. Look down. I can't. Look at her. I won't. The carnal pleasure in her big brown eyes.

When they left I followed her laughter out onto the street. Into the night and along Botanic Avenue I followed it. As I slowed amongst the fighters and the chip-laden masses it called me onwards. When I lost sight of her back or her hand in his I could still always hear her laughter. When my journey finally ended I lit a cigarette and smoked it in the shadows outside a house on India Street. I watched their two figures silhouetted in an upstairs window as they became one. There was no doubt now, no chink of light creeping through their union. He laughed for the first time then, and after one final gift of music from her throat he lowered Betty Boo slowly out of my sight and onto the bed as Leonard Cohen's band started 'Paper Thin Hotel' inside my head.

I finished my cigarette, thanked my father and Mr Cohen for their infinite wisdom, and walked back to the pub, marvelling at how the apples fall so close to the tree.

'You staying for the match?'

'I'm off, mate. Gimme a quick Jack Daniel's and Coke there, no ice.'

'You getting the curly finger?'

'Young, free and single, mate.'

'Way to keep it, kid. She has my head melted.'

I use only an inch of Coke. I want to dull the whiskey's edge, not drown it in sugar. Ice is nice but it slows down the delivery. I hold the mixture in my mouth but I miss the burn.

'Give us one more there without the Coke.'

'Yeah, you've plenty in the bottle.'

'I'm leaving that. Sure I couldn't taste the whiskey.'

'If you want to taste the whiskey you can forget that American shite and have a Bush.'

'It sends me mental.'

'Bushmills?'

'Any Irish or Scotch.'

'You're not alone.'

Round two and the burn comes out swinging. I let the flames move along the ridge of my tongue, biting into the ulcers at the back and sides before washing the skin of Guinness from my throat on its way to my guts.

'The bourbon mellows me out, you see, but even one Bushmills and I'd start to twist.'

'Drink enough of any spirit and you'll end up somewhere dark. You should stick to the beer, kid.'

'You're probably right.'

'It has been known.'

I leave without passing her. I'm not nervous or shy or sad. I just couldn't give a fuck. At the door I turn for a final look and see her throat exposed and her head between her shoulder blades as another mirth quake ripples through her. Does she ever stop giggling? It can't all be real. I wonder where she goes to when the laughter dies. In the off-licence I buy two litres of cider, six cans of Castlemaine XXXX, twenty fags and a packet of Rizlas. This time I enter the university through the front gates. If I'd finished school I would have been entering a university somewhere via the front entrance every day now for the last three weeks.

Would I have come here, to Belfast? No chance. Manchester, London, Edinburgh, Glasgow. Why the fuck would anyone stay in Northern Ireland when they could go to university anywhere else in the world? That's the problem with 'our wee country'. Not enough people have the imagination to leave and have their horizons broadened and their brains rewashed. There is no point lingering in the impressive entrance hall waiting to field questions on my dubious-looking offie bag of books, so after a quick glance around I shoot through into the gardens and take a seat under my tree.

There is no one around. The silence bathes me. The beer is so cold that it takes my breath away. It takes two long pulls to empty half of a can, which I then top back up to the brim with Dr Cider's sweet sticky medicine. The Snakebite doesn't mess around. Before the first concoction is finished life takes its foot off my shoulders and I lean back and allow my torso to be swallowed by the trunk of the tree.

The hash is dark and pungent and oily. Pure Moroccan black, the dealer said. 'You don't even need to burn it. Break bits off and roll them into balls, or even into a wee black sausage.' There is a drought on in south Belfast. None of the students or kitchen workers have seen any gear for weeks. A shipment seized down in Cork is the word. A fishing trawler, its hold stuffed tight with big blocks of marijuana. It's an improvement on the fishing trawlers whose holds had been stuffed tight with big blocks of plastic explosive. A chef from west Belfast called the Gypsy Nolan sorted me out. 'You'll get gear off the boys,' he said. 'There's always a bit somewhere, if you know who to ask.' He brought me to a bar in the New Lodge just north of the city centre, where I met two serious-looking men my father's age. We sat opposite them, clinging to pints while they checked my credentials.

'Why are you here?'

'I want to buy some hash.'

'I know that, but why are you here?'

'I don't know what you mean.'

'What's your name?'

'Vincent.'

'Vincent what?'

'Vincent Duffy.'

'You're fucking vouching for him. Take him to Charlie, and if I see either of you back here again . . .'

Halfway up a tower block we did business through a hatch with a metal grille in a reinforced door. To make it worth the dealer's while I was buying for a lot of people. When we got out of there alive I chopped and weighed on some scales in the kitchen, and when I'd divvied out and cashed up I was smoking for free myself.

I break bread and crumble it onto the Rizlas that I have stuck together in a little rectangle. The stuff is so wet that it stains my digits, and I hold finger and thumb to nostrils and savour North Africa. It's a strong smoke. On its own I would freak but the booze blends with it, mellowing the recipe and evening out the blow. Getting dark now. Last time it was getting light. I search the stained glass for traces of the morning show. Funny how somewhere so illuminating can look so cruel when the lights go out. The smoke fuses with my blood and I follow the buzz as it travels the circuit of my body, dulling my brain and choking my thoughts. I lie down beside my tree and scan the sky. There is just enough light left to make out my bats. Funny little bastards are always with me. Creepy little night birds never let me down. I close my eyes and reach out towards you. The joint falls from my fingers into the grass but I know that you will pick it up. It's your turn now. You never miss your turn.

'So what do you think of Belfast?'
    'About as much as you do, Vincent.'
    'I'll give it another month.'
    'Then what?'
    'London.'
    'Told you.'
    'You did.'
    'How's the arm?'
    'Bad at night.'
    'When you float away?'

'One wing.'

'Could be worse.'

'How?'

'McGullion.'

'One leg?'

'Exactly.'

'Maybe he's why.'

'Standing in front of a bomb is why.'

'How are you?'

'How do you think?'

'One of the four.'

'Immortalised.'

'Bet you can't spell that.'

'Beats being a mere statistic.'

'Bet you can't spell that either.'

'"One of the thirty-seven" doesn't even have a fuckin' ring to it.'

'Wish I could say the same for my ears.'

'Is there a new girl in your dream yet?'

'Yes. Every night she lies on the carpet in front of me and bleeds to death.'

'Not ideal.'

'Through her eyes.'

'You'll get over it.'

'She won't.'

'You should get up and find a party, Vinny.'

'I'm happy here, Jonty.'

'You're lying outside wasted.'

'You could have left me the money.'

'Unbelievable.'

'Five hundred quid eviscerated in your Dunnes Stores jeans.'

'They were Levi's.'

'And I'm the fucking Pope.'

'Get up, Vinny.'

'The boys all came to your party.'

'I was touched.'

'The entire riot showed up. Turnip and all the lads!'

'Get up now, Vinny, please.'

'Chalky and Barry, Bingo and Mickey, Davy and Jim.'

'All the lads.'

'We cried when they put you in the hole.'

'Like girls.'

'Your ma's sandwiches were shite.'

'As always.'

'Your sister was looking well.'

'Wanker.'

'Jonty?'

'What?'

'I miss you.'

'Vinny?'

'What?'

'Fuck up!'

Author's Note

All of the characters in this novel are fictional but clearly some of the historical events mentioned actually took place. I have adapted some of these from real life and have woven them into my story with an inch of poetic licence. The 'Big Bomb' in Enniskillen took eleven lives on Sunday, 8 November 1987. A twelfth victim died some years later from his injuries.

The Provisional IRA ceasefire, generally thought of as the beginning of the final chapter of 'The Troubles', was announced on Wednesday, 31 August 1994. By the end, over three and a half thousand people had died. Not one of them is forgotten. Peace and love.

Ciaran McMenamin

Vinny's Soundtrack

The Who, 'Baba O'Riley' (Townshend)

The Stone Roses, 'Elephant Stone' (Brown/Squire)

Happy Mondays, 'Step On' (Kongos/Demetrious)

Van Morrison, 'Moondance' (Morrison)

The Cure, 'Just Like Heaven' (Smith/Gallup/Thompson/
Williams/Tolhurst)

AC/DC, 'Thunderstruck' (Young/Young)

Leonard Cohen, 'Famous Blue Raincoat' (Cohen)

Leonard Cohen, 'Paper Thin Hotel' (Cohen/Spector)

Bob Dylan, *Highway 61 Revisited* (Dylan)

Pet Shop Boys, 'What Have I Done To Deserve This?'
(Tennant/Lowe/Willis)

Erasure, 'A Little Respect' (Clarke/Bell)

Rage Against The Machine, 'Killing In The Name' (Commer-
ford/de la Rocha/Morello/Wilk)

REM, 'Nightswimming' (Berry/Buck/Mills/Stipe)

The Clash, 'I Fought The Law' (Curtis)

Carl Cox, *Fantazia Presents The DJ Collection Vol. 1* (Various/
Cox)

Jam & Spoon, 'Follow Me' (El Mar/Spoon)

Roy Orbison, 'Working For The Man' (Orbison/Melson)

The Velvet Underground, 'I'm Waiting For The Man' (Reed)

Kenny Loggins, 'Footloose' (Loggins/Pitchford)

The Stone Roses, 'This Is The One' (Brown/Squire)

Primal Scream, 'Higher Than The Sun' (Gillespie/Innes/ Young)

Pink Floyd, 'Time' (Mason/Waters/Wright/Gilmour)

Pink Floyd, 'The Great Gig In The Sky' (Wright/Torry)

The Smiths, 'Please, Please, Please Let Me Get What I Want' (Marr/Morrissey)

Billie Holiday, 'Summertime' (Gershwin)

Frank Sinatra, 'Strangers In The Night' (Kaempfert/Singleton/ Snyder)

The Human League, 'Don't You Want Me Baby?' (Callis/ Oakey/Wright)

Michael Jackson, 'Bad' (Jackson)